THE LOST GIRLS

A MOIRA FOSTER MYSTERY

CAROLINE CLARK

MANOR HOUSE BOOKS

First published by Manor House Books 2023.
©Copyright 2023 Caroline Clark
All Rights Reserved

License Notes
This story is a work of fiction any resemblance to people is purely coincidence. All places, names, events, businesses, etc. are used in a fictional manner. All characters are from the imagination of the author.

To my mum who gave me my love of reading on the darker side and the confidence to follow my dreams.

Thanks, Mum. I miss you.

LOST IN THE SHADOWS

SOPHIE ANDREWS PLONKED down on her pink bed. *Pink was so over. She was thirteen, after all.* She let out a sigh, leaned back against the pink and once-frilled headboard, and closed her eyes.

"Are you flipping stupid...."

The shout came from the other side of her door. Sophie covered her ears before the bad words could start. She knew the reply to her mum would be Biaaach, followed by her mum shouting back, but she didn't need to hear it. She had her own annunciation, or at least she thought that was the word, for all the bad words. Changing them in her head made it easier, but the sick feeling in her stomach wouldn't go. Why did they have to do this? Why couldn't they just get on with each other? Why did they have to fight?

Parents were the worst!

Then she thought about the word annunciation. Was it right? Did it start with a P? Maybe, as in pannunciation, no, it was pronunciation. It didn't matter. No matter what she called it, it didn't make the hurt go away. Tears formed in her eyes, and she shut them so tight they hurt. She wouldn't cry, not again.

The shouting was building to a crescendo. She cowered against the headboard, covering her ears as much as she could.

The bed moved, and a furry body cuddled up next to her. For a moment, she took her hand away from her ears and stroked the cloud-like coat of her dog, Dig. She remembered how happy she had been when her mum let her go to the pound. Then, closing her eyes, she let her mind drift back to that happy day.

So many dogs were at the rescue center, all barking and excited, but none seemed right. She walked up and down the kennels, wanting so much for a dog of her own, but none of them called to her. Somehow she knew that her dog would... that she would know it, and it would know her.

Then, there in the corner of one of the kennels, was this little matted and pitiful ball. "That one," she had said, for he lifted his head, and brown eyes found hers, and she could see he was in the same pain she was.

This little one was let down by his family. He needed someone to be on his side. Together they could make a home and keep each other safe. She wondered if the people who loved this puppy had split up like her parents had. Had he suffered the shouting and the rage, and had he hidden away like she had.

"It's very scruffy, love," her mum said.

"That one only just came in. It's a cruelty case," a man said. "But he can be adopted if you want. We can show you how to clean him up and care for him." The man seemed nice, but he was old to Sophie, in his twenties, she thought. Not as old as her mum, but still old.

"Would you do that?" Sophie asked.

"Sure."

"Does he have a name?"

The man shook his head. "No, they never named him. Do you have a name for him?" The man smiled, and the fact that he had asked her opinion was amazing.

As Sophie looked in the cage, the dog tried to dig into its bedding. "Dig," she said. "He's Dig the dog."

That had been a year ago, and now they were inseparable, especially when the bad times came. Sophie bit back her tears and hugged Dig to her. He leaned against her, and she could tell he was shivering. The atmosphere in the house was toxic, and she hated to see him so scared.

"I've got you, Dig."

A door slammed. "Don't you walk away from me!" Came through the walls. It was her mum, and she just wished she would shut up.

"What you gonna do about it, B...."

"La, la, la, la, la," Sophie sang. "Let's go for a walk, shall we?"

Dig jumped off the bed and barked, spinning on the spot. It brought a smile to her face. As she passed the mirror, she pushed her mousy brown hair behind her ears and stuck out her tongue. She hated how she looked. Tired and cheap, she'd heard her dad say once. It still brought a tear to her eyes. But she loved these black leggings and the pink hoody with a paw print on it. It was her favorite.

The shouting started again. Humming in her mind to drown it out, she crept down the stairs and opened the door, sneaking out and staying close to the building until she could dart for the hedge. Dig was at her side, racing when she ran. The wind lifted his honey-brown ears and teased through his coat. Finally, they were through the gate. She turned sharp right, hidden by the hedge, and then let out a sigh.

Their street was two back from the main road. Sophie raced down the path with Dig at her side. He yipped in delight, and she let the tears fall. She knew they would soon burn out if she didn't try to hold them in. Then she could escape onto the common and forget home. One day she was going to have a house with land. Somewhere that she and Dig could walk for hours without seeing anyone. No mean girls would laugh at her clothes or lack of phone. No one would be shouting, look at the pauper, and sneering.

No boys would ignore her. It would be just Sophie and her dog, Dig, going on adventures.

Maybe they would find treasure or meet a prince and win his heart. That would show them. Then her mum would not have to work two jobs and beg dad for money. It didn't matter as long as she had Dig.

Sophie had always found comfort in the expansive fields of Lincoln Common. Today was no different. Her parents, Carly and Jack, were back at it again. Their raised voices had destroyed the otherwise tranquil Sunday afternoon air. She'd heard enough. She needed to get away.

Sophie and Dig ventured deep into the park, where urban noises gave way to rustling leaves and the distant chirping of birds. She picked up a stout stick and slashed at the bushes like an adventurer. Feeling like Indiana Jones or Lara Croft, she fought across the landscape with her trusty sidekick Dig. It was liberating and peaceful, yet as the sunlight started to wane, she knew she had stayed too long.

Dig turned and barked at something running back along the path. It was getting dark, and the sun had gone down. A chill set in, and it was not the thought of going home this time. Her parents had never argued for this long, but would she be in trouble? Probably. Maybe she should run away. She could become Lara Croft. Traveling and solving mysteries.

Dig stopped and barked again. His fur was raised in a dark line down his back. "What is it?" she asked.

Dig whimpered and turned back to her.

It was quiet. An unnerving stillness had set in. Sophie looked around. The once familiar landscape now felt remote and unfamiliar.

Then Dig growled, his body stiffening. Sophie followed his gaze. There was a figure in the distance, shrouded in the thickening twilight. Sophie's heart punched against her chest, and the hairs on her arms stood on end.

"Keep back, creep," she called. "My dog'll have ya."

Maybe they were just walking but a shiver ran down her spine. She turned to hurry back. They were a good five minutes' walk from the road, and no one else was around. Sophie increased her pace but glanced back as the feeling of someone there was overwhelming. The figure was closer. Dig's growl turned into a bark, his small body trembling with protective fervor.

Sophie's heartbeat quickened as she dragged Dig along. The man was tall, his figure obscured by heavy clothing and a hood. As he got closer, she could hear his labored breathing, a chilling sound in the gathering gloom. Fear squeezed at her heart, but she fought the urge to run. She was sure someone had told her never to run. Just look confident and keep going. She did. "Come on, Dig." He followed, and she walked faster and faster. Swinging her arms and pushing her legs as quickly as they would go without giving in to the urge to run. Should she run? Maybe? The path took her through some trees. It was so dark beneath them. Her feet were going so fast, her heart raced, and she needed to pee. Fear squeezed her heart and froze the blood in her veins. Why had she left the house? "Mum, I want to come home," she whimpered as her breath caught in her throat.

She was out from the trees. It was lighter, but not much. She could see the road. The houses all had lights on. The cathedral and castle were lit up on the distant hill. So beautiful, a place of sanctuary but out of reach. She was in trouble. Was he still there? When she finally mustered the courage to turn around, the man was gone.

She let out a nervous chuckle, scolding herself for letting her imagination run wild. "Come on, Dig," she said, her voice shaky, "Let's face the music."

As they approached the road, she noted a van parked haphazardly on the side. It was nearly dark now. Sophie felt a twinge of anxiety, knowing her mum would be angry, assuming she'd even noticed her absence. Nevertheless, she quickened her pace, eager to get home and out of the growing dark.

The van was next to the gateway, and she dodged around it, not paying much attention, until Dig stopped and barked again. Fear clamped onto her heart and squeezed it tight.

A strong arm snaked around her waist, pulling her off her feet. She screamed, the sound muffled as a cloth was pressed over her mouth. Dig yelped, straining at his leash and snapping his teeth in the air, but his barks gradually faded into the terrifying silence.

Sophie's world tilted, her senses overwhelmed by fear and a sickeningly sweet smell from the cloth. The last thing she remembered was the sight of the van's back doors slamming shut, and then... all was black.

THE CALL

IT WAS A CHILLY TUESDAY EVENING, and Moira Foster curled up next to the fire. Her feet ached as she skipped through a file, not because she had walked too far but because Rose, her 30-kilo brindle boxer dog, was lying on them. Shuffling, she placed the file down next to her chair. There was nothing else she needed to add, and a sense of dread overcame her. Tomorrow she had to tell her client that her husband was indeed cheating. For a moment, she longed to be back on the force. Only a shiver went down her spine as an old memory surfaced. No, she couldn't face that again.

Her phone buzzed, and she reached over and picked it up. The caller ID displayed Jonny Chandler's name, his mugshot from their training days grinning at her from the screen.

"Jonny," she greeted, cradling her phone against her ear. Rose was now sitting next to her, and she absently stroked the dogs broad and silky head. The Boxer's tail beat a melody against the side of her chair.

"Moira," he replied, the warmth in his voice softening the blow of what he was about to ask. "I need your help."

An icy prickle of anticipation ran down her spine. "Missing person?"

"A kid, Sophie Andrews. Thirteen years old. She was walking her dog and never made it home last night."

Moira swallowed hard, the fear of the past threatening to consume her. *Last night!* "Any... particular reason you're calling me?"

She heard him sigh on the other end of the line. "Our K9 is on another case. We're spread thin, Moira."

MOIRA HESITATED. She knew this was not the first time she had helped the police, and she regularly did search and rescue. They had found many a missing person and had only just returned from helping out after an earthquake. That had been grueling but satisfying as everyone they found was brought out alive. Could the same be said for this job? An image of Lily flooded her mind, replaced with Sarah's heartbroken face when she received the news that her daughter was never coming home. Moira had stepped away from that world, unable to face another dead child. Dread sent bile up her throat. Could she do this? Could she not, when there was a chance she could help? She looked at Rose, the dog's dark eyes meeting hers. "And you want Rose." She needed to lighten the moment, and her ex-partner's derision of her dog would do the trick.

Jonny laughed, the sound echoing in her ear. "Well, I wouldn't mind seeing you, too. But yes, we could use Rose."

Moira chuckled, her heart lightening at his good-natured banter. "A Boxer, Jonny? Really? You remember saying that she's practically got no nose, right?"

"Well, I did say that, but she's proved me wrong on more than one occasion," he said, his voice teasing. "Reminds me of someone I used to work with."

There was a pause, a moment of silence stretched between them, filled with unspoken words and memories. "We'll be there," she finally replied, her voice filled with a quiet determination that matched Rose's eager gaze. As she took the details, she forced down the old memory of Lily. That was eight years ago now, and she needed to forget it.

THE EVENING WAS FALLING, and the search site was abuzz with activity when Moira arrived. Uniformed officers moved with grim efficiency, the seriousness of their task creating a heavy atmosphere. Moira and Rose drew a few sideways glances. Some wore expressions of respect; others, predominantly from the ones who still resented her departure, carried clear disapproval.

"Private eye and her mutt," one of the officers sneered, but a sharp glance from Jonny shut him up.

"Why so late in the day?" Moira asked. "I thought you said the girl went missing last night?"

Jonny raised his eyebrows. They were lost under dark hair that was a touch too long. Detective Inspector Jonathan Chandler was an unassuming man from this side. Of average height and build, his dark hair was always a touch too long and frequently fell over his serious blue eyes. He dressed modestly, favoring worn-in jeans and shirts that look like they've seen more of the world than most people have. He was to her left. As he turned, she saw the scar. It seemed to glow as it did sometimes when it touched the light. It traced from across his left cheek to his mouth. Some called him Smiler because of it. It never bothered Moira, they had come through training together, and she remembered the early days when he seemed to get in so much trouble. Their boss used to say he was a magnet for the bad ones.

"The parents are divorced and were fighting." Jonny shrugged. "The mum didn't notice Sophie was missing until this morning and then thought she was out with the dog. I think the woman had drunk a bit too much the night before. It was only when she found the dog outside that she started to panic."

Moira looked at the light. They had a couple of hours. "Did you get a scent article?"

He nodded and handed her a plastic bag carrying a pink sweater. It made her heart churn. It was something a young girl would love. She didn't need to ask if Jonny had followed procedure and ensured that the only scent on the article was Sophie's. He understood and would have done right by her.

Another comment about her was muttered, but Moira ignored it and focused on her task. Sophie's scent would be captured on the piece of clothing. Moira put Rose's tracking harness and line on her. The dog began to wag her tail with joy, her whole body shaking in anticipation of using her nose.

Moira dropped the sweater and let the dog circle it. Rose took in big sniffs, walking round and round, then raised her head. She had the scent. Moira took her to the park entrance. Rose dropped her nose, taking a deep sniff. Her body tensed, nose quivering as she searched the entrance to the common. Working back and forward. It took her less than a minute to find the trail.

Moira cast a look at Jonny, catching the ghost of a smile on his lips as Rose set off on the trail. But his eyes were serious, filled with concern – not just for the missing girl, but for her too.

Rose was pulling fast, tracing Sophie's steps through the park. Moira kept well back, her heart racing in anticipation of what they would find. It had been too long. A happy outcome was unlikely. She stayed clear of Rose in case the boxer needed to double back; this way, Moira would not foul the scent more than had already occurred. After all, this was a public park, and who knew what had been over the ground since Sophie's last walk. *Don't think like that.*

Behind her, Jonny followed. Silently, there as support but never intrusive. It was as if they were still a team. Moira pushed the thought away. She had given up that life, and a few on the force were still sore about it. Maybe, she had laid a little blame when she left. That last case.... She shook the thought from her mind; this was different.

As Rose led them further into the search area, Moira couldn't help but feel a chill of foreboding. The memories of the past - of Lily, of a taunting note, and her skin-crawling fear - whispered at the edge of her consciousness. The nightmare about to unfold remained unknown, but one thing was certain:

Moira was walking back into the world she had tried so hard to leave behind.

She prayed tonight would not be a rerun of one from eight years ago.

ON THE CORNER OF A NARROW, winding street at the top end of Lincoln, just below the nice area of town, stood a row of houses not often frequented except by those who lived there. It was tucked away, close to the cathedral but far enough away to feel forgotten. This grand old neighborhood, nestled in the heart of the city, a historical architectural testament to the 1800s. It was a picturesque lineup of three-story terrace houses, each emanating the charm of an era gone by. The buildings stood shoulder to shoulder, their facades red weathered brick. The wooden windows and doors reflect hues of pastel blues, greens, and creams.

A careful observer would notice that the houses were meticulously cared for. Their antique charm was maintained and enhanced by the proud residents who dwelled within. The scrubbed sills, polished iron railings, and meticulous tiny front gardens perpetuated the feeling of care and pride.

A house that told a different story was at the end of the row. Attached to the terrace but out of place. It was narrower and shorter than its neighbors, a little hunched as if carrying the weight of many years on its tired shoulders. If one took the time to look at the row, you would think it was an afterthought. Slapped on without care or consideration. Its bay window, a distinctive feature not shared by the others, was marred by faded white paint peeling off in large flakes, revealing the worn, rotting wood beneath. The bay protruded across the tiny front gardens, almost onto the street.

This house wore a cloak of dereliction. It didn't gleam like the others. Instead, its roof sagged a little, the brickwork was discolored, and the front door, once a shiny black, faded to grey and peeled like the windows.

The windows were smudged with the patina of time, a stark contrast to the sparkling panes of its neighbors. Net curtains stained yellow hung behind the dirty panes. At one time, this house had a charm of its own, a character shaped by the relentless passage of time. Amid the row of polished perfection, it stood as a testament to endurance, its weather-beaten face narrating a tale of the centuries it had silently observed. It might have been worn and tired, but it was far from defeated. Instead, it was a living piece of history, a silent sentinel to the passage of time in this grand old neighborhood.

Above the bay window, a board was fixed to the wall. It had once been a sign, but the paint had peeled away, and the writing was no longer legible. All that could be seen is ' t s o l Emp. ' The once vibrant lettering weathered by time and neglect. The step up to the house is stone and worn to a curve. A testament to the once bustling shop, now a deserted relic of a time long past.

Grimly with decades of dust and neglect, the ground floor windows displayed an eerie tableau. Popped in front of the grimy curtains were two dolls, Poppy and Isobel. Beautifully made, with meticulous detail, dressed in velvet, one blue, one crimson Victorian gown. With a bonnet over their curls, they peered out onto the street. Their glassy eyes stared at the passersby with an unnerving constancy. Some would call it creepy, yet there was an undeniable fascination with attention to detail. People hurried past, averting their eyes, a shiver running down their spine when they dared a glance. With their ever-staring eyes, the dolls seemed to follow their movements, their presence seeping into the dreams and nightmares of the locals.

Behind the curtain of the first-floor window, a solitary figure huddled, almost perfectly still. The soft glow of a table lamp illuminated her work - Clara Sutton considered herself the last of the Sutton line and the owner of the once Emporium.

Clara was a relic herself, a remnant of the past clinging to the present. A shawl draped her slender shoulders, her grey hair meticulously braided and wound into a neat bun. Her frail hands worked deftly on a doll's dress, stitches meticulously threading their way through the delicate fabric. Her eyes, sharp yet somber, flitted between her task and a shadow in the corner of the room. It was there, the pain of her life, hulking, grunting, and destroying her peace. She pulled her eyes back to her work. Her children had to be perfect.

THE SEARCH

THE CHILL in the air had grown sharper as night fell over the city of Lincoln. Moira and Rose moved cautiously through the darkening park. No streetlights reached here, and the night had come down suddenly. Jonny switched a torch on behind her, distorting Moira and Rose's shadows. The dog didn't need light, her nose was her eyes, and she could follow the scent with a blindfold if needed. She was nimble too, fit and athletic; she would not put a foot wrong. That was more than could be said for her human companions. A twisted ankle would not help, and Moira was grateful for Jonny's presence.

Rose stopped for a moment. Moira was not worried. The scent of Sophie Andrews was imprinted in

Rose's mind. Sometimes she would lose the scent, but if she did, she would work until she found it again. If Sophie was lying somewhere injured... or dead... *don't think like that*, then Rose would find her. The boxer worked with single-minded determination, never seeming to tire when she tracked.

Moira watched with bated breath as Rose tracked to their left, came back, and to the right. She lifted her nose and sniffed the air. Moira's heart pounded in sync with the Boxer's panting breaths. Each moment was another moment Sophie was missing, and the urgency was etched deep in Moira's heart.

Rose was moving again, fast, sure, and confident. Moira let out a breath of relief. They moved further into the wooded area behind the park. All lights from the city were hidden from them now. As she tracked on, Moira realized they had moved in a semi-circle and were heading back towards the city. As they cleared the trees, the magnificent cathedral lit up the sky, dominating the city. Soon they could see the flashing lights of the police cars and, behind them, the neon lights of shops and takeaways throwing garish splashes of color onto the wet pavement. Had it rained? Moira realized that both she and the dog were wet. She had been concentrating so hard she hadn't noticed. A flush of panic rocked Moira. The rain could wash away the scent. It was not quite what the movies depicted. A dog could air scent over water and could scent something beneath it. However, Moira wanted this to be easy. She wanted Rose to find the girl alive and quickly.

On the street, people walked by, their faces blank and wary. Lincoln was becoming a city of strangers, and she wondered what its inhabitants would do if they were haunted by the specter of the missing girl, as she was.

A deep sense of disappointment was growing inside Moira, for she realized what was happening. They had walked in a circle and were returning to the road, three hundred yards away from where Sophie entered the park; it looked like she left it again. So why hadn't she returned home?

As they came through the gate into a car park, Rose came to an abrupt halt, her body rigid as she stared at the road and the lack of scent ahead. Her tail drooped, her gaze flicking back to Moira. The scent trail had ended abruptly, like a story cut off in mid-sentence.

"No..." Moira murmured, her heart sinking. She looked around the silent street. It was an area devoid of CCTV - an ideal location for an abduction.

Moira knelt beside Rose, her hand running over the dog's short, silky fur. "Good girl," she murmured, her voice trembling. "Good girl, Rose." She reached into her pocket mechanically, pulling out a pot of food for the dog's work.

A hand touched her back, and she jumped and turned.

It was Jonny, his voice tense. "Why are we here?"

Moira relayed what she suspected, that Sophie had done a circular walk around the park and that her trail went missing here.

"Can't the dog track her on the tarmac across the road?" Jonny asked; his scar looked garish when he was worried.

Moira's stomach twisted at the implication of what she had to tell him. "Yes, she could, but the trail ends here. I think she got into a vehicle."

Jonny's eyes narrowed. "You think she was abducted?"

Moira shrugged. She was no longer a detective. There is no way to tell if it was voluntary or forced.

"Give me something," he said, his voice rising.

"She didn't cross that road, I'm sure of it. Maybe the dad picked her up, maybe a friend, or maybe...."

"Oh frick, I hope not." He activated his radio. "Get unis across the road, find me a witness or CCTV." He turned to Moira. "Stay put for a little longer, Moira."

She nodded, and as he walked away to organize the uniformed officers, she looked around the desolate street. Few people were walking on this side. The shops were too far away and across a busy road. No one would see anything. Moira felt a shiver crawl up her spine. Rose whined softly, her brown eyes meeting Moira's.

"We're not giving up, girl," Moira said, her voice firm. "Not yet." She reached into her pocket and pulled out a gravy bone for the dog.

But as the sirens wailed in the distance and the echo of Sophie's scent faded away on the night breeze, a sick feeling of dread twisted in Moira's stomach.

They were searching for a needle in a haystack, and time was running out.

The search was supposed to bring hope, a promise of rescue. But as the night wore on, it seemed to bring nothing but a chilling echo of the past, of lost girls with a killer still at large. It was an echo that would haunt Moira's dreams, whispering of a guilt that once again began to creep into her heart.

Because Sophie Andrews was missing, Moira had led them to a dead-end. The failure was a bitter taste on her tongue that could only be washed away with the discovery of the young girl.

And yet, as the city of Lincoln slept, Moira knew one thing was certain: this was only the beginning of a chilling journey. A journey that would lead them into the very heart of darkness.

A PLEA FOR SOPHIE

2 DAYS Since Sophie Went Missing

THE TELEVISION SCREEN flickered with the somber images of a distraught family. Carly Pierce, a stout woman with tangled blonde hair, sat uncomfortably under the harsh studio lights, her mascara-streaked face pleading with the camera.

Next to her, Sophie's father, Jack Andrews, maintained a facade of stoic determination, his short-cropped hair greying at the temples. His knuckles were white, where he clenched his hands together, the only outward sign of his turmoil.

The estranged couple had come together in the face of a shared nightmare - their daughter, Sophie, was still missing.

Carly spoke first, her voice thick with restrained tears. "Please," she pleaded, her gaze never leaving the camera, "if you have our Sophie... if you're watching this... just let her go. She's just a little girl."

She broke off, sobbing, a trembling hand pressed to her mouth. Jack put a comforting arm around her, his voice hoarse as he added, "We just want her back. No questions asked."

The strain between them was palpable - two people were pulled together by a love for their missing child, even as their relationship lay in shambles. No doubt, guilt lay heavy on their shoulders. Moira wanted to tell them it wasn't their fault. Yes, they argued, probably too much, but that was families. It was too late for recriminations now; they must stay together for the love of their girl. If only her own head could get that message.

Suddenly, a soft whine filled the studio, drawing all attention to a fluffy honey-colored mongrel making its way onto the set. It was Dig, Sophie's faithful companion, who had returned home alone after Sophie disappeared.

Seeing the dog without Sophie sent a fresh wave of gasps through the studio. The studio presenter, a big man called Daniel, blinked back tears.

Carly clung to Dig, her sobs muffled in his fur, while Jack stared blankly at the dog as if trying to glean some clue from its whines.

"If anyone saw anything, please contact the police at the number below. Calls can be anonymous. Please, folks, check your dash cams and check your CCTV. Let's find Sophie and bring her home." Daniel said.

The broadcast ended with a shot of Sophie's bright smile, a stark contrast to the grim faces of her parents. As the screen faded to black, viewers across the nation held their breath, their hearts echoing the desperate plea: bring Sophie home.

But in her quiet living room, Moira Foster watched the broadcast with a sinking feeling in her stomach. The public appeal was a sign of increasing desperation, indicating that the police were no closer to finding Sophie than when she completed the search.

Moira glanced at Rose. The Boxer's head cocked inquisitively. The dog could feel her pain, of that she was sure, but she couldn't understand the reason for it. Rose backed up to the chair, sitting at the side of it, and Moira put her arm around her. Stroking the silky coat was soothing; it gave her comfort. The search had led them in circles, ending abruptly on a dead-end street. Now, they were back at square one. What could she do to help?

But as Moira stared at the television screen, now showing some soap, she made a silent vow. Sophie's disappearance echoed a past Moira had tried to leave behind, but she couldn't ignore it. She wouldn't.

She had to dive back into that chilling past and confront her deepest fears for Sophie's sake. The next move was uncertain, but one thing was clear: this was far from over. There were dangers ahead, and Moira braced herself for a rollercoaster ride into the abyss.

THE FOLLOWING MORNING, Moira still struggled to concentrate on anything but Sophie's sweet face.

Her phone rang, and she saw it was Jonny, maybe checking on her or giving her an unofficial update. She felt her stomach roll, hoping it was not bad news.

"Hey," she answered.

"How are you doing? he asked. He sounded tired, exhausted even. But that was understandable. No one would be sleeping until Sophie was found.

"I'm okay; any news?"

"Not really, we're doing another appeal tonight, but Carly Pierce, the child's mum, wants to speak to you."

"I know who she is," Moira said, "but why?"

Jonny sighed. "You know parents, they clutch at anything, and she heard that you were there that night and that you are a private investigator, a rare commodity in our little cathedral town,"

"City," Moira corrected. It was a running thing between them. She did it automatically and knew that he had used the word to make her smile.

"I think she wants to hire you. The problem is, she doesn't have two bob to rub together. I can tell her you're too busy."

"No," Moira didn't even hesitate. She couldn't imagine the pain the woman was going through. Nothing could be more important than that; she would do her best. Her last case was a high-profile divorce. There was enough in her account to take a few days on this. "I'll do it." After she hung up, she wondered if she was being a fool. This would raise Carly's hopes, and in reality, there was little she could do to help. This felt like a lost cause, and maybe she should keep clear.

JONNY HAD ALREADY BRIEFED Moira over the phone when she pulled up outside Carly's house, a small, semi-detached just across from South Common. The house stood out with its well-tended front garden, starkly contrasting the grief and confusion within. Rose, attuned to Moira's somber mood, sat quietly on the passenger seat, her soulful eyes watching Moira's every move. Usually, the dog traveled in the back of the van. It was an ex-police canine van fitted with state-of-the-art crates and air-conditioning to keep Rose safe no matter the conditions.

As Moira and Rose entered the house, she was hit by the scent of strong tea and the undercurrent of anxiety. Carly was waiting in the living room, her face pale and drawn under her blonde hair. The wrinkles around her eyes were more profound than Moira remembered from the television appeal, and her blue eyes were bloodshot from crying.

Carly led Moira upstairs to Sophie's room, a girlish haven of pink and white. Posters of pop stars and animals adorned the walls, and the room was filled with a familiar teenage scent of perfume and unwashed laundry. The headboard had seen better days, but the house and this room were clean and neat. It looked cared for, like a loving home.

The sight of the room – so vibrant yet so silent – was a poignant reminder of the missing girl.

Carly stood in the doorway, clutching the frame for support, her gaze distant. "I'll sell me car, anything, just help bring my baby home," she said her voice barely a whisper.

Jonny was right; the rusty Ford outside wouldn't even cover a week's work. But as Moira watched Carly, the desperation in the woman's eyes tugged at her heart. It wasn't about money; it was about a mother's love for her child, a love that was willing to give up everything. But maybe, it was also about redemption. One had got away, but not this one.

"Forget about the fee for now," Moira said gently, her gaze meeting Carly's. "Let's see where this goes."

Relief washed over Carly's face, but it did nothing to mask the underlying dread. Moira felt a stab of empathy for the woman; despite her brash exterior, Carly was living a parent's worst nightmare.

Moira didn't know why she had brought Rose, but it seemed to cheer Dig up, and Carly hugged Rose, crying into her neck. If only the boxer could speak, maybe she could find another clue. As it was, she was there for support.

"I walk the common twice a day," Carly said. "For as long as I can, you know, just in case."

Moira nodded. As she left the house, she couldn't shake off a chilling feeling. It was the gut instinct that had saved her more times than she cared to remember during her days in the force. And right now, it was telling her one thing: they would not find Sophie alive.

As she got back in her car, Rose whined softly, picking up on Moira's heavy mood. She reached over and petted her faithful companion. "We've got a tough road ahead, girl," she murmured.

The sun was setting, casting long shadows over the city of Lincoln. As Moira sat in her van, her eyes wandered to the silhouette of Lincoln Cathedral, standing tall and majestic against the darkening sky. Like a beacon of hope, it shone in the distance, reminding her of the resilience and faith of a city that had seen its fair share of turmoil. Its gothic architecture, dramatic spires, and stunning stained-glass windows were a testament to the artistry of the craftsmen who had built it centuries ago. *How did they do that without machines?*

In her mind, she traced the cathedral's history, recollecting the tales she had read and heard. Completed in 1311, its central spire towered an impressive 160 meters high. The spire had once made it the tallest building in the world - a title it held for 238 years, surpassing even the Great Pyramid of Giza. That was until a storm brought the spire down in 1548. If the spire had remained, Lincoln Cathedral would have held the title until the completion of the Washington Monument in 1884. Five centuries after it was built.

Moira mused at the might of human endeavor and the irony of fate - the tallest structure, undone not by man but by the forces of nature. Yet, despite the loss of the spires, the cathedral remained a symbol of magnificence, strength, and faith. Its walls held stories of times gone by, of faith, hope, and resilience. At one time, it was home to one of the four remaining copies of the original Magna Carta, a testament to a pivotal moment in human history. This was now securely displayed in Lincoln Castle, next to the cathedral.

Every time Moira looked at the cathedral, she was reminded of life's transient nature, victories and losses, and histories written and unwritten. She found comfort in its presence, an assurance that the city, like the cathedral, would endure no matter what. Sitting there, the words of the Magna Carta echoed in her mind - 'To no one will we sell, to no one deny or delay right or justice.' It was a promise she held close to her heart, a promise she intended to keep in her search for Sophie.

As Moira drove away, she was filled with a sense of foreboding. Somehow she knew it was too late for Sophie. She wasn't looking for a missing girl anymore; she was searching for a ghost. And that search would take her down paths she had sworn never to tread again.

She pulled the van to the side of the road and let the tears fall. Too many girls had died on her watch. First, Lily was let down because she couldn't save her, and now Sophie. What if this crime remained unsolved? What could she do?

Though it was years since Lily's case, she kept searching, kept looking. Maybe one day, a clue would come to light. But life wasn't as easy as the movies. The killer knew what they were doing, they were careful, they were cleverer than she was, and they had won.

Rose reached over with a silken muzzle and touched Moira's arm. The dog whined softly, understanding that Moira was stressed but not knowing why. Stroking the boxer's soft head, Moira knew she wouldn't give up. Lily's killer had got away with things so far, but as long as she didn't give up, there was still a chance she could solve that crime, and she would solve this one too.

Beneath the watchful eye of the cathedral, she promised that she would stop the beast who was prowling their city and that she would bring them to justice.

THE UNVEILING

THE MORNING **of 4 days missing.**

The morning was breaking, casting long shadows across the desolate playground, when Moira received the call.

"I hate to tell you this, but we found Sophie," Jonny said.

"Oh, no." Her heart dropped, for she could tell what was coming. Jonny's voice held a chill.

"Yeah, she's gone. I know it's hard, but would you come and have a look?"

"Jonny, I don't think I can add anything. So maybe I should stay away." She couldn't face another dead child.

"It's a weird one, he said."

Moira felt her stomach flip, and her veins were filled with ice. "Even more reason to stay away."

"Not like that. Look, I can't explain, it's just a feeling, and you have experience with serial killers, please."

"Detective Chandler," Moira head over the phone.

"I have to go. The body is in the playground, not far from the search area. Get here now."

The phone went dead, and she closed her eyes, dreading the next few hours. But there was something inside her; she couldn't turn Jonny down. She couldn't let Sophie down.

Rose was in the back of the van this time, with water and a comfy bed. This could take a while, and she doubted she would need the dog, but it was worth having her in case.

She arrived to find the area swarming with police activity, their faces grim under the pale dawn light.

Moira closed her eyes as she stopped the van. Taking a moment to steady her pulse and work up to this.

She got out into the frigid morning air. A shiver ran down her back, but it was not the cold. The playground was surrounded by yellow crime scene tape, uniformed officers and white overalled crime scene officers swarmed all over. Nestled within the playground's eerie silence, next to the rusty swings that creaked gently in the morning breeze, was a white tent. That innocuous structure filled her with dread.

Swallowing, Moira ducked under the tape. An officer nodded at her and pointed rather pointlessly at the tent.

Moira pulled back the flaps to see the lifeless body of Sophie Andrews at the far edge of the tent. Jonny was kneeling over the body, deep in thought. The playground, usually filled with the laughter and joy of children, was now a chilling crime scene.

Moira approached slowly, her heart pounding in her chest. This was a sight she had witnessed countless times during her career, yet it was a sight she could never get used to. Each victim was a brutal reminder of humanity's capacity for darkness and of its frailty.

Bitter bile rose in her throat as she took in the heartbreaking sight before her. Sophie lay still, her eyes open in eternal terror. The terror of her final moments. A terror that was mirrored in Moira's eyes as memories of Lily Parker threatened to surface. But now was not the time for personal demons, she reminded herself. Now was the time for justice.

Apart from her face, her body looked perfect. She was dressed in a plain white linen robe, her hair combed. Something caught Moira's eye, an object clutched in Sophie's hand. It was a doll. An antique doll about a foot tall. Oddly dressed in a modern outfit of black leggings and a pink hoody with a paw print on it. Something about it niggled at Moira, but she pushed it aside for now.

Before her was a nightmare, a sharp contrast between the innocence of the playground and the grim scene before her.

Moira donned her gloves. "Can I?"

Jonny jumped as he looked around. His eyes focusing on Moira. "Yeah, the crime scene guys are done for now." He handed her some gloves and pulled them back as he realized she had come prepared. "I guess old habits die hard."

Moira nodded and squatted down, carefully extracting the doll from Sophie's lifeless grip. As she studied it, she felt an unsettling mix of familiarity and dread. This beautiful doll should be a child's delight, not this mockery of life left by a murderer playing a twisted game. Anger surged through her at this mockery of innocence.

She pulled out her phone, her hand steady despite the turmoil within her, and began taking pictures, but only of the doll. She held it up against the stark white of the tent, giving no indication of the grisly scene below. Each click seemed to echo loudly in the unnerving silence. She would decode this clue and unravel this puzzle. That was her vow to Sophie.

Standing, she stepped back. Jonny joined her, his usual banter replaced by a severe and grim expression. His eyes met hers, a silent understanding passing between them. The loss of Sophie was a blow to them both, but it also hardened their resolve. They would find her killer and bring him to justice.

As they left the playground, the eerie image of the antique doll dressed in its modern clothes, lying next to the body and the silent swings, was etched deeply in their minds. It was a grim reminder of the task ahead of them.

"What makes you think this will be a serial killer," she asked, for there was nothing to indicate that. Well, apart from the creepy robe.

Jonny froze for a moment. The scar prominent on his face as he clenched his jaw.

The wind blew through the deserted playground, stirring the stillness that shrouded it and lifting Moira's chestnut ponytail. It pulled her eyes as a crisp packet skittered across in front of them. Moira found herself staring once again at the tent by the swings, her eyes drawn toward the spot where they had found Sophie. A lump formed in her throat as the memories replayed. The white silk robe, the doll in modern clothes, the lifeless eyes of the once vibrant teenager.... It was all too cruel.

Jonny's voice broke her reverie, returning her to the harsh reality. "There was a note with the doll on Sophie's body," he said, his voice heavy with a mixture of dread and determination. "Come, you need to see this. We need your input on what it means."

Moira nodded, but she already knew what it meant. The look of desolation in his eyes told her that this was a brag and a threat. *You don't know that*, a voice said in her head, but she pushed it down, for she did.

He led her to a SOCO Scene of Crime Officers white high-top transit van parked nearby. The cold metallic interior of the vehicle seemed to amplify the gravity of the situation. He stepped in the back doors and beckoned her to follow. There was a box on the counter with a tablet next to it. Evidence was logged and scanned since she had left the force. No more spidery handwriting.

Pulling on his gloves, he sorted through and pulled out a plastic evidence bag. Moira felt the bile rise in her throat. How much more could she take?

He showed her the evidence bag, and she took it, her own gloves still on her hands. The plastic revealed a simple piece of cheap, lined paper. Her heart pounded in her chest as she read the chilling message:

'Unveiling 1,

more to follow.

😊'

A chill ran down her spine as the implications of those words hit her. It wasn't just a message. It was a promise, a grim vow from a monster who intended to strike again. The audacity of the killer, leaving such a brazen message, made her blood run cold.

Jonny's face was ashen. The playful banter and the lighthearted camaraderie that had once defined their relationship seemed far removed now. Instead, the air between them was tense, heavy with unspoken thoughts and fears. There was a killer on the loose, one who had taken Sophie's life and was promising more victims.

"Does it mean what I think it does?" he asked.

Moira nodded. This was what she had trained for. With a degree in psychology and a postgraduate course in forensic psychology as well as a lot of on-the-job experience she had a unique insight into the criminal mind. "This is a promise of more to come and a taunt. He thinks he is better than us. That smacks of a personality with something to prove. He is probably an underachiever."

Anything else?"

"He's most likely white, male, in his mid 30's to mid 40's, and he feels as if the world is laughing at him. So this is his way of laughing back."

"Why the white robe?"

"That is more difficult." Moira found that now she had started to analyze the killer, her intuition and training took over. It was a case now, and she could control her emotions for a while. "It could be remorse. It could be a symbol of innocence. His belief that she is a victim, or it could be part of a ritual, the robe could hold some meaning." She shook her head. The robe felt wrong. "It could simply be misdirection, or there was something on her clothes that would lead back to him."

"Such as?"

"Was she?" Moria stopped as horror filled her mind.

"No, he said, understanding her. "She hadn't been touched that way. At least, that is one blessing."

Moira wondered why that had come to her mind. "Did Sophie have any defensive wounds?"

"Just a bit of bruising. It was over very quickly for her."

"Maybe she cut him. Maybe his blood was on her." Moira shrugged. "At the moment, this is all conjecture. I would have more information...." The words stopped; she couldn't say it.

"I understand," he said and patted her shoulder. "Let's hope it doesn't come to that."

The scent of sterilization fluid and the sight of evidence bags made Moira feel queasy, and she walked away from the van.

"Jonny," a Police Constable called.

"It's Detective Chandler, or DI to you." Jonny turned his face at the young bobby and watched him quake. When his blood was up and his scar shone bright, he was a force to be reckoned with.

"Sorry, Sir, the boss wants you."

Jonny shrugged. "Tell him I'll be a minute."

Moira's hands clenched into fists, her nails digging into her palms. Fear filled her veins with ice. It wasn't just a fear for the safety of others in Lincoln; it was also a fear that echoed past traumas. The memory of Lily Parker's skinned body flashed in her mind, and a shiver coursed down her spine.

"Moira..." Jonny's voice wavered, pulling her back from the edge of her memories.

"We'll catch him, Jonny," she replied, forcing determination into her voice. "We will."

There was a cold certainty to her words. They had to catch this killer. For Sophie. For Lily. For every potential victim out there.

And with that grim determination burning inside them, they went their separate ways, leaving behind the haunting message and the chilling memory of the doll. The note was a dark promise, a terrifying prophecy. But it was also a call to action, a challenge that Moira and Jonny were more than willing to take on.

UNSPOKEN WORDS

MOIRA KNOCKED LIGHTLY on the open front door of Carly's small terrace house, her heart pounding in sync with the persistent tick of the wall clock in the hallway. She noticed the unopened mail and discarded shoes that told a story of a household abruptly disrupted.

"Moira," Jonny's voice was a dull edge of weary frustration as he approached the door. His face was a storm of conflict, fatigue lines etching deep crevices in his forehead. He looked as though he hadn't slept. The signature-worn jeans and t-shirts he wore always looked like they had seen more of the world than most people. She guessed they had, and he had to face this sort of scene regularly. It was one part of the job she didn't miss. Moira was not good around emotions. She did her best to keep her own bottled up. It was the only way to do the job. On the other hand, Jonny was able to be hard and soft at the same time. He felt everyone's pain deeply, but he could push it aside when needed. That scared Moira; if she let the emotions fully in, would she ever escape them?

"I need to speak to Carly," she said softly, holding his gaze. She was firm, unyielding, despite the dread that knotted her stomach.

"Can't it wait? We failed; what more does she need to hear?" He flashed an apology with his eyes. He hadn't meant to be that harsh.

Moira sighed and ran a hand across her face; her hand felt the small scar on her left eyebrow. It seemed she and Jonny were matched in more ways than one. The scar was a reminder of a fall on a rescue mission, a sweet reminder that life was short and could end suddenly. She pulled her mind back to the present. "It might be important. I want to ask her something about Sophie."

"She doesn't need this now, Moira," Jonny's voice was a harsh whisper, his eyes pleading. His frustration wasn't directed at her, she knew, but at the helpless situation that had engulfed them.

"I... I failed her, Jonny. I failed Sophie." Moira's voice was strained, a tear escaping her eye. She quickly wiped it away, reminding herself she wasn't here to grieve. "I have questions... and a photo. I need to know if Carly recognizes the doll. It's crucial."

The words hung in the air between them, and Moira watched as Jonny clenched his jaw. He took a deep breath, his anger fading, replaced by the shared weight of their failure.

"Don't do this, not yet," he said.

Carly shuffled to the door. "It doesn't matter what it is," she said. I want to help. "I failed my Sophie, but maybe I can save another child." She turned and walked away, her head bowed, broken, and defeated.

"You'll go easy," Jonny said, not a question but a solemn promise. He stepped aside, allowing her to enter.

Walking into the house, Moira took in the somber silence, the kind of silence that echoed in the aftermath of catastrophe. Carly walked before her into the living room, a pale ghost amidst the shadows, her eyes vacant and red-rimmed. Moira felt a pang of guilt as she looked at the grief-stricken woman. It felt like an intrusion, a violation of sacred pain. But she knew she had to push forward. Something told her this was important. It was the detective part of her. The part she missed now she was doing private work. There was not a lot of thrill in following cheating spouses.

Carly slumped onto the sofa. She was wearing pajamas and a peach fluffy dressing gown. They seemed wrong for this grief, she should be in black, but somehow they were right. Carly was unable to step into the normal, to forget this had happened; she hadn't even dressed. No doubt, she woke each morning, forgetting that Sophie was dead.

Jonny cleared his throat.

"I'm sorry, Carly," Moira began, a slight tremble in her voice. "Could you look at this?" She handed over her phone, showing the photograph of the doll found with Sophie.

Carly took it hesitantly, her eyes widening at the sight. It was a moment that both broke and steeled Moira's resolve. They had a killer to catch, and this grief, raw and potent, was a reminder of why they must.

Carly's fingers traced the outline of the doll on the screen, her hand trembling as if the photograph itself held an electric current. It was more than recognition in her eyes; it was the realization of a nightmarish truth. The air in the room grew thick, charged with her palpable grief.

"Those... those were Sophie's clothes..." she choked out the words, her voice barely a whisper, barely holding onto the thread of composure she had left. She was shaking now and dropped the phone onto her lap. Her head hung as she sobbed out her pain.

Moira felt a knot tighten in her chest, her throat closing at the sound of Carly's despair. This was significant, a tangible connection to Sophie's death and a clear insight into the killer's mind. They were meticulous, patient, and rooted in detail. What did it mean? Where did it lead them?

Moira closed her eyes at the realization of what she had done. This was a devastating blow to Carly, which she should have expected. Jonny would have! Seeing the doll must be like seeing her dead daughter. It was a mockery of Sophie's death and a sight that would stay with Carly for life.

Moira felt guilt like acid eating away at her stomach. What had she done? Couldn't she have just asked what Sophie was wearing?

But, now they knew. This was also a lead, a piece of the puzzle gnawing at her mind to be solved.

"That's what Sophie was wearing," Carly repeated, louder this time. Her breath hitched, her chest heaving with unrestrained sobs. The phone slipped from her knees, fluttering down to land on the carpeted floor. The room filled with the echoes of Carly's grief, her wails punctuating the silence like shattered glass.

Jonny moved first, a comforting presence wrapping Carly in a brotherly hug. Moira could see his eyes, the same pained sorrow reflected in her own, the hardened detective facade crumbling under the weight of the situation.

Carly clung to Jonny, her sobs muffled against his shoulder, her body shaking with the force of her despair. He held her, a rock amongst her storm of grief, his own guilt concealed behind a mask of stoic duty.

Dig came across the room and leaned against Carly. Her hand reached out and stroked his head. Could these two ever heal?

Moira felt the tears prick her own eyes, but she blinked them back. She was the outsider here, the one who had promised to help and failed. And yet, she knew this was a pivotal moment. This was a clue, a lead in their case, a signpost pointing them in the direction of the killer. As much as it pained her, she had to hold onto that.

The room felt heavy, the specter of Sophie's loss looming large. The grief was a tangible force, a tidal wave of emotion that threatened to sweep them under. But beneath it all, Moira felt a spark of determination ignite within her. Finally, they had a lead, and now more than ever, she felt a renewed sense of resolve. They would catch this killer. For Sophie. For Carly. For all the lost girls.

CLARA'S CHILDREN

STITCH AFTER STITCH, Clara sews until her arthritic hands ache, and she takes a break. Closing her eyes momentarily, she places the doll on her worktable, next to the ancient sewing machine and on top of scraps of fabric. A grunt pulls her eyes open. She looks up. "Enough," she shouts before her eyes are drawn from the lump to an antique wooden cabinet. A smile eases the tension from her face. The cabinet nestled against the wall in pride of place in the living room. It's a striking piece, its mahogany frame weathered by age yet holding an elegant aura. So tall and imposing that it almost touches the ceiling.

Though slightly smudged and speckled with age, the cabinet's glass front allows a glimpse into the world Clara cherishes. The shelves inside are home to her precious children, each standing in its designated spot. Their eyes seem to glint in the dim light filtering through the room, and their porcelain faces a myriad of different expressions - some joyful, some serene, some lost in thought. Dressed in meticulously tailored Victorian-era clothing, they present a parade of fading times and fashion.

Right before this imposing cabinet, like a stage before an audience, rests a petite table and chairs. The setup is quaint, reminiscent of a bygone era. A delicate lace cloth drapes over the table, which is adorned with an exquisite tea set. Each piece, from the teapot to the cups and saucers, is a marvel of miniature craftsmanship, reminiscent of the delicate nature of the dolls themselves.

Sitting at that table are four of her current favorites, Edith, the leader and head of the house, Daisy her sister, a little rebellious, Sophie the clumsy one who spilled her tea yesterday, and Cora, the shy girl who needs encouragement or she will be back in the cabinet.

In her mind, her dolls chatted discreetly, talking of the day. The sound of the chatter almost drowned out the ominous silence that Peter carried with him.

He cowered in the corner, his large frame almost merging with the darkness. His face, usually masked by shadows, held a strange intensity, an unsettling mix of confusion, with an inexplicable undercurrent of something darker, something malevolent.

Yet, Clara continued to sew, her attention locked onto the dolls. She poured love into every stitch and little detail of her dolls as if the love for these inanimate objects could balance the unease and tension she felt towards her flesh and blood.

In his corner, Peter was like an unplayed note in a symphony, a figure perpetually on the periphery, unseen yet undeniably present. His presence was a constant reminder of Clara's past, a reminder she sought to ignore but could never truly escape. As she sewed, she turned a blind eye to his ominous silhouette, focusing on the task at hand, pretending to be alone in her solitude.

Talking softly, she addressed the dolls as though they were her children. She guided them through the life she envisioned, weaving intricate tales of imagined adventures and grand balls, quiet afternoons in the garden, and warm nights by the fireplace.

"This one," she murmured, lifting a doll with soft curls and painted blue eyes, "you are Amelia. You'll live in a grand house with a large garden filled with the scent of old English roses." Then, as she sewed a petite dress from a scrap of lace, she told Amelia about her character - a quiet, thoughtful girl with a love for books.

Clara cherished each doll as if they were a part of her, a fragment of her soul molded into porcelain and fabric. Each was an individual, a unique entity birthed from her creativity and companionship. However, to keep the lights on and her world alive, she had to part with some of them. This reality tugged at her heartstrings whenever she had to hand one over to a buyer.

"Remember, my darlings, this is your home," she whispered to them, her voice echoing in the hushed room, "You mustn't leave. But some of you... some of you, if you betray me... you will journey elsewhere," her voice raised as fury filled her at the thought of such betrayal. Although her heart ached as she said the words, the thought of an empty spot in her family was always a source of sorrow.

In their silence, the dolls stared back with their glassy eyes as if acknowledging her sadness. Yet, they understood, or Clara liked to believe they did. They were her children, her family, and she loved them, one and all. Each night, she kissed each of them goodnight, promising them that she would always be there, even when distance separated them. Clara found solace, purpose, and joy in their silent company. And as the sun dipped below the horizon, painting the sky with the hues of twilight, Clara's house came alive with the whispered tales of her doll children, their lives playing out in the depths of her vivid imagination.

IN THE SHADOW OF A GHOST

THE COLD NIGHT air wrapped itself around Moira, whispering tales of dread and despair as she stood outside a police cordon. The strobe of blue lights painted the darkness with a grim luminescence. Somewhere in the distance, an ethereal melody drifted in the wind, a voice as angelic as it was haunting. It was just a hymn on someone's radio, but it transported Moira back in time. Her throat tightened, and she heard Lily Parker's voice, a heartrending aria filling the quiet night. Even though she knew the voice was only in her head, it felt real and tore at her heart.

Moira dug her nails into her palms, and Sarah Parker's face came into focus, etched with the unspeakable sorrow of a mother who had lost her child. It was doubly cruel for Moira, for she had known Sarah since their school days, but the woman standing before her now was a stranger. The grieving mother's eyes held a silent accusation stabbing Moira's heart – 'Why couldn't you save her?'

A chilling image flashed before Moira, a tableau of horror so stark that it seemed to drain the warmth from the world around her. It was Lily again, lying motionless on a cold steel table in a dimly lit morgue. The sight of the young girl, a girl she had known, mutilated and lifeless, was a cruel testament to the world's brutality.

Suddenly, the scene shifted, the world seemed to spin, and a cold jolt surged through her body. Moira jerked upright in bed, her body slick with sweat, her heart pounding against her rib cage. The chilling echoes of her past receded, leaving her with the aching void of reality.

Rose's tail thumped against the duvet, and the dog placed her broad head on Moira's leg.

It was just a dream!

Just a haunting visitation from her past, a brutal reminder of the scars that marked her soul. The lingering sorrow in her heart was joined by a fresh wave of despair as the reality of Sophie's death crashed over her. The memory of Carly's anguished face returned, the image superimposing itself onto that of Sarah's from eight years ago. Another young life snuffed out, and another mother was left to grieve. Another soul she had let down.

A sense of dread clung to Moira like a shroud. Would she fail again? But within the heart of that dread burned a spark of resolve. The monsters of this world had taken away one too many innocents. Moira wouldn't let Lily's tragedy replay itself. She would not let this murder go unsolved. She would find this beast that stalked her city, and she would make him pay for his atrocities.

Leaning against the headboard, she stroked the boxer's silky head and tried to push the images from her mind.

THOUGH MOIRA HAD DRESSED in a smart black trouser suit, which had seen better days, she still found her mind on the dream. Rose had been fed and sat at her side. The dog whined and pushed her with her nose. She wanted to help as she could feel the emotions that stormed through her partner, but she didn't understand them, didn't know what was causing such grief.

The soft light of morning filtered through the blinds as Moira sat at her kitchen table, a half-eaten piece of toast slowly drying on her plate. The aroma of her brunch hung heavily in the room, mingling with the faint echo of past conversations, past lives, and past losses. Moira's mind was far away from the mundane comforts of food, caught up in the turmoil of emotions left in the wake of Sophie's death.

Beside her on the table lay a file, the case of a divorcee seeking help, a tale of broken vows and shattered hearts. Or possibly vengeance and greed. It was often hard to tell. She looked at the documents, seeing the words but not really reading them. She was expected at the client's home in an hour, but the prospect of listening to another tale of human frailty felt like a weight pressing down on her. The thought of going through stacks of financial records and listening to the bitter disputes that always surrounded these cases left her feeling drained. The he said, she said, the petty quarrels, it was all too much. Her heart wasn't in it, and she wondered if she could put the client off.

Could she cancel? Reschedule? The echoes of Lily's and Sophie's faces filled her mind, their stories left unfinished, their lives cut short. Suddenly, the petty grievances of divorce seemed so trivial, so inconsequential. Her gaze fell to her lukewarm cup of tea, the once-steaming liquid now as cold and still as her resolve.

Just as she was about to reach for her phone, it buzzed, startling her out of her thoughts. An unknown number flashed on the screen; the area code was the next town over. Newark. In a different county but still close. She had no work there. What could it be?

She answered the call, her voice steady despite the surge of dread that knotted her stomach. A man introduced himself as Calvin Pierce from the Newark neighborhood policing team. "We have a missing child, and your details are on the search and rescue rota. Can you attend?"

"Of course," she answered. *Another missing child!*

"We don't think it is anything traumatic at this point." His voice was unnervingly calm as if he was discussing the weather.

Moira's heart pounded in her chest, echoing the urgency of his words. Images of Lily and Sophie flashed before her eyes, their memory searing through her like a bolt of lightning. The taste of the black tea in her mouth suddenly turned bitter, the pain of their loss resurfacing like a raw wound.

"I will set off now. Text me the address."

"It's probably nothing," Calvin said, his words shattering the ghostly images. His attempt to downplay the situation, likely a means to keep his own fear in check, only stoked the flames of her anxiety. She wondered if Sophie's parents had initially thought the same, their hope now a cruel irony in the face of the horrifying truth.

"Maybe, but I will be there as quick as I can. Keep people off the scene and get me something the child touched that no one else has. Place it in a clean plastic bag without touching it."

He agreed, and she ended the call. Another child was in danger, and she had a chance to make a difference. To right the wrongs of her past. To save a life where she had failed before.

Breakfast was forgotten, and the divorce case a faint memory. Moira rose from the table, the specter of the past trailing behind her. The sunlight streaming through the window did little to warm the chill in her bones. But in that moment, she realized something vital, a truth that gnawed at her very soul.

Haunted by her past, she was now walking in the shadow of a ghost. Every missing child would bring back the faces of Lily and Sophie. Every unsolved case would weigh on her like an unseen burden. But as chilling as this realization was, it came with a flicker of hope. She had been given another chance, an opportunity to change the outcome. She would find this child. She had to. To do so, she had to push the ghosts of the past into the darkest recesses of her mind and seal them there. If she spent too much time on the past, she would mess up the future.

"Come, Rose." As she grabbed her coat and headed for the door, she couldn't help but feel a strange sense of purpose. It was a cruel irony that tragedy had to be the catalyst. Still, as she closed the door behind her, she knew she was stepping into a battle where every second counted. She would not let another child be claimed by a monster.

This time, Moira thought, as she raced towards Newark, this time things would be different.

THE LOST BOY

THE DRIVE to Newark was a tense one, and she broke the speed limit as she streamed down the A 46. The images of Lily and Sophie played on a loop in her mind, but she knew she had to move on.

It was almost lunchtime when she arrived at the Marsh home, and yet she still felt half asleep. Today had been surreal. She stopped next to a police van parked outside a semi-detached house at the end of a sleepy cul-de-sac. As she climbed out, the house was shrouded in an eerie silence. The garden looked like a scene from an apocalypse movie. A table set for a party. Balloons fluttering in the wind, but no children, no laughter, just somber parents praying this would end.

The birthday cake in the shape of a football with its unlit candles was a stark contrast to the police cars parked haphazardly along the street. Steven Marsh, a five-year-old boy, was missing. The joyous preparation for his birthday party had turned into a desperate search.

Moira's heart pounded in her chest as she walked towards the garden, Rose trailing behind her. Could this be similar to Sophie's case? Newark was a neighboring town in a different county, but it was possible, wasn't it? She wondered if she should call Jonny, but the local police wouldn't welcome him. County lines always complicate matters.

"Who's in charge," she called, dumping her tracking bag and putting Rose in a sit.

A tall, distinguished man in a grey cardy and grey trousers came over. The look on his face, as he stared at Rose was a picture of doubt. "I expected... well... a dog with a bigger nose."

"Don't worry, Mr. Pierce, I presume? Her nose works just fine."

He nodded. "The article you wanted is on the table over there. It is his pillow case, and I removed it with gloves and placed it in the bag. The parents are over there. Mrs. Judy Marsh and Mr. Paul Marsh."

"Great, I may appear rude, but I need to get Rose on the trail. Have you any idea where the boy may have gone?"

Pierce pointed to the corner of the garden, where there was a hole in the wooden fence. It was not big enough for Moira to fit through. "Get me a crowbar and apologize to them over the fence."

He walked away.

As Moira pulled Rose's tracking harness out of her bag, she could almost feel the pain of the two anxious parents waiting on the lawn. The mid-morning sun cast a harsh light over the domestic scene, illuminating the worry lines etched deep into their faces. It was a sight that was becoming all too familiar to her.

She observed the couple as she snapped the harness in place. Her scrutiny was deep, checking to see if there was subterfuge in their movements and faces. They would not be the first couple to cry missing child when they had killed said child themselves. Moira hated having such thoughts, but it was part of the job.

The harness was on, and she was nearly through her routine. Every time she tracked with Rose, they went through the same procedure. Harness on at the scene, take scent, track, reward.

While she prepared the line and harness and got Rose ready, she studied the parents. Mrs. Marsh was a petite woman with disheveled brown hair and bloodshot eyes. Her floral print dress bright, beautiful, and a reminder of the fun that should be happening. She was wringing her hands incessantly, her gaze darting between the officers and the entrance to their property as though expecting her son to appear at any moment.

Beside her, Mr. Marsh, a tall man with thinning hair and a weather-beaten face, stood with his arms crossed, eyes glued to the ground. His jaw was set firm, the muscles twitching in silent anxiety. The stark silence between the two hinted at the strain of the situation, their shared fear hanging heavy in the air.

With her harness on, Rose was ready to track. Pierce handed Moira a crowbar. "Do you want an officer with you?"

"If they can stay back, also someone the child knows but not the parents."

"Surely, they would be the best person."

Moira hated this part. The parents would want to come, but the chances of them interfering with the search were high. "It needs to be someone emotionally steady."

Pierce nodded, understanding, and walked away.

Moira didn't wait. Her mind was screaming for her to hurry. She picked up the bag and took Rose over close to the hole in the fence. It was possible that Steven hadn't left this way, but they had to start somewhere.

Pierce was back. It looked like he was coming, and there was a short chubby man with him. His face was white, but he looked in control. "This is Martin. He is Steven's uncle."

"I can do this," Martin said.

"Great, these are the rules. Rose is in front. I will be 15 feet back. You will stay 15 feet behind me. The reason for this is to stop us from contaminating the trail if she has to track back. Can you do that?" Moira gave them her most earnest glare as her heart screamed hurry; a five-year-old can't survive forever.

They both nodded.

Moira took a moment to share a reassuring glance with the parents. It was a silent promise, a vow to do her utmost to reunite their family. The stakes were high, and every second counted. She knew they had a challenging task ahead, but they were on the scene relatively quickly. The scent should be easy for the dog to follow. Unless he was taken? She pushed the thought aside. One last look at the desperation on the face of the Marshes; she was their lifeline. They were clutching at the thin thread of hope.

Moira opened the bag and dropped the pillowcase on the ground. "Take."

Rose was already on it. Looking forward to the game that used her best sense and filled her with joy. She breathed in, again and again, and then began to circle the article. It was only seconds before she went to the fence.

"Wait," Moira called. The hole was large enough for the dog, but she wanted to go through it at the same time.

Taking the crowbar, she enlarged the hole. All the time, her mind screamed to hurry. Once it was large enough, she checked it was safe and pointed Rose in the direction. The dog needed nothing else. She was on the scent and eager to follow it.

Moira turned to the men. "Count to 20, and then come to the fence. If I am far enough away, follow." Without waiting for a reply, she went through the hole, for Rose was tracking fast. Did this mean good news or bad? At this stage, Moira didn't want to guess.

With Rose's tracking line securely in her hand, Moira let it pull through, giving the dog her space. Then she followed at a distance. As she worked, Rose was a vision of canine beauty. Her striking coat, a rich tapestry of warm browns and deep reds in tiger-striped brindle hues. It was glossy and sleek, fitting tightly over her muscular frame.

The hole in the fence led to a small lane that went between the two rows of houses. It was not well used, being access to garages at the rear of the properties. The surface of broken asphalt was easy for the dog to track on, and Rose was moving fast and confidently.

The dog moved with an agility that belied her size as she sniffed at every leaf and blade of grass, every discarded crisp packet, and a cigarette butt. There was an intensity in her movements that showed her determination and professionalism. Her nostrils flared as she drew in a lungful of air, determined to follow the scent that would lead them to Steven.

Moira stayed the same distance behind Rose, keeping the line taut but not impeding the dog. Her heart was pounding in her chest, her mind swirling with the grim possibilities. She watched her trusted companion as she seemed to dance between air and ground scenting, her movements precise, almost balletic in nature.

Behind them, Calvin Pierce and Steven's uncle, Martin, kept a respectful distance, their eyes trained on the pair leading the search. Moira could feel their anticipation, their hope, their anxiety. The weight of their expectations hung heavily on her, but she knew she needed to focus on the task at hand. The life of a child was at stake.

After just a few minutes, they reached a junction, and Rose paused. She lifted her head, scenting the air, her body alert and tense. She circled, moving right, then left, her nose hovering over the ground. For a moment, Moira's heart dropped, fearing they had lost the trail. Had this been another child abducted? Taken in a vehicle, would the trail end here and reappear in 3 days with another doll?

But then, Rose's body stiffened. She turned left and moved at speed.

Moira almost had to run to keep up, her mind racing as fast as her pulse. Rose's increased pace was a good sign - she had picked up something strong. They darted down the street, past rows of identical houses, until Rose abruptly stopped in front of one with a decent-sized garden.

Moira's heart pounded louder in her ears as Rose continued into the garden and down the side of the house. This was strange. Had the owner of this unassuming house taken the boy?

Rose stopped at a gate. This was private property, but Moira didn't hesitate. She came to the dog and opened the gate. Rose was off again, over a lawn surrounded by flowers, past a small garden pond, and then towards a wooden shed in the corner of the garden. The dilapidated structure looked untouched, almost forgotten. But Rose went straight to the door, her body rigid as she barked to say she had found the unsub and expected her reward.

She turned to look at Moira, her eyes almost human-like with their message: he's here. I did it!

"Good dog," Moira said as the owner of the house came out.

"What are you doing?" he shouted.

Pierce went to him, and Moira indicated for Martin to wait.

As they approached the shed, the relief was palpable, but they were yet to see if the child was safe. The air hung heavy with trepidation as they neared the door, the culmination of their search just a heartbeat away.

Moira's heart thudded in her chest as she approached it. She took a deep breath and pulled open the door.

And there he was. Steven Marsh, hiding in the corner, scared but unharmed. A black cat ran out of the shed and disappeared over the fence. It looked like he had followed a cat into the shed and got locked in.

Relief washed over Moira, her knees nearly buckling under the weight of it. This wasn't like Sophie's case.

This was an innocent accident, not a sinister crime. For a moment, she allowed herself to breathe, to let the weight of Sophie's case lift.

As she led Steven back to his parents, safely held in his uncle's loving arms, she thought about Lily and Sophie. Their cases were still unresolved, and their killers were still out there. This moment of relief was just that, a moment. But at least for today, she had made a difference.

A CLUE AMIDST THE CLUTTER

WITH A SIGH of relief still resting on her lips from the morning's success, Moira found herself driving back to Lincoln with Rose nestled securely in her crate. When she looked at her phone after the search, she found a slew of angry messages from her client. That was one job she had lost.

She sent them a sarcastic text saying she was out searching for a missing child and left it at that. Now she was hungry, and Rose could do with a proper run.

The verdant English countryside blurred past as her mind gently churned through the day's events.

Halfway into the journey, she pulled over at a footpath flanked by rolling meadows. After the morning's tension, both she and Rose could do with a breather. As Rose bolted out of the car, Moira looked around, her eyes landing on a bustling car boot sale in the neighboring field.; rows and rows of people with tables in front of their cars selling everything from junk to cakes to stationery. She thought back to the photo of the doll found with Sophie, the incongruity of the outfit nagging at her. Perhaps someone at the sale might have some insight.

With Rose enthusiastically bounding at her side, Moira strolled towards the hubbub. The air buzzed with the chatter of haggling buyers and sellers, mingled with the smell of worn books, musty clothes, and the faint trace of sizzling burgers.

Before she got there, she clipped the dog onto a lead and hoped there was a burger van as her stomach rumbled and complained about the missed brunch.

She passed stalls of weathered trinkets, boxes of pre-loved books, piles of old clothes, and an assortment of antique furniture. All the while, she carried around the photograph of the doll, occasionally showing it to the stallholders, always hoping for a glimmer of recognition.

At a stall selling vintage records, an elderly man with a handlebar mustache squinted at the photo, then shrugged, "Don't know much about dolls, love. More of a vinyl man, myself."

A young girl with a pink dress and her hair in pink ribbons stopped when she saw Rose. "Oh, I don't know," her mother said.

"She's gentle," Moira offered.

The girl approached, she was not much taller than the boxer, and she stared at her for a moment with wide eyes. Rose's face bore the characteristic boxer look – the broad, blunt muzzle, strong jaws, floppy jowls, and that distinctive, wrinkled brow that gave her an almost human-like range of expressions.

The girl began to grin and then rushed forward and put her arms around the dog's neck. Rose stood still, only the thumping of her tail telling how much she enjoyed the cuddle.

"That's enough, Courtney," the woman said and mouthed a thank you to Moira.

As they walked away, Moira felt like today was a good day. She walked a little further, and there was a burger van. She bought a cheeseburger and a sausage for Rose. They took a seat and watched the world walk by. People were so happy, so content, not knowing that a killer may walk amongst them. That at any moment, it could all be over. Moira chewed on the burger and decided she needed to get a life. She was becoming much too morose.

The sausage was cool, and she fed pieces to Rose while she finished her tea. Now, it was time to go home. No, she would ask a few more people about the doll.

A young woman selling handmade jewelry giggled at the photo, "Looks creepy. No idea where it's from, sorry."

As they wandered, Rose was a source of delight for many stallholders and customers alike. Kids giggled as they patted her. Adults admired her physique and playful nature. Rose, basking in the attention, greeted everyone with a wagging tail and enthusiastic licks.

At a stall dedicated to heart research, a middle-aged woman with kind eyes and a weathered smile took the phone from Moira. She examined it for a moment, her brows furrowing. "I think I've seen this type of doll before," she mused, handing it back to Moira.

Moira's heart quickened. "Do you remember where?"

The woman frowned in concentration, her gaze distant. "It was a while back... at a small shop... but the clothes aren't right. They sold antique effect dolls, quite like this one, but in old fancy dresses."

Moira felt a spark of hope. "Do you remember the name of the shop?"

The woman shook her head, apologetic. "I'm afraid not. It was years ago. And these little shops have a way of disappearing, don't they?"

While it was not the breakthrough she'd hoped for, it was a clue nonetheless - a step forward when all she'd been doing was treading water. Should she share it with Jonny? Part of her knew there was not enough and that he would already, no doubt, be looking into the doll. He had greater resources than her and would probably tell her to back off. After all, she was not officially on this case. She could use the excuse that Carly had hired her, but it would not go far with the force. However, in her mind, she had made a promise, and she would follow it through.

As she walked away, she glanced at Rose, her heart swelling with gratitude for the canine's unwavering support. And in the crowd of chattering shoppers and trinkets from the past, she felt a renewed determination. Tonight she would do an online search for the shop. She would find the answers she was looking for, for Sophie and for herself. After all, every great mystery began with a single clue.

SHADOWS AND ECHOES

MOIRA SPENT long hours that night searching for an old doll shop, but she found nothing. Finally, she went to bed and slept fitfully.

Blinking awake, the sterile ringtone of her mobile phone was like a klaxon in the heavy silence of Moira's house. She fumbled for it on her bedside table, squinting at the name displayed on the screen. Jonny. It was nearly midnight; he wouldn't call this late if it wasn't serious. Swallowing the knot of dread rising in her throat, she answered.

"Moira," Jonny's voice was a strained whisper, "We have another missing girl."

The news landed like a punch to the gut. Her heart pounded in her ears, drowning out the silence of her bedroom. The memory of Sophie's lifeless eyes flashed in her mind, but she pushed it down.

"Same area?" she managed to choke out.

"Three miles from where Sophie was taken."

Moira closed her eyes, feeling the weight of her past bearing down on her. Another girl, another family in the throes of agony. And all the echoes of Lily taunting her from the shadows. Shaking off the creeping chill, she forced herself to focus.

"Is this just a courtesy call, or do you want me?" She hoped it was the latter but realized she had no right to be on the case. She had given that up when she walked away from the police.

"We could do with you and Rose. I got the boss to agree that having an expert trained in profiling serial killers would not hurt. If you want it, you are a consultant on this case."

"Do I get paid?" she asked with a chuckle as she grabbed her jeans. Anything to lighten the mood and lift her mind out of the darkness.

"You do. Are you with us?" There was tension in his voice. He knew this would be difficult, but he should have known she could never let this girl down.

"I'm on my way."

The end of the call punctuated the quiet. She pulled on her jeans and a fleece, staring blankly at her worn but comfortable boots by the edge of the bed. Her gaze fell on Rose, the brindle boxer, looking at her with concerned brown eyes. Moira managed a weak smile for the dog before the weariness drained away, replaced by the hard-edged focus she needed.

"We're off to work," she said.

Rose was up and at the door, her whole body wagging with anticipation.

THE DRIVE WAS a blur of familiar sights under an unfamiliar sky. The trees seemed gnarled beneath the streetlights. The houses shadowy, each hiding secrets behind their blank windows. They all seemed to bear witness to a narrative that was playing out yet again in this small town that she loved so much. Moira couldn't help but feel the ripple of fear that undulated beneath the calm exterior of the sleepy streets. The night was quiet, yet each passing moment screamed the reality of the situation – another young life hanging in the balance.

Arriving at the scene, the house was already swarming with police. Yellow tape cordoned off the area, and lights from police cars bathed the place in an eerie glow, casting long, foreboding shadows. As she stepped out of her van, a gust of chilly wind picked up, sending a shiver down her spine. It felt as if the town was holding its breath, awaiting the fate of its missing child.

It was a silly thought. The news would not have broken yet. The only ones that knew were the people and the killer... abductor.

It was a nicer house, a nicer area. On one side, it faced the street, but the back of the houses opened onto farm fields and tracks.

Jonny came over. He looked tired but otherwise exactly as he always did. "This is what we know. Another girl went missing last night. Mandy Bradford, just 13. The parents are Dr. James Bradford and Professor Elaine Bradford. Both are academics, well-respected in their respective fields."

Moira listened as he explained the events that had led to this search.

"Dr. James Bradford is a renowned neurologist known for his groundbreaking research in cognitive disorders. He's often engaged in international medical symposiums. In addition, he spends a significant portion of his time either at the hospital, in the lab, or on research-related travels.

Professor Elaine Bradford is an esteemed figure in the world of anthropology, with several books and research papers to her name. Her work often takes her to far-flung parts of the globe, excavating ancient human civilizations and deciphering cultural complexities."

Despite their demanding professions, both have always endeavored to provide a nurturing environment for Mandy and her older sister. However, the nature of their work often requires them to be away from home, entrusting the care of their daughters to a string of nannies over the years and, more recently, relying on Mandy's older sister."

As Jonny continued, Moira got Rose out of the van and prepared her tracking gear. The tub of food went into her pocket, and her nerves screamed hurry, even as she knew this information was vital. They might be looking for another missing child, not an abducted one.

"Last night Mandy went missing, James and Elaine were at a charity function, raising funds for an initiative close to their hearts - scholarships for underprivileged students in the sciences and humanities. They had coordinated with their older daughter, who was supposed to be home earlier, to care for Mandy."

He let out a sigh and ran a hand through his dark hair, pushing it out of his eyes. "A miscommunication, and the sister, Grace, got stuck in that traffic jam on A 15. This left Mandy alone longer than expected."

"I see. Let's go talk to them."

The parents were outside the front door of a large house. They huddled together, their faces pale under the unforgiving glare of the flashing blue lights. Elaine's eyes held a wild look of desperation, James's stoic façade betrayed by the twitch of his clenched jaw.

"Do you know what happened?" Moira asked.

"This is not normal," Elaine began. "We always ensured that Mandy is cared for. It was just...." The guilt of this oversight weighed heavily on them, adding to the torment of their daughter's disappearance. They are clearly anguished, their high-profile statuses providing little solace in a situation that's every parent's worst nightmare. Moira did not think they had any involvement in this.

"Do you know where your daughter was?"

"She left a note. Mandy had been returning from the corner store around 7 pm. She loved her chocolate and couldn't find any in the cupboard. When Grace got back, she didn't check her room. It was 9 pm before she looked in and then she checked near the phone and saw the note. She called us straight away."

"I understand. Do you have a picture and a scent article?"

They showed her a picture, one of many on their phone. Moira could see that Mandy was a beloved child. Her vivacious personality was a beacon in the quiet suburban community. Bright, sparkling eyes stared back at her from the picture, a stark contrast to the terror-filled eyes of her parents. In many, she was painting. Mandy was a budding artist and had her whole life ahead of her. Moira wondered if she had been thinking about her latest drawing or the dinner she was going to have when... She shook off the thought, not allowing herself to think about what might have happened.

The sun was setting when Mandy disappeared. It was the perfect time for shadows to come out and play.

"I have her nightgown," Jonny lifted the plastic bag pulling Moira's mind back to the search.

"Bring her home," Elaine clasped onto Moira's hands.

"I will do all I can." As she turned away, she felt her heart break, for she hoped it would be enough.

THE TRAIL OF UNCERTAINTY

"TAKE ME TO THE SHOP," Moira said.

"It's a quarter of a mile that way. They expect that Mandy would walk on this side of the street going there and the other side of the street coming back. It was something she always did. This side going there, that side coming back," he repeated, showing his own fears. "We know she got to the shop."

"Okay, even so, we will track from here."

"There's been so many people, can she?"

"Yes, don't worry about that." Moira led Rose a little up the street, away from all the hustle and bustle. She put on her tracking harness. The boxer began to bounce in anticipation. Her brown and red striped muscles rippled under the streetlights.

"Calm," Moira said and stroked her soft head.

Taking a breath to calm herself, Moira took the plastic bag from Jonny and tipped the contents onto the pavement. "Take."

Rose sniffed the nightdress. Moira pushed the sight of it from her mind. It was pretty, pink, a young girls. Would this life be cut short too?

Rose set off toward the shop, her tiger-striped coat bristling under the crisp night air. Moira let the line play out across her fingers as she whispered words of encouragement. She felt a wave of trepidation wash over her, her heart pounding in her ears. Yet, she knew she had to hold on, to focus. She had a job to do. For Sophie, for Lily, and now, for Mandy.

Before she followed the dog, she looked back, her gaze landing on Jonny as he nodded that he would follow. She read the unspoken plea in his eyes – Help us, Moira, for Mandy's sake.

Fueled by a quiet resolve, she nodded in return. She'd do her damned best. She had to, and she began to follow the boxer as she tracked the girl to the shop and prayed this was not her last taste of chocolate.

Rose was working fast. She seemed more anxious. Moira wondered if the dog knew their mission tonight wasn't ordinary. It was another search; the scent of another lost soul filled the air. Was there an unseen cry for help that only Rose could discern?

Rose tracked past the police cars that lined the street, their blue lights painting the scene in an eerie, disorienting palette. The dog covered the ground to the shop easily and quickly. Moira was almost at a run to keep up. Finally, they came to the road, and Moira shouted, "Wait."

Rose stopped, and Jonny ran ahead and stopped the traffic.

"Track," Moira said, and Rose crossed the street. On the other side was the shop. Its lights a beacon of hope in the night. Moira could see the shop's owners, a middle-aged couple, huddled together by the entrance. Their faces were a blend of concern and fear. Their store was never supposed to be a crime scene.

Rose rushed towards them; Moira was close but still behind her on the line. The couple understood what was happening, their eyes mirroring a glimmer of hope. Moira felt her heart twist. The girl, Mandy, was just fourteen. She had disappeared on her way home from their shop. Though it wasn't their fault, they felt a sense of guilt.

Rose tracked up to the shop, and Moira nodded. A uniformed PC opened the door. It was your typical shop, narrow alleyways, shelves lined with everything bad for you. The dog ignored the tasty treats and went around the store, to the till, and then back to the door.

Now it got interesting. They already knew that Mandy made it to the shop, but what happened next.

Rose soon found the scent when she came out of the shop and headed around a uniformed PC under some crime scene tape and back along the opposite path. The dog's nose worked rapidly, deciphering the myriad scents as Moira followed her lead. Rose was thorough and methodical. She traced Mandy's steps along the pavement. It appeared that Mandy had veered off the most direct route. Rose led them across a small city park, even stopping at a quaint bridge where Moira imagined that Mandy loved to sketch the flowing river. The scent was strong here; Rose sniffed up and down the bridge. It looked like Mandy had most likely lingered for a while.

As they neared the halfway point to Mandy's home, they were back on the pavement next to the road. Rose slowed down, and Moira noticed a man standing in the shadows of a tree. She felt a shiver run down her spine. What was he doing? Was he watching them, was he involved. She pulled on the line, and Rose stopped, whining gently. Moira felt her skin crawl as she thought of the lost girl out here alone and afraid. She took a breath and whispered a prayer for all the lost girls in trouble this night.

Looking around, she nodded to Jonny and pointed in the direction of the man. Jonny shook his head, and Moira searched the shadows. The man was gone, disappeared into the night. Had he just been a watcher, a lookie-loo? Had he just been out for air, or was he involved?

"Track," she said, and Rose pulled forward, but the trace of scent must have grown fainter. The houses were more spaced out here, and the traffic was heavier. Were vehicle fumes interfering with the trail?

Moira could feel an acid burn in her gullet as the dog took her time. No longer rushing forward, pulling Moira along but stopping every few steps to reacquire the scent.

She already knew what would happen, but she tried to will the dog to find a scent. Maybe Mandy had gone to a friend's or was in the park or on the common drawing?

These things were unlikely to be true; Mandy hadn't taken anything with her. Not even a coat, and it was now the early hours of the morning.

Rose stopped at a small patch of grass at the edge of the pavement, snuffling back and forth at the ground and the air. But then, after a few minutes, she sat back on her haunches, her amber eyes meeting Moira's. That look, one of frustration and confusion, told Moira everything. The scent ended here.

Moira felt her heart drop. This wasn't like Steven's case. This was far too similar to Sophie's. The lack of CCTV, the abrupt end to Mandy's scent… It didn't bode well.

With a sinking heart, she had to admit they were likely not dealing with a lost child but another abduction.

She turned to see Jonny's grim face behind her.

"I'm sorry," she managed as she opened the food packet and gave Rose her reward. "I'm sorry, this is where the trail ends." The words tasted bitter as she voiced her findings. This was becoming all too familiar, a haunting echo of the past. The specters of Sophie and Lily hung heavy in the air, a grim reminder of the dark reality they were facing.

"We expected this," he said. "We hoped, but inside we knew."

Moira nodded and took comfort in the determined look in Rose's eyes. She knew they couldn't afford to dwell on their fears. They had a job to do. They had to find Mandy.

If the killer kept to the same timing, the bright girl who loved to draw had three days to live.

DECREPIT AND DESOLATE

ON THE WALK back to the Bradfords' home, Moira's mind was a turbulent sea, teeming with a whirlwind of thoughts. Could she have done more? The familiar pang of guilt gnawed at her. Yet, logically, she knew there was nothing she could do. Rose could not track a car, and even if she could, how many miles had Mandy been taken?

Jonny walked at her side, silent, a statue of professional stoicism. Only the heaviness of his steps told her of his frustration. It was something she picked up on after years of working with him and only discernable if you were really listening. When he was frustrated or angry, he planted his feet heavier. "There was nothing you could do," he said.

"Do you have any leads?"

"No, no one saw anything, no one remembers anything. No one has come forward with dash cam footage or something from their doorbell cameras, and believe me, we have canvassed over and over.

Meanwhile, the Bradfords' house was abuzz with frantic energy. Moira could feel it as they approached, the tension palpable in the night air. Outside, the house was lit up like a beacon against the stark darkness, a harsh reminder of the reality within. Uniformed officers, locals whispering hushed prayers, and worried neighbors adorned the scene. The raw fear was infectious.

Moira was not ready to face another pair of terrified, bewildered parents yet. She wasn't ready to see their hope-filled eyes clinging onto her every word; their lives paused in anticipation and then shattered when they realized Mandy hadn't been found. It felt like the walls of the house would close in on her, suffocating her with the weight of their grief and despair.

Making a decision, Moira turned to Jonny, "I think I need a moment. I'll stay back here with Rose." *Was she being a coward?*

JONNY LOOKED AT HER, understanding filling his eyes, and nodded. He continued into the house, for he couldn't avoid the dreadful conversation that was to come. He had to tell the parents that their daughter was missing. They would cry and scream and maybe blame him. It didn't matter; he was strong enough to take it. But, unfortunately, Moira wasn't.

Moira needed the quiet solitude of her van and time to think. She made a quick trip to a cafe for a Styrofoam cup of coffee and retreated back to the van.

Sitting in the van, with Rose on the front bench seat, she leaned her head against the dog's sturdy frame. She stroked Rose's brindle chest, the rhythm soothing her jumbled thoughts, allowing her to focus. Rose's warm presence was a comfort she had come to depend upon. She needed to think, to strategize, to find Mandy. This wasn't about her. It was about a young girl lost and scared, possibly in the hands of a monster.

She closed her eyes, allowing the darkness to wash over her. She began piecing together a mental map of the surrounding area, marking all the places a child could be taken without raising alarms. She let her instincts guide her, her years of experience painting a canvas of potential hideouts.

Then a location sprung to her mind. A derelict barn on the outskirts of town, a forsaken place where society's outcasts once sought refuge. It was sometimes frequented by the homeless, the addicts, and those running away from life. It was a known place for drug deals. Even Charity workers occasionally showed up, offering solace in the form of hot meals and blankets.

It was not an ideal location, too dirty, the chance that the killer would be seen. Yet, it was secluded, relatively off the law enforcement's radar, a den of the desperate. Could that be where Mandy was? Could that be the lair of this insidious predator?

Taking a quick gulp of her coffee, Moira resolved to explore this possibility. She knew it was a long shot, but she couldn't afford to leave any stone unturned. She owed that much to Mandy, to Sophie, to Lily.

Sipping slowly at the coffee, she tried to think of other places. Her mind wanted to wander down a rabbit hole of despair. The most likely place was a private residence, and that would be hard, if not impossible, to find. What more could they do? They had to hope that someone saw something. A van, a car, anything that could lead to who had taken Mandy. But until then, she would get Jonny to come with her to the barn, or she would go alone.

FOLLOWING his interview with the parents, Jonny emerged from the house, his face drawn and haggard under the harsh porch light. His steps were slow and heavy as he approached the van, his ordinarily bright eyes clouded with exhaustion and concern. As a seasoned detective, he'd seen more than his fair share of heartbreaking cases, but missing children always hit him hardest. He knew all too well the lifelong scars they left on families.

Moira watched him from the driver's seat, her heart aching for the burdens he bore. A tang of guilt roiled in her stomach for leaving him to face it alone. She pushed it back. If her idea found Mandy, the betrayal of letting him face the family without her would be worth it.

Their shared history had seen them through thick and thin, and they'd always managed to pull each other back from the brink of despair. This would be no different.

The idea of the old barn still lingered in her mind, tugging at her gut instinct. She knew it was a shot in the dark, but she had to follow this lead, no matter how slim. Jonny came around to the driver's side and leaned on the open window.

"How did it go?" she asked, then bit back a curse. How could she be so stupid?

"Great!" he said and sighed. "They are afraid. They gave me more information, too much. They are grasping at straws.

"I had an idea. That old barn on the edge of the common. Is it still frequented by druggies and the homeless?"

He shook his head. "Not so much. It was sealed up with Harris Fencing as dangerous. The floor gave way. There's a gaping hole into the cellar."

"I wondered if it was worth a look?"

Jonny frowned, "The barn? Really, Moira? It's probably just another dead end."

She could see he was tired, and that was stopping him from thinking. "I know it's a long shot, but it's remote, desolate. The cellar could be a good place to hide someone."

"I don't know. It's late, and I have paperwork. The team to direct."

"I know. The team already knows what they are doing. You are probably right. It is probably a waste of time. But, I'm going, Jonny," Moira retorted, her voice firm. "It's close, desolate, and it's worth a try. I'm going with or without you."

For a moment, he just looked at her, a playful glint sparking in his eyes despite the situation. "I forgot how pretty you are when you're angry," he said, a smirk tugging at his lips.

Moira rolled her eyes, but she couldn't suppress a smile. "I should slap you for that."

He chuckled, "It wouldn't be the first time. But when does a guy get slapped for a compliment?"

"It's a strange world," Moira shrugged, suppressing a grin. Her heart pounded in her chest. It was this camaraderie, this shared understanding, that made working with Jonny bearable, even in the most dire of situations. "Are you coming?"

He gave her a nod, "Yes."

"Jump in."

"Aren't you going to put the dog in the back?"

"No, she'll put up with you, or I can put you in the back!" Moira assured him, patting Rose's head.

Jonny walked around, slid onto the bench seat next to Rose, and buckled his seatbelt.

Moira buckled Rose into the other belt, took a moment to gather herself, and then started the van. As they set off toward the barn, her mind raced, and her gut churned with a swirl of anxiety and determination. Was she making the right call? Was this trip going to lead them to Mandy, or was it merely a distraction from the real investigation?

Only time would tell, but for now, she would follow her instincts, as she always did. And Jonny, ever the supportive partner, was along for the ride. So together, Moira, Jonny, and Rose, each carrying their silent hopes and fears, ventured into the unknown.

Because at the end of the day, they were all driven by the same unwavering desire - to bring Mandy home.

THE OLD BARN

DESPITE THE MOON'S GLOW, the night was dark and ominous. Moira maneuvered her van along the unkempt road, her headlights cutting through the encroaching darkness. Rose was perched on the bench seat between Moira and Jonny, her alert eyes following the van's movement as they journeyed into uncertainty.

"Let's keep our expectations in check," Jonny warned, his deep voice vibrating through the interior of the vehicle. "This place is ram shackled and likely too public to suit our guy." He looked worn out, his eyelids heavier than before.

Moira knew he was right, but she had to look. Why were her instincts pulling her here?

The barn came into view, standing like a monolith from a forgotten era, its decrepit structure veiled under the moonlight. As the headlights of the van shone on the entrance, Moira saw a blue Vauxhall race past them, its wheels kicking up a cloud of dust.

Her gut tightened. "That car, Jonny," she said, her gaze locked onto the fleeing vehicle as it disappeared in her mirror.

He squinted into the twilight, tracking the car. "Damn, it's too fast. By the time we spin around, it'll be gone."

Moira was torn between giving chase and investigating the barn. She was in the driver's seat, yet it felt like she was not in control. Was the answer driving away or waiting inside the barn? Each decision seemed to hold a consequence that she wasn't sure she was ready to face.

Jonny flicked on his radio and relayed the car's description. "Blue Vauxhall, leaving the vicinity of the barn now. Stop and search. Over."

The radio buzzed with affirmations, the local units promising to intercept.

Moira let out a sigh. They were close, still at the scene. She trusted them to do their jobs, and she had her own to focus on.

With a sigh, she directed the van toward the barn, parking it with the headlights illuminating the cavernous entrance. It looked eerie in the artificial light. The shadowed corners seemed to hold sinister secrets. She could almost taste the bitterness of fear in the air, an invisible fog of dread. She looked over at Rose, the loyal dog meeting her gaze with a determination that eased her tension slightly.

"Ready, girl?" she asked, her hand brushing over the dog's brindle coat. Rose nuzzled her hand, a silent agreement. She was always ready.

As they got out of the van, the barn seemed to grow in size, a titan made of old wood and weathered stones. The smell of decay and damp earth filled Moira's nostrils, and the taste of rust lingered on her tongue. Joined by a melody of whispering trees and a fading horizon. The barn had seen better days; now, it was a husk of what it used to be, left to rot in solitude.

Moira moved first, Rose at her side, Jonny just a step behind. This time there was no tracking harness.

This was a search, not a track. She held out the bag and let Rose sniff once more. There was no need for commands. The dog understood that this was a different setup and began to sniff the air and ground.

The barn door creaked under her touch, a mournful sound that echoed in the stillness. She could feel the cold seeping in through her fleece and could almost feel the damp earth beneath her feet. She let Rose of the lead, and the dog began her search. To a casual observer, she looked like she was having fun, and Moira guessed she was, but she was also serious. Testing every drop of air and every surface for a trace of Mandy and the chance to win her prize.

The barn was filled with discarded remnants of what once might have been a prosperous place. Broken tools, shrouded furniture, and other relics of the past. A shaft of moonlight entered through a crack in the ceiling, spotlighting the dust motes that danced in the air. The scent of old hay was pungent, a reminder of the barn's past life.

As they moved deeper into the barn, Moira felt her heart pounding in her chest, every creak of the old wood, every rustle of the wind outside amplifying her senses. She watched Rose stop in a corner and then move on. The steady rhythm of the dog's breathing providing a strange comfort.

Was the barn just an empty structure, or did it hide something more sinister? She could feel her skin prickling, her pulse thundering in her ears. Every step seemed to bring a new wave of anticipation. The shadows danced in the corners of her eyes, making her see things that weren't there.

She was not alone in her fear. She could see the tension in Jonny's posture, the way his hand unconsciously balled into a fist. Despite his previous comment about keeping expectations in check, his body language suggested he was bracing himself.

They continued their search, the barn now a labyrinth of shadows and mystery. The fear was palpable, a living entity amongst them. But Moira knew better than to let fear control her. She had Rose, she had Jonny, and above all, she had her determination.

The barn held its secrets well, but they were resolute in uncovering them, one creaking floorboard at a time. As they made their way deeper into the barn, their flashlights casting long, looming shadows, the silence felt heavier, suffocating.

Then, Rose paused, her muscles tensing as her gaze fixed on a shadowed corner. Moira felt her heart skip a beat. She crouched down beside Rose, her hand on the dog's back, and shone her flashlight in the direction Rose was looking.

"What is it, girl?" she whispered, her voice barely audible in the silence of the barn. There was tension in the air, a charge that prickled on the back of her neck. The dog's muscles were shaking with anticipation or fear. She didn't know. And then, they heard it. A soft, muffled sound came from the corner.

They moved toward it, Moira's breath hitching as her flashlight fell upon a discarded blanket. She reached out, her fingers trembling as she pulled away the material to reveal...

It was empty. Nothing but a trapped bird that flapped its wings and took off into the night, its terrified chirp echoing in the quiet barn.

Her heart still pounded in her chest, but it was not the discovery she had feared. She exchanged a look with Jonny, and they shared a breath of relief.

They moved on. Moira's heart pounded a relentless rhythm in her chest as she observed the dog weaving in and out of the maze of darkness.

Rose's lean, tiger-striped form glided like a phantom through the spectral light. Her nostrils flared, tasting the night for any hint of the missing girl. Moira could only marvel at her dog's intense focus despite the distractions surrounding them. Needles, empty laughing gas canisters, discarded bottles, and other evidence of clandestine activities littered the ground. The barn was less a derelict structure and more a refuge for those existing on society's fringes.

At the barn's darkest corner, they came upon a couple of disheveled figures huddled together against the biting cold. The sharp smell of desperation hung heavily in the air. Jonny approached them. His expression was both stern and sympathetic. His words flowed in a low, soothing murmur, blending with the wind's soft whispers. "Have you seen a young girl?"

The inhabitants of the barn mumbled incoherently, their eyes vacant and lost, but one thing was clear: no young girl had sought shelter here recently. Jonny, drawing on his years of experience and contacts, resolved to help get them to a hostel. As he moved away to make a call, Moira found herself admiring his compassion within such grim circumstances.

Moira heard his radio and caught the last half of the conversation. "Just a couple of kids making out."

He cursed and turned to her with a wry smile. "Romantic," Jonny scoffed, his voice heavy with sarcasm. "Hey love, fancy making out at a drug den?" Moira couldn't help but laugh, her anxiety momentarily quelled by the absurdity of the situation.

But their levity was fleeting. The hours were slipping by, and Rose's search had yielded no scent of Mandy. With each passing minute, each fruitless search hammered another nail into the coffin of hope. Despair was a bitter pill to swallow, and as the night advanced, it began to take root in their hearts.

Despite the creeping fear, Moira never wavered. She continued to traverse the shadowed landscape, encouraging Rose while exchanging updates with Jonny. The barn was a dead-end, but it was only one of many places Mandy could be. They had more ground to cover and more darkness to penetrate. For Moira, giving up was not an option. As long as there was a shred of hope, she would chase it. No matter how elusive, no matter how terrifying the journey.

THE COMING STORM

THE NEXT DAY all Moira did was walk around with the picture of the doll. She stalked the high street and then the posher shops on Steep Hill. Rose was with her, the dog patiently following wherever she led. In Moira's head, there was a ticking clock. Her mind tried to wander to what Mandy must be thinking, how she must be feeling, but she dared not go there. That way lay madness and inaction, for it threatened to freeze her heart.

She approached another group of people, university students enjoying the sunshine on their lunch breaks. Their carefree faces laughing and happy. "Do you recognize this doll?"

A girl with pink hair laughed. "No, but it's creepy."

The other girls crowded around, almost jumping over their friends to look. Giggles and shakes of the head, and they were off, heading for a lunchtime drink. Moira walked on, her day an unyielding tapestry of faces and voices, the city's streets acting as her canvas. She'd walked the breadth and length of Lincoln, the doll's picture gripped in her hand, desperately seeking someone to shed light on its origin. The words of rejection had begun to blend into a hum of discouragement, and she could feel the weight of each "no" pressing down on her.

It was nearing 3 pm when she felt the buzzing of her phone, a lifeline in a sea of dead ends. It was Jonny suggesting they meet at a pub near the Brayford Pool, a break she desperately needed. He knew about Rose, of course, but reassured her that the place was dog friendly.

The wear of the day tugged at the corners of Moira's eyes as she rounded the familiar corner near the Brayford Pool. The water of the inland dock was a beautiful sight dotted with pleasure boats and gleaming in the sunshine. It was quieter here, and the city's insistent buzz reduced to a dull thrum in the distance.

Turning her back on the pool, she pushed through the door of the welcoming pub, Rose padding in step beside her, her fur blending seamlessly with the weathered wooden floors.

Across the room, a pair of familiar eyes locked with hers. Jonny sat at a corner table, a half-eaten sandwich abandoned in favor of a thin stack of papers. He looked up, his gaze momentarily drawn to her. In the corner, his back to the window, he was haloed in the dim light, and a flicker of something passed between them. It was gone as soon as it appeared, replaced by a shared sense of determination, the unspoken reality of their grim task.

Their lunch was a dance of conversation and shared glances. Jonny's voice washed over her, an island of calm in the tempest of her thoughts, his words intertwining with the steam from their coffees. The trivial details of their shared meal, the texture of the bread, the crunch of the lettuce, and the succulence of the meat, became an interlude, a sweet suspension of the gritty reality outside.

His gaze fell on her, an undercurrent of shared affection mirrored in the low hum of conversation around them. As he looked, his hand went to his scar, and she wondered if it bothered him. It was a silly question. Many of his colleagues had teased him over the years. When he first brought in arrests, he would be asked who was arresting who. He took it all well, and she wondered if it was why he never courted for long. A series of one-night stands could hardly be called courting.

Moira pulled her eyes back to the conversation. A question remained unasked as Jonny's eyes lingered on her face a moment longer than necessary before darting back to the papers. It was a dance they had mastered, weaving affection with professional necessity, preserving the precious space they occupied between the unspoken and the acknowledged.

The evidence, however, was almost nonexistent. The case had gone nowhere. All they had was that witnesses had seen a possible van, its color shrouded in uncertainty as though it was a chameleon fading into the crowd. "Could be brown, blue, black...transit, Renault, Peugeot," Jonny rattled off, his voice a steady stream against the increasing tension.

Moira's response was automatic, "And the driver?"

Jonny merely shook his head, their shared silence amplifying the weight of their unanswered questions.

"It hasn't hit the papers yet," Moira said.

Jonny rubbed a hand across his scar. The pain in his eyes was deep. The words hung in the air between them, and the mood shifted. Anxious anticipation of a media frenzy once another body dropped. The coming media storm would be brutal for them and for the parents. It could, however, be useful for the investigation. Still, they both wanted to avoid that, both the media circus and the body. However, a media call for dashcam footage and witnesses might break the case. Jonny was no doubt happy that the decision to make that call was not his. Tension knotted the air as their half-eaten sandwiches curled at the corners, a tangible reminder of the ticking clock.

The reality of the situation was clear - they were not just battling against a villain but also against time. And each passing second was a step closer to the horrifying truth hitting the news or the more horrifying sight of Mandy's body if they didn't break the case in time.

They avoided the topic, tiptoeing around the precipice of what it would mean. A city in fear, parents clutching their children tighter, streets filled with the echoes of a nameless dread. The unspoken 'if' had silently morphed into a dreadful 'when.' A silent agreement passed between them, their eyes reflecting the shared dread of an impending storm. It was the dread of knowing the terror that awaited, the shattering silence before the city's heartbeat echoed with the news of another lost child.

THE COLLECTOR

IN THE MEAGER daylight seeping through the grime-coated window of Clara's home, the shadows danced with an eerie quality, and they made Graham Lawrence's heart sing. It was time.

The scene was uncanny, the house's peeling paint revealing a past no longer reflected in its present. Part of him wanted to buy the place, to restore it to its original glory, to fill it with dolls to buy, but he had to be careful. People talked, and he was a respected accountant. He forced himself to limit his visits to Clara. However, he had stayed away long enough, as long as he could, and the three dolls that peered from behind the grimy window filled his heart with joy. Their glassy eyes were an echo of innocent childhood companions, and he couldn't wait to meet them.

Graham licked his lips and swallowed as he stepped over the threshold into the once-doll emporium. The aroma of the place was a strange brew of dust, old fabrics, and faint traces of mildew. He loved it here and was always so excited to come back.

Clara Sutton, a diminutive figure shrouded in a frayed floral print dress, sat in her chair by the window already talking, her reedy voice twining around the room.

"Them three, they've been bad," she said, a spindly finger jabbing towards the window. "They need new homes... or something dreadful will come upon them."

Graham, a rotund man with a ruddy complexion under a thinning cover of brown hair, approached the trio in question. His eyes, always a touch too wide, seemed to hold a hungry quality as they assessed each porcelain face. His pink tongue darted out, wetting his thin lips in a reptilian manner.

Graham moved with an unhurried grace, stopping before the window, delaying his gratification just a few more seconds. It was best to take your time to check everything, and his eyes glanced around the room. Nothing had changed. The table with dolls, materials, and an old-fashioned sewing machine. Clara's faded chair and the lump in the corner. He ignored that and looked back at the window. The anticipation was too much now, and his hand reached out as a sigh passed his lips.

His pudgy fingers gently cradled each doll, assessing its weight, texture, and details. Stroking the soft velvet of the dress, taking in the scent of each doll and relishing the feel of it in his hands. Strong, real, solid, and soon to be his.

The doll's glassy eyes bore into his, and he seemed to search their depths for something only he understood. Which should he have? Could he take them all? Should he take them all? They needed homes, better homes, and he could give that to them.

His breath was coming fast now with the anticipation of making a choice. It was so delicious, but he would hold back. One was all he would take — today.

In the corner, hidden in the shadow, Peter Sutton let out a grunt. An oversized, misshapen figure, Peter was Clara's son, a product of an unforgiving past. His low grunts echoed around the room, an eerie accompaniment to the tableau.

Oh, which one? Graham licked his lips almost tasting the dolls, but he couldn't decide. There had never been this much choice, and he wanted them all. No, hold back. You must be cautious, a voice inside warned.

After much contemplation, Graham selected one of the dolls. Its Victorian garb was impeccably crafted, the stitched lace and red satin radiating a timeless charm. He cradled it gently in his arms, his movements almost reverential, as if he was holding something infinitely precious.

"Ah, my dear," he crooned, his voice barely above a whisper. His eyes were locked onto the doll, a strange, affectionate smile tugging at the corners of his lips.

"Isobel was naughty," Clara said as she watched him. "She pushed Daisy and knocked her over. She will need discipline."

Graham's eyes widened with anticipation. "I can give her that," he said in a raspy whisper as he handed over a crisp £20 note.

Graham watched Clara as her hand shot out to take the note. His sharp eyes missed nothing. Her fingernails were long and filled with dirt. A chill ran down his spine at the thought of those nails touching his girls, but he ignored it. She needed the money; the dolls needed homes. As he hugged Isobel to him, Clara looked away from Graham and his new purchase, focusing instead on the cluster of dolls waiting patiently in the cabinet and the four sitting around the table waiting for their tea.

As Graham left the store, he glanced back, the doll cradled securely in his arms but beneath his jacket. She would be safe there. No prying eyes could see his girls.

The two remaining porcelain faces stared back at him from the window, a groan left him at the thought of leaving them, and he almost turned back. Almost but he managed to walk away. One thing he was very good at was self-control. He had been taught that lesson well.

With a final nod to Clara, he disappeared into the twilight, leaving the Suttons in their decaying home.

ONCE GRAHAM WAS GONE, Clara sank into her worn armchair, the hush of the room pressing in on her. Peter grunted again, his dark silhouette looming larger in the corner of her vision. The faint echo of Graham's voice lingered in the room, a chilling reminder of the visitors who sought comfort in Clara's creations.

Anger surged through her at the thought of letting her children go. She picked up the doll she was working on and threw it across the room, screaming as she let it go.

The day drew to a close, the dwindling light giving the room a desolate air. Clara's eyes rested on the dolls once again. Their innocent expressions seemed to waver in the dimming light, leaving her with a gnawing sense of unease. Something felt off, but she pushed the feeling away, disappearing back into her world of porcelain children.

THE SECOND DOLL

MOIRA AWOKE to the harsh trill of her mobile phone. At first, she pushed the sound away, stretching out her legs and catching the lump that was Rose lying at the bottom of the bed. The dog grunted but didn't move.

Curling into the duvet, her brain shrieked for the noise to stop. It stabbed into her skull like a knife, and all she wanted was just a few more minutes. Then she realized what the ringing meant. A wave of nausea rolled over her, and she bolted upright, fumbling for the phone.

It was still dark, the quiet hours of the early morning interrupted by the digital shrieking that had torn her from a fitful sleep. She reached again, a lack of coordination from lack of sleep making her fingers clumsy. The cool brick slipped away, and she couldn't grasp it. The noise seemed to grow more incessant, and her heart pounded in time to its rings. At last, her fingers gripped the slippery, shrieking herald of doom. Blinking to clear her fuzzy head, she pulled the device from beneath the pillow she'd buried it under to help her forget the inevitable call. She knew what today was. The 4th morning since Mandy went missing. That was why she was so tired, why her mind would not switch off last night.

"Yeah," she said.

The voice on the other end belonged to Jonny, his words curt, clipped with urgency. "We found Mandy."

The sentence hung in the air like a guillotine, its weight bearing down on Moira. The reality of it was a sharp jab to her already weary heart. She ran a hand over her face, the taste of dread sour on her tongue. They were too late. Another life was gone. Another failure.

She let out a sigh that carried the resignation of a soldier heading back to the front lines when they knew the battle was lost. "Where?" she asked, already knowing the answer. Why hadn't she thought of this before? If she had, they could have staked the place out.

"The same playground as Sophie," came the stark reply. It was clear that Jonny bore the same guilt. They shouldn't have. No one would expect him to use the same place.

The silence that followed was pregnant with unspoken horror. They both knew what this meant. The confirmation of their worst fears was a bitter pill to swallow. The knot in her stomach tightened, the all-too-familiar metallic taste of fear filling her mouth. She reached over to her bedside table, her fingers fumbling for her light.

"I'm on my way," she responded, her voice carrying a grim resolution.

AS SHE DROVE to the playground, Rose safe in her crate in the back of the van, the sky began to lighten. Few cars were on the road, and the haunting sight of the cathedral hovered above the city.

Usually, it gave her solace, but today it seemed to be mocking her.

Stop this!

The sky changed from pitch black to a murky gray, and the sun behind her was no doubt resplendent, but in front, the reluctant dawn was hesitant to illuminate the gruesome tableau that awaited.

Moira drove her van past police vans and was waved into the car park of the playground. She wondered when the media would get wind of this. The police had released very little about Sophie's death, it had hardly made the columns, but some journalist would notice a second vast police presence at the playground on the West common. The story would be out before long.

The playground was swarming with uniformed Police Constables. Milling around like ants, their faces white, their expressions grim. Many would never expect to see this in Lincoln. It was a small place, rural, and relatively crime-free. They expected to be dealing with parades and traffic offenses. No doubt, this had been a harsh awakening.

Vehicles, some with their blue lights flashing, were a stark contrast against the innocent backdrop of the swings and slides, their flashing lights painting the scene in a grim, surreal glow.

Moira crossed the boundary marked by the police tape, past a pasty-faced young PC. He waved her on, and she gave him a nod. She was closer now, her heart pounding an uneven rhythm against her rib cage. As she approached the foreboding white forensic tent at the center of the playground, it felt like walking toward a dreadful inevitability. For a moment, she wondered if this was how the condemned felt when they were walking to their death. It was something that had always intrigued her. How did a man walk to their death? Shaking her head, she blew out a breath. Her mind was doing a normal human coping behavior, escaping the horror awaiting it by concentrating on trivia, but it didn't help. Now she had to think about Mandy and the other lost girls that would surely follow.

Jonny came out of the tent to meet her, the pallor of his face a testament to the horrors that lay within. He nodded at her in silent acknowledgment, his eyes heavy with exhaustion.

"Same as before?" she questioned, pulling on the latex gloves handed to her by a PC.

Jonny's confirmation came in the form of a nod. He seemed too weary for words.

Moira took a breath and steadied herself. Here they went again down the rabbit hole into the mind of a psychopath.

Stepping into the tent was a descent into a nightmarish reality. Mandy's lifeless body lay mercilessly before them. For a moment, Moira's vision closed down to a dot, and she wondered if she would faint. Closing her eyes and biting her lip, she pulled herself back. No matter how she felt, this was not about her, and she owed the victim her best.

She opened her eyes and took in the horror. Like Sophie, Mandy was wearing a plain white linen robe. She was lying on the bright blue and red merry-go-round, a spot of purity against the garish colors, all now covered by the tent.

The sight of her white-clad body against that implement of fun was like a punch to the guts. Moira swallowed down bile and took a breath, closing her eyes. A young life had been snuffed out too soon. There was no time for her to fall apart, and yet she felt it hard not to. Closing her eyes, she bit her lip again.

Hold on, you can do this.

Opening her eyes, she looked at Mandy not as a young girl, her hopes and dreams ripped away from her too soon, but as a piece of evidence.

Mandy was holding the inevitable doll. This one had blonde ringlets, a hair fashion left in the 1800s. The doll was dressed in an unnerving mimicry of Mandy's last attire. Blue jeans and a flowered top. The clothes were a perfect match for the photo of Mandy's clothes they had been shown. Was that why the girls were dressed in white, so he could dress the dolls in their clothes? Or was the gown to remove evidence?

The doll's face bore a scratch, a disconcerting discrepancy as Mandy's face was perfect and bore no such mark. The sight sent an icy shiver skittering down Moira's spine. Evidence, she reminded herself and bit back a cry. *Sorry, Mandy, but I have to think of you as evidence.*

Did the scratch mean something, or was in coincidental?

The dimly lit tent seemed to close in on Moira as she studied the doll's face. It was an unnerving facsimile of Mandy, and that scratch—it couldn't be a mere coincidence. She felt her mind race, churning like the uneasy feeling in her stomach. Was it deliberate? A message? Or merely a coincidence?

"Moira," Jonny's voice pulled her back to the present. "What have you seen?"

"It's the doll," she replied, her voice barely above a whisper. "There's a scratch on its face. Mandy's face is perfect. I don't know... is it a random defect; it feels intentional."

Jonny was silent for a beat. "Could it be a message?"

"I don't know," Moira admitted, frustration lacing her voice. "It could be deliberate. It could be coincidence. We need more information, Jonny. We need more dolls."

The room seemed to drop several degrees; she couldn't believe she had said that. She didn't mean it, for more dolls, would mean more dead girls.

Silence stretched between them. The words hung heavily in the air, their implications sinking into Moira's bones. She felt sick, regret gnawing at her.

How she wished she could take back those words, but they were the ugly truth.

"We'll find another way," Jonny finally said, his voice soft, understanding the torment in Moira's mind. "We won't let it come to that."

"I hope so," Moira murmured, her eyes still fixed on the doll's scratched face. The evidence was there, a puzzle missing pieces. They had to solve it before another life was lost. But the scratch, the message—if it was a message—left them with more questions than answers.

The bitter bile of frustration burned in the back of her throat. They were back to square one, despite their tireless efforts. They had no tangible leads, no fingerprints, no stray DNA. The killer was precise, deliberate, and seemingly untouchable. There had been nothing on the previous body, and Moira would lay odds on there being nothing on this one.

Moira glanced at Jonny. He was staring at Mandy, a haunted look in his eyes. She knew he was thinking the same thing. They needed evidence. A break. Something.

"Thoughts?" Jonny asked, his voice low and strained. He, too, was grappling with the helplessness of their situation.

"Was there another note?"

He nodded and turned to a table at the side of the tent where evidence was stacked in boxes. There were bags and bags of rubbish, all neatly tagged. Most probably, nothing would be obtained from this, it was simply here at the scene, but everything would be fingerprinted and checked. Jonny pulled a bag from one of the boxes. Inside was the same paper as the first one.

'Unveiling 2,

Are we having fun?

☺

Anger surged through Moira, but she bit it down. The sick beast thought this was fun. Was she dealing with a psychopath?

She sighed, rubbing her temples. "Whoever we're dealing with, they're thorough, meticulous, someone who enjoys staging these scenes and playing with us. Or this is a compulsion that they have to carry out.

The dolls... there's a narrative here, a story he's telling us, something he's controlling. The notes are a game and a brag. He is better than us," she mused aloud. "But we need more than theories, Jonny. We need evidence."

"I know." He wrung his hands.

"Do we know how Sophie died yet?" Moira asked for the bodies were so clean, no bruises, no obvious sign of trauma.

Jonny nodded. "The autopsy came back. It was cyanide."

Moira felt a flush of hope. "You have to be able to find the source of that."

"So far, we've had no luck. There are many sources in the city, industrial, labs, colleges, and apparently, you can make the stuff or buy it on the dark web."

"We have to find something," she said.

He met her gaze, a quiet determination flaring in his eyes. "Then we'll find it, Moira. We have no other choice."

As she exited the tent, the horrifying image of Mandy and her dollish counterpart remained etched in her mind. This was more than just a killing spree. This was a grand performance, a cruel game orchestrated by a puppet master who was all too content watching his dolls dance on their strings. It was a stark reminder that time was of the essence, and right now, the killer was winning.

Moira walked to her van, feeling out of control. She could go home, but Mandy never would. Glancing back, the tent was a haunting reminder of the killer's twisted game and the invisible clock ticking away in the background.

The game was far from over, but for Mandy, time had run out. And for the killer? Time was just another tool, a weapon to wield in a twisted game of life and death. And right now, he was winning.

ENDLESS HOURS

THE EARLY MORNING light was the color of molten gold, spilling across the operations room at police headquarters. Its brightness hurt her eyes as it streaked across the cluttered desk where Moira sat, hunched over a notepad and staring at a screen. The 48-inch flat screen on the wall was broadcasting the news, the reporter's voice nothing more than white noise in the background of her frantic thoughts.

The words "These two lonely girls will not be forgotten" from the journalist on the TV punctured the air like a bullet, shattering her focus. Her blood ran cold. Rage swelled up inside her, a hot and pulsating fury at her own failure. She gripped her pen so tightly that it shattered in her hand. The guilt and regret tasted bitter and metallic on her tongue.

Dropping the pen, she turned to the TV. Tired eyes scanned the countless faces that flickered across the screen - all the missing, all the lost. Every child became Mandy. Every parent's pain was her own. She felt a knot tighten in her stomach as she realized that all she could offer was empathy, but what they needed was answers. She had been so sure she could make a difference and save these girls from the monster that lurked in the shadows. Yet, here she was, feeling like she was drowning in a sea of unknowns.

The scent of stale coffee wafted in the air as Moira turned back to her desk, her eyes straining to make sense of the blurry CCTV images, the countless number plates caught on the Automatic Number Plate Recognition cameras or the ANPR for short, and the myriad of faces recorded by dashcam and doorbell footage. Every van, every suspicious figure, and every unfamiliar face was scrutinized, analyzed, and cross-referenced. It felt like looking for a needle in a haystack.

A team of special police officers was already doing this. She had given them pointers on what to look for. Not that it was rocket science, vans, cars stopping, suspicious behavior, but there were no cameras in the area they needed, and the further they went away, the more they had to look at. Her notepad had over 50 vehicles to check, and her heart told her that none of them would be the killer. It was just endless hours of wasted time.

Next to her desk, her trusted companion, Rose, lay sprawled on her jacket, her snout buried in her paws. The Boxer's deep, rhythmic breathing was a comforting soundtrack amidst the chaos. A fleeting smile crossed Moira's face as she watched the dog sleep. It was a slice of normalcy in an otherwise warped world.

Her mobile rang, the shrill tone echoing in the room. It was Jonny. His voice was strained, laced with the same sense of fatigue and frustration that weighed on her own shoulders.

"Anything?" he asked, though the defeat in his voice suggested he already knew the answer. Moira shook her head, forgetting he couldn't see her. "No," she replied, her voice barely a whisper. "Lots of vans, 4 x 4's to check, but nothing to point at any of them."

Moira rubbed at her temples, the throbbing ache there a cruel reminder of sleepless nights and relentless worry. Each second that passed was another second the killer remained on the loose, another second their monster was free to take another life. When would he choose the next girl? How could they stop it?

"How about you?" she asked.

"The canvass has brought up nothing so far. I've looked into the local pervs. They all have alibis. We're pulling a few people in for questioning but reviewing their files... none of them call out to me on this one."

He stopped; she knew he wanted her to give him a magic bullet. To provide the answer, but she couldn't, not yet, maybe not ever. *Stop it!* She pushed the defeat away. Mistakes would be made, and they would find this monster; the only problem was when. "I'll take a look at them," she said. "I think they should release the dolls to the public. We need to find out where they are coming from, and that would help."

"The boss doesn't want to do it. He thinks it will be the way we prove who it is."

Moira shook her head and closed her eyes. "I understand, but... we need the public to help us, and if they know about the dolls, they could help us find their origin. I think it's important.

"Ok, I'll talk to him."

"Good." Moira felt as if she was getting somewhere, and there was silence between them. For a moment, she wondered if he had gone.

"What could make a man do this?" Jonny asked. She could almost see his clenched jaw, the scar more prominent because of the tension in his face.

"It's not that easy. Sure, there could have been a catalyst, a death, a rejection, but some people just have urges that are wrong." She swallowed and tried to lubricate her dry throat. "Some people just like to see others suffer."

He let out a long whistle. "I'm glad I'm not in your mind."

"Be glad you're not in his."

"It's definitely a man?" he asked.

Moira wasn't sure about much, but she was sure about this. Though the attention to detail could have pointed to a woman, as could the dolls and the doll's clothes, which the killer had obviously fashioned themselves, she still knew it was a man. "It's a white male with a chip on his shoulder, but I can't tell you much more than that."

"What makes you think he has a chip on his shoulder?" Jonny asked; the dread had left his voice, replaced by a hint of excitement. If he could find something to help the case, he was all over it. You could hear the fatigue lifting with the promise of a clue.

"He wants us to see how clever he is. That was why he went back to the same place. That won't happen again; however, steak it out anyway as he could visit it for thrills. To relive the moment. It's why he leaves the notes." She had no more, and her voice trailed off. Most of what she was coming up with was instinct.

The sound of voices on the line. "Okay," Jonny said but not to her. "I have to go; call me if you get anything else. We must stop this." Then he was gone.

An icy chill ran down Moira's spine as the magnitude of their situation settled over her. She had always known the job would be hard. She had braced herself for the long hours, the constant uncertainty, the crushing weight of responsibility. But nothing could have prepared her for this - the all-encompassing dread, the overwhelming helplessness, the desperate need to solve the puzzle that was one step out of her reach.

As she stared at the cascade of vehicles flickering across her screens, she made a silent vow to herself. She would find this monster, she would bring him to justice, and she would ensure that no more 'lonely girls' would be forgotten.

AMONGST THE SHADOWS

THE ONCE BUSTLING town was now a ghost of its former self, transformed into a barren landscape of fear and suspicion. As Samuel pulled his trolley along the street, things looked different. Parents held their daughters close. Worried looks filled their eyes as they scanned the shadows. The echoes of laughter from the playgrounds had been replaced by the eerie silence of deserted streets. The swings left empty creaked and rattled as the wind moved their vacant seats. The merry-go-rounds were silent and still.

It made him sad, for all he wanted was everyone to have the same chance. He picked up another bag of clothes left on the doorstep for him. Samuel Fletcher, a tall and lean man in his early fifties, had been working these streets for twenty years. He moved through the quiet streets with an air of resignation. Another bag, more promise for his cause. What cause was it today? He looked at the bag; the writing was red. That was a heart disease charity. The bag was thrown into his trolley on top of many more. Each treasure was to be sorted, washed, and sold in the shops that relied on the good heart of the city's people to keep themselves and their causes going. For a moment, he wondered if the bags contained better clothes than he was wearing. He pushed the thoughts aside; he would be allowed to take his pick. That was something.

Sammy, as some of his regulars liked to call him, sported a thin beard. He caught his reflection in a window and stood a little taller. The beard was new this year; it gave him a touch of bohemian flair that he believed fit his chosen career. As he picked up another bag off a doorstep, the owner came out.

"Sammy, it's good to see you."

"You too, Mrs. Wilkins. How are you?"

"I'm good... terrible business... terrible. You keep an eye out; you hear me. You make sure all the girls get home, and if you see anyone suspicious, you tell the bobbies."

"Don't worry, I will do. This is our city. No one can get away with this for long."

She nodded and retreated inside.

Sammy felt a touch of warmth. It was good to be liked and respected. To be considered the community protector. Was that what he was now?

For so many years, he had merely blended into the backdrop, the kind of man you could pass in the street without a second glance. But now, people were glad that he was there, keeping a watchful eye on the girls and streets.

It was boring walking up and down, so he developed a game. He liked to imagine what was going on behind the curtains. What secrets were hidden from view? Some of the ones he imagined were quite saucy. Mrs. Wilkin had been a widow these last five years, and he often imagined that she had a liaison with the milkman. A chuckle escaped him. The street no longer had a milkman.

His hands were calloused from years of labor, his eyes bearing the weariness of a man who's seen too much of life's harsher side. As a charity worker, his life was devoted to helping others, a calling he fulfilled with quiet dignity, or so he told himself. He was a champion, and he would ignore the looks people gave him. He was doing good, clearing up the streets. Recycling things into something better.

He passed a poster telling people to recycle, and he chuckled again. The youth of today were fools. They blamed his generation for all the wrongs, forgetting that we never had wet wipes or plastic milk bottles. No, the milkman was the first really green industry, and it had gone for the sake of convenience. He wondered if the milkman would have seen the killer. A shudder went down his spine, and he realized he had stopped. There were another six streets to do. At this rate, it would take all day.

With a roll of his eyes at the poster, he walked on. His routine had changed little despite the escalating terror. Each day, he either dropped charity bags through letter boxes or collected the bags of clothing left outside the doors of the houses he passed. His brawny arms heaved the weighty bags with ease, though his back was starting to grumble at the heavier ones.

The only difference now was the suspicious glances, the lingering stares from behind curtained windows, and the hushed whispers that seemed to follow him.

On the corner of Park Street, a group of teenage girls huddled together on a bench, their giggling whispers breaking the hush. Samuel paused, studying them from a distance. They were a little older than the girls that had gone missing... died... murdered. Maybe 15 or 16. He saw the fear beneath their brave smiles, their youthful recklessness battling against the harsh reality that had infiltrated their sanctuary. But they would not admit it. Their laughs were a little too much, their smiles a little forced, but they always came here, and no creep was ruining their lives. They had that arrogance of youth that believes it never happens to them. That it's someone else's problem.

A small frown tugged at his lips, and he moved towards them.

"Best head home, girls," Samuel said, his voice gruff yet imbued with a protective undertone. "Ain't safe out here no more."

The girls glanced at him, their giggles dying abruptly. One by one, they nodded, gathering their things with a newfound seriousness before scampering off down the street. It was as if his words had been a relief. They gave them the excuse to leave when not one of them wanted to be the first to admit they were afraid.

He chuckled. Before this, they would have given him a mouthful of abuse if he had dared to tell them to leave. Maybe, there was some good in the situation.

He grabbed another bag and threw it into the cart he was pulling. *Oh, that one was heavy.* His back twinged as he hauled it over the side. The trolley was nearly full. He would do the three houses to the end of this row and then return to his van.

A POLICE constable named Davies had spent the day knocking on doors and asking if anyone had seen anything in the area. His feet ached, and his brain felt as if it had melted. No one had seen anything. Half the houses were empty, the people were out at work. Of the others, he got three reactions, indifference, annoyance, or the lonely ladies who invited him in, gave him tea and cake, and wanted to talk for hours. He grimaced, remembering the third house he had been invited into today. It was nearing lunch, and he had accepted the offer of tea and an Eccles cake. The tea was good and strong, but as he bit into the cake, a strange musty taste flooded his mouth. When he looked at the cake, blue mold was growing on the bottom. He spat the mouthful out, much to the annoyance of the woman.

"What are you doing?" she shrieked.

"It's moldy." He couldn't believe it, was it dangerous?

"No," she said and then turned her own cake over and saw the blue mold growing there. "Oh, sorry, my children don't come to see me anymore, and I still bake for them."

Davies hadn't known whether to be sorry for her or disgusted at that point. And, of course, she had seen nothing to help him.

It was nearly the end of his shift when he saw the guy pulling the trolley. He stopped to watch Samuel's interaction with the girls. His trained eyes observed Samuel, taking in the details. Just for a moment, he wondered if this could be the killer. Only all Samuel did was tell them to be on their way. A sigh escaped him. The weight of his badge felt heavy against his chest, a constant reminder of the responsibility he bore to protect and serve.

"Mr. Fletcher," he called, nodding towards him. "You around here last night?"

Samuel shook his head, a flash of regret passing over his features. "No, officer. Terrible business, terrible... I'm 'round these parts often enough. I'll keep my eyes peeled. I promise I will."

Davies noticed something in his gaze, telling him that Samuel, the simple charity worker, had now become part of a much larger narrative. But in the midst of fear and suspicion, life moved on.

Davies continued his route, carrying the burdens of the town in his heart while the silent specter of dread lurked in the shadows, waiting for the right moment to strike again.

THE WATCHER

THE RHYTHMIC CHANT of schoolyard games echoed across the playground. A chorus of young voices, oblivious to the shadow that loomed on the periphery of their innocent world. Two boys chased each other in playful abandon, their laughter filling the crisp afternoon air with a sense of normalcy that belied the underlying tension.

Graham Lawrence sat alone, the chill of the steel park bench seeping through his impeccably tailored trousers. He was not interested in the boys and pulled his eyes from their shrieks. The girls were what he came here for.

His plump fingers caressed the porcelain face of the doll he cradled in his arms, a hint of obsession flickering in his hazel eyes. Ragged breath caught in his throat as three girls approached the fence. Now, his fingers stroked the crimson velvet of Isobel's dress. Enjoying the silky feel of it beneath his fingers. Crimson was a bad color. It said look at me, see me. I am vivacious. He let out a gasp.

Graham was a compulsive collector of Clara's dolls. She named this one Isobel. He liked it; the name felt full on his tongue. He rolled it around his mouth as he stroked the silky velvet, and another gasp escaped him as the three girls let out a shriek.

He looked at them for a long time, drinking in their differences. All had long, straight hair, unlike Isobel, and he imagined the girls in the red dress with ringlets. It was such a wonderful vision that he started to pant. Knowing he was being too obvious, he pulled his eyes back to the doll. Graham was instantly enthralled by her delicate features, her glassy blue eyes that seemed to mirror his own longing.

The gossiping girls had moved, and he wondered what naughty secrets they had whispered over, and his hands grasped the velvet dress. Two girls were skipping to his right. The sight of the skipping children stoked a burning desire within him. He watched their lithe forms, his gaze trailing the flutters of their uniform skirts, the innocent gap-toothed smiles that lit up their faces, the careless toss of their pigtailed hair. He imagined the scent of their innocence, the powdery fragrance of their youth, a longing to touch, to feel, gnawing at him from within.

His tongue darted out to wet his lips, a private, primal reaction that was unbeknownst to the world beyond his narrow focus. His heart pounded in his chest, his breath hitching as a group of girls skipped past the perimeter fence, their laughter almost tangible. He could almost taste their mirth in the air, so close and yet so far.

His fingers tightened around the doll, the porcelain face pressing into his clammy palm. The boundary of the fence seemed painfully evident, a tantalizing touch of reality that restrained his burgeoning fantasies. An involuntary shudder passed through him, the desire to sniff the air, to breathe in their presence, clawing at him. The desire to reach out and clasp his hands on the fence, maybe one day to cut through it and touch the girls. Oh, it was delicious, and he felt his breath coming faster, faster, so fast it was hard to breathe.

Suddenly, a harsh voice tore through his reverie. "Oi, you! Clear off!" A stern-faced teacher, her eyes brimming with suspicion, gestured angrily toward him.

His face flushed under her accusatory stare, the stinging rebuke a cold splash of reality. He had stayed too long, been caught, and knew that he would have to vacate the bench for at least a month. There were other schools, but this was his, the closest. Graham rose hurriedly, cradling Isobel closer as he scurried away from the schoolyard. Luckily, he didn't have far to go.

His heart pounded in his ears as he reached his pristine home just across from the schoolyard. The prim lawn, the white picket fence, and the neatly arranged flowers all belied the tumultuous storm raging within him. Walking past, he went around the back and came in that way. The last thing he wanted to do was let the teacher know where he lived. That way lay trouble. No, this was better.

With Isobel still cradled in his arms, he shuffled up the steps to his back door, his plump form lumbering heavily with each step.

Once inside, he crossed the kitchen to the living room and sunk into the soft cushioned chair by the window, Isobel still clutched tightly in his hand. His eyes flickered towards the playground, the distance no barrier to his longing. A sense of breathless anticipation filled him, his every sense on high alert, as he resumed his silent vigil.

The world outside remained oblivious to the turbulent desires that whirled within Graham's mind. The loneliness often crushed him, but this and the dolls gave him hope. He just had to be careful, his existence camouflaged by the seeming normalcy of his life.

The children continued their play, their laughter echoing hauntingly across the distance, while Graham, their silent observer, licked his lips and stared hungrily at their small faces, hands, and legs. He clung to the edges of his own distorted reality, veering dangerously close to releasing his obsession.

IN THE STAFF ROOM, Marianne Thomas, the vigilant teacher who had spotted Graham, sat hunched over her cup of tea. Acid burned in her gut, her mind racing with thoughts she wished she could dismiss. The image of the man from the schoolyard, the one with the doll and that odd, lingering gaze, refused to fade from her memory. What was he doing there?

She had seen him before; she was sure of it. That same out-of-place figure lurking in the vicinity of the school, always with a doll, always watching; today, however, had been different. She knew that was probably because of the awful killings, two girls taken and murdered in their small city. It didn't bear thinking about.

Her mind came back to the plump man. His gaze seemed more intense, his presence more pronounced. And those eyes, they were like icy shards that seemed to pierce the very fabric of their innocent playground.

When she had seen him before, she thought he was a little slow, that he was looking for friends, but could that still hold true now the world had changed?

The words of the news reporter echoed in her mind, their warnings reverberating in the quiet room. Two girls were gone, just like that. And there was no guarantee there wouldn't be a third. Marianne clenched her hands around the steaming mug, her knuckles white with tension. The children's laughter seemed to sound a little more distant now, a little more fragile.

Could the staring man be the killer? The question gnawed at her, the weight of the thought making her feel sick. He had done nothing. He was back from the fence, just taking a moment to rest... with his doll! Should she call the police? It seemed ridiculous and maybe discriminatory. The rules were so hard to follow now. You had to be so careful. Was she judging him because of his mental capacity? That way led to her losing her job, and she couldn't afford that. Not now, she was divorced.

Yet dismissing him as harmless also seemed equally perilous. She had to do something.

Sliding her phone towards her, she pulled up the number for the local police station, her fingers hovering over the screen. With a deep breath, she dialed the number. The room seemed to fall silent as she waited for the call to connect.

She wasn't sure if he was a threat, but Marianne knew that her responsibility was to her students. Their safety was her primary concern. It was better to be safe than sorry, she reasoned, her heart pounding as the call connected. She steeled herself to speak, ready to step up for the children under her care.

SHADOWS OF DREAD

IN THE DAPPLED shade of the Brayford Wharf's Garden, Moira Foster found herself locked in a battle of her own thoughts, each one darker than the one before. With each bite of her medium-rare steak, her senses were consumed not by the succulent taste but by the gnawing dread of the unseen killer she sought.

Across the table, Detective Jonny Chandler, his face creased with a hard weariness only she could truly understand, nursed his chicken tikka, the mirthful conversation around them a far cry from their own.

"Progress?" she asked, breaking the silence.

He shrugged, a grim resignation settling on his features. "Still going through CCTV, nothing yet. The arsenic leads... they've all turned out to be dead ends. And the TV coverage... that's just made it worse. Calls are flooding in, every crank, everyone who has a creepy neighbor, everyone with a vendetta. You know what it's like. We have to sift through them all, but the chances of one of them being him... it's a long shot." He rubbed his hand through his hair. "In other words, so far, nothing substantial."

Moira felt a shudder ripple through her. A labyrinth of faces, a city of shadows, and somewhere among them, a wolf stalked, undetected, ready to strike again.

Rose shuffled at her feet and whined slightly. It was as if the dog felt her anguish.

Trying to break the pall of gloom that had settled between them, Jonny cast a glance her way, "You could always come and have a drink with me tonight."

"Now I know you're struggling." She laughed, but she understood. They both craved the feeling of being alive that another person could bring. It was not exactly gallows humor but a way to feel alive and connect. Jonny was handsome, despite the scar. In fact, it gave him an air of mystery. She wished she could pull her mind out of the killers and take advantage of the offer. They were adults, and it would be nice to forget for a while.

"Or you could come back to mine after this. Help me unwind."

Under different circumstances, she might have welcomed the idea. It had been a while since she'd allowed herself that kind of distraction. He was a kind, caring man despite his gruff manner. She imagined he would be a considerate lover, and maybe she could do with the release. But today, the suggestion didn't land as intended. The image of the murderer, cold and calculating, the perverse pleasure he derived from his deeds, overshadowed any possibility of escape. Though part of her needed to fall into someone's arms and let the horrors go, she couldn't.

"Not this time, not with where my head is," she said.

He grimaced. "Yeah, I get that."

An awkward silence stretched between them. She knew Jonny meant well, but her mind was too engrossed in the predator's psyche. To catch him, she needed to think like him, to understand his motivations. She found herself repulsed at the prospect of tapping into such a dark, twisted mentality.

"How are you doing with that," Jonny asked, a fork full of Tikka on the way to his mouth. That made it so casual, and Moira looked down at the blood seeping out of her steak. It had never put her off before, but for a moment, she thought that she would vomit.

"It's a work in progress. I'm not sure I've got anything else that I can put into words."

"I know it's hard," he said. "Don't make yourself ill with this."

Moira nodded and ate a few of her chips, trying to keep her eyes off the blood. The problem was she had to think like this man to really understand him. Understanding him might help them catch him, and yet she hated to think like him. She closed her eyes for a moment. What would he be doing now?

She imagined that he was an obsessive personality but was probably clever with it. She doubted that anyone was aware of his obsession. His intelligence would be animal or at least a certain type of cunning intelligence. This man was not an intellectual, and she even thought that he felt slighted by those better than him... in his mind.

When he saw the girls, his heart would race in anticipation. It would be like a secret pleasure, a thrill. She doubted he got aroused, for the girls had mercifully been untouched. At least there was that!

"How's the steak?" Jonny asked, his tikka almost gone.

"It's a little tough," Moira lied, for she had pushed it around her plate.

"I understand, he said, and she could see it in his eyes that he did. Though he had managed to eat, it did not make him heartless. He was feeling this every bit as much as her, but he was exposed to more horror than she was and knew that if he didn't eat, he would be less effective.

"When do you think he'll strike again?"

Moira hoped he wouldn't but knew in her heart that he would. There had been five days between finding Sophie and Mandy going missing. That was fast. "It depends. Mandy might have just been opportunistic. Something too tempting to ignore." Moira shuddered, normal people, saying that would be talking about ice cream or chocolate, not murdering a young girl. "It's too early to tell, and with the press coverage, he might be driven underground. It could even be enough to stop him." Moira closed her eyes and chewed a mouthful of steak. It tasted good, and she swallowed.

"But you don't think so," Jonny asked, his voice no longer flirty but flat and exhausted.

"No, I don't. It all depends if he is stalking them or if he simply sees an opportunity. Hopefully, there will be fewer girls out alone, at least for a little while."

"Amen, to that."

"Yeah. Maybe I should look at some of the leads you're getting from the public?"

Jonny nodded. "I will let you know if we get any likely suspects. Every known pedo has been looked at. They all have alibis. Do you want another drink?" He held his glass up. "I could have a coke."

Moira was about to say no, but the shrill sound of Jonny's airwave broke the lull, the urgency in the dispatcher's voice cutting through the hum of the pub.

"Control to 390, over."

"390 to control, over."

"Report of a male subject, seen watching a school with a doll in hand. Do you want to take it? Over."

The steak on Moira's plate suddenly seemed much too red. Ice traced down her back as the question hung in the air between them. Could this be a beacon among their sea of dread? A lead, possibly nothing, possibly something. But in their line of work, every call warranted attention.

"Yes, yes, confirm we will take it," Jonny said, his jaw clenched.

Control quickly gave him the details, and they both forgot their flirtation, their meals, and anything but bringing the killer to justice.

"Let's go," Moira said, pushing away her unfinished meal. The mostly untouched steak stared back at her, a grim reminder of the task ahead. It was a cruel world they were a part of, but as they left the pub, the dread was momentarily replaced with determination.

A new lead, a new direction. They were not done fighting yet.

THE DOLLMAKER'S RUSE

THE MIDDAY SUN shone brightly as Moira and Jonny met with Marianne Thomas outside the imposing iron gates of the school. The schoolteacher was tall and thin, wearing a plain blue shirt and a white blouse, her shoulder-length brown hair in a ponytail. She wore no makeup and looked tired and jaded, but there was a slight breathlessness as she welcomed them.

With Rose at her side, the delicate scent of fresh-cut grass filled Moira's nostrils as they spoke. The teacher was flustered, her voice wavering as she explained her concerns about the man with the doll.

"I'm not sure if I should have called you. He never did anything, never approached the fence. I thought he was watching the girls, but I could be mistaken."

"What did your instincts tell you?" Jonny asked.

Marianne looked at her worn loafers before meeting his eyes. "He was breathing heavily and he looked... hungry. It was as if he was devouring the children with his eyes. I found him quite disturbing, and with what has been going on... I thought it best to call you," she finished, a shudder running through her.

"You did the right thing," Jonny said. "Can you describe him?"

Her mouth opened for a moment, and she shook her head.

"Take your time," Moira said. "Was he tall, short, thin, fat, facial hair?"

Marianne took a breath and closed her eyes. "He was plump with a round face, he had a beard and was wearing a nice suit. It looked expensive. I don't know his height as he was sitting down."

"Do you know his name or where he lives?" Jonny asked, his notebook in his hand as he scribbled down the details.

"No, I'm so sorry. I'm not much help."

Moira had a thought. "You said he was sitting on a bench. Can you show me which one and then which direction he headed?"

That made Marianne smile, and she nodded, leading them around the fence surrounding the playground to a bench on the opposite side. "It was this one on the left-hand side," Marianne said. "Then, when I chased him off, he went down that street, there." She pointed to a street between the houses that were just across the road.

Moira looked, and she could have sworn she saw the curtains twitching in the house on the corner. Was it a coincidence? Did she believe in coincidences? Her pulse stepped up. Could this be the lair of their killer?

Jonny asked another couple of questions, but Moira was lost in her darkest thoughts. If the killer stalked this playground, what was he thinking when he sat here? Was he enjoying the young nubile limbs of the girls, anticipating getting one of them alone? She pulled her mind out of the killers and let out a sigh.

"Thank you so much," Jonny said, and Marianne walked away.

"You, okay?" he asked.

"Yeah, I just hate getting in these sick minds. Let's see if Rose can track him."

"Sheeze, I never thought of that. I was all deflated, and you pulled that out of the bag. Go girl go." His face was split into a broad grin.

"Hold your horses, guard the bench while I fetch her tracking harness."

Jonny nodded, but it was clear that he wanted this to move faster. Moira understood.

Minutes later, Rose was wearing her harness, and Moira pointed to the bench. "Take."

The dog sniffed the bench, taking her time going over and over the metal surface, and then her body stiffened. Moira let the line play out over her fingers as the dog dropped its nose to the pavement and began to track in the direction Marianne had pointed. This was good. Rose was moving fast.

Jonny ran ahead, pulled his warrant card from his pocket, holding his police credentials in front of him, he stopped the traffic. Rose went straight across the tarmac and down the street in the direction the man had taken.

Could this be it? Moira was filled with hope to stop this before another body. That would be something.

Rose followed along the pavement and then down the street. She stopped at the first door, a white PVC door, and let out a bark.

Jonny's face reflected the tension that hung in the air. The house was nondescript, indistinguishable, yet to Rose, it stood out.

"Control, 309."

"Go 309."

"We have located the suspect at 60 six zero Planter Street. We intend to speak to the suspect. Over."

"Yes, yes, information confirmed. Out."

Moira had forgotten the code on the airwave radio. They always said yes, yes to confirm, and you only had seven seconds and then had to say so far. It could be slow, but it was done to make sure that mistakes were not made. That all information was received correctly. It worked well. Jonny had let control know where they were in case of trouble. If they did not report in again soon, backup would arrive.

Jonny knocked on the white door.

A man in his late fifties answered the door. As Marianne had said, he was plump with a beard. His face was as ordinary as his house, the eyes a little too bright, a little too eager. This was defiantly the man from the bench. His surprise at seeing them quickly smoothed into a facsimile of friendliness.

"I am Detective Inspector Chandler, and this is my colleague, Moira Foster. We tracked you from the bench, where a teacher said that you were watching the children. May we come in and talk?"

"Come in," he invited, though there was hesitation in his voice, a subtle wariness that hinted at his reluctance. "Oh, the dog as well. Could we do this here?"

"I would rather come in, and she is a police dog. She won't cause any harm," Jonny said, stepping a little closer to the door.

The man stepped back and invited them in. There were stairs directly in front of them and two doors leading off. He took them through the righthand one at the back of the house. It was a kitchen, small, nondescript, with cream units and a small oak table.

The man pointed at the table, and he sat down heavily. "How can I help?"

"What is your name?" Jonny asked, pulling out his notebook.

Rose sat and watched the man, which seemed to make him nervous. His eyes flicked from her to Jonny and back again.

"Oh, forgive me. It was quite a shock seeing you here. I'm Graham, Graham Lawrence." He held out a pudgy hand, and Jonny raised his eyebrows. The hand hung for a moment before dropping to the table, where he tapped his fingers against the wooden surface.

Moira noticed that his nails were manicured and even painted with clear varnish. That was unusual. Was it creepy? Perhaps a bit. The fingers were like fat sausages drumming on the table.

"What were you doing on the bench?" Jonny asked.

"Taking a rest and enjoying the sunshine," Graham said. His eyes looked a little haunted, and now they were flicking from Jonny to Rose to the door into the hall. He didn't want them going in there.

"Do you always have a doll with you?"

Graham laughed. "No, it was a present. I had just bought it." He shrugged, but it didn't look genuine to Moira. He was hiding something. She just couldn't decide what.

"We were told you were watching the children and that you had a doll that looked like this," Jonny said. They showed him pictures of the doll found with Sophie.

Moira watched his reactions closely. There was a flicker of desire in his eyes, changing to anger, then a moment of indignation, all quickly veiled. He seemed almost offended by the dolls, but why?

"Let me see. I guess I was watching the children. They were having such fun... oh... just normal watching... I'm not like that!"

"Well, a grown man staring at children, you can see why the teacher called us."

"No, not really. The bench is a nice and sunny place to sit. I was looking forward to sitting there. It would be hard not to watch the children. I've done nothing wrong."

"But you were watching the children, carrying a doll, and breathing heavily. Had you been rushing, or were you finding the children exciting" Jonny asked, and he leaned forward, angling his scar at Graham.

Graham's eyes widened, and he looked as if he might poop. The scar had really gotten to him. For a few moments, he blinked rapidly, and then he changed. His fear seemed to have gone and was replaced with reptilian confidence. "Yes, as I said, the doll is a gift for my niece. I had just bought it. Was I puffing? Maybe, you can see, I'm not as fit as I used to be, and I walked from town. Have you ever come up that hill on foot."

Moira felt the weight of disappointment pushing down on her. Somehow she knew he was going to get away with this. Her instincts said he had something to hide, but she didn't know what. Was he a killer? She couldn't say, but she wouldn't like him watching her children, that was for sure.

"So you admit you had the doll," Jonny said again.

"Doll? Yes, I was holding one," he admitted, his chuckle a touch too forced. He walked over to a nearby cabinet, opened a door, and pulled out a modern doll wearing a bright red dress.

"As I said, I bought this for my niece. A gift," he added, holding it up for them to see.

Moira felt a pang of disappointment surge through her, threatening to engulf her. Beside her, Jonny's face mirrored her sentiments. Their promising lead seemed to be falling apart.

But as they left the house, a sense of unease lingered. Lawrence had been too quick, too ready with his explanation. His eyes still haunted her, the way they had darted to the door of the room when they'd shown him the photos, the hidden anger that flashed momentarily.

Back in Moira's van, as they watched Lawrence's house shrink in the rear-view mirror, Moira sighed, stroking Rose's head. She thought back to Lawrence's house. The place was too clean for a man. Something was wrong, the eagerness in his eyes, the doll in the red dress. But they had nothing on him.

This was not the end. It was just the beginning.

A ROSE BY ANY OTHER NAME

MOIRA LOOKED DOWN at the police file that had, until now, monopolized her attention, the chilling facts about the doll-killer case looking back at her. She felt a tremor of unease crawl up her spine, her mind a whirl of theories and suspicions.

The more she tried to get into the killer's mind, the worse she felt. It was like stepping into the sewer and taking a big swallow. It was awful, but she had to do it.

The shrill ring of her phone interrupted her ponderings. She glanced at the screen. It was Jonny, always eager for an update, she thought, always trying to pierce the gloom of the investigation. She took a deep breath, readying herself for another conversation with him. They were both hit by disappointment earlier. Only Jonny was sure Graham was not involved; she was not so sure. He knew something. He recognized the doll. Now she had time to think; she was sure of it.

Jonny's voice buzzed with his usual enthusiasm, but she could hear the undercurrent of worry. "Any breakthroughs, Moira?" he asked. There was a pause. She could imagine him, nervous but trying not to show it. It was his way.

"No, Jonny," she said, the frustration clear in her voice. "Not yet."

"Me neither, but we will keep looking. I might have a couple of suspects for you to look over tomorrow. I'll shout if I do. You sure you don't want that drink... just the drink?"

"Thanks, but not tonight. I have a lot to go through. Okay."

"Sure, I'll touch base tomorrow."

She hung up and took another long sip of her tea, its malty taste somehow comforting within the tangled maze of the case. Her gaze wandered, settling on Rose, her faithful companion, asleep in her corner.

Her chestnut stripes shone under the weak afternoon light seeping through the window.

Seeing Rose there, a beacon of loyalty in the uncertainty surrounding the case, her mind took her back to the fateful day they met.

She had been on a road trip, seeking some quiet away from the chaos of her job. The endless expanse of the motorway had begun to blur, the harsh afternoon sun making her eyes water. She decided to pull into a service station. It was a nondescript place, nestled between green fields, the kind of place where life seemed to slow down.

She had ordered a burger and a cup of tea, the lukewarm liquid was a far cry from comforting, but it served its purpose. The burger and chips were a little plastic, but they took away her hunger. As she sat there on the patch of grass outside the service station, sipping her tea and nibbling on the last few chips, a pitiful whimper drew her attention.

She looked around, and under the shrubs, a brown dog, short-nosed, coat all matted and barely more than skin and bones, lay hidden. She held out a chop, and the dog crawled up to her. Its eyes, shimmering with fear and hope, pulled at Moira's heart. She offered her hand, and the dog sniffed it tentatively before licking it, a faint wag in her frail tail.

The dog's eyes seemed to say, 'Help me.' And at that moment, Moira felt a strange bond forming between them. She named her Roselee, Rose for short, a nod to their first encounter over a cup of tea.

Rose had crawled from the bushes and wolfed down the remaining chips. Moira had taken her to the service station and asked if anyone had lost the dog. However, if anyone had come forward, they would have been in serious trouble. Not only had they starved the dog and left it in terrible condition, but they had dumped it at a motorway -service station.

It didn't bear thinking about. If Rose had run onto the carriageway, many people could have lost their lives.

Over the weeks that followed, Rose transformed under Moira's care. She wasn't chipped, and the local vet said she would recover but slowly. She had been weak and mistrustful initially, but Moira's unwavering patience and kindness won her over. In Rose, she found a loyal companion, a silent confidante who eased her loneliness.

In return, Rose found in Moira a savior, a friend who gave her a second chance at life. From being an abandoned, suffering creature, she became a part of Moira's world, her constant shadow, her confidante. The dog was intelligent and had a great nose. It didn't take Moira long to train her to track, and in time she had qualified as a search and rescue dog. Moira was thinking about doing a cadaver training course with her, it would have to wait until after this case, but it could be worthwhile. Moira shuddered. Not for police work, though, just for rescue.

Moira's reverie was broken by Rose's soft whine. She walked over to her, running her hands over Rose's silky fur. The dog leaned into her touch, her tail thumping against the floor.

"Got your back, girl," Moira whispered, her resolve hardening. Rose seemed to understand, her eyes meeting Moira's with a determination that matched hers.

With renewed energy, she walked back to the table and picked up the file again, ready to plunge into the case. They had a killer to catch, and they were going to do it together.

THE PUPPETEER

THE ONCE BUZZING city lay cloaked in an eerie silence, with a sense of dread seeping into every corner. Rumors swirled like autumn leaves in the wind, settling on each doorstep and painting every heart with fear. Everyone kept their daughters close, under their watchful eye, fearing the worst. A serial killer was at large, and a local accountant, Graham Lawrence, was now under the spotlight.

Moira leaned back in her chair at the station, the unsettling image of Graham when he first saw the picture of the doll playing on a loop in her mind. His eyes had been transfixed, and a spark of unsettling delight ignited in them, making Moira's skin crawl. Only, it had changed in an instant. Anger seemed to bubble below the surface before it, too, was extinguished. All of this happened in a fraction of a second, and she wondered if she had seen it at all. Was she just looking for something and thereby finding it. Confirmation bias was a powerful force, and she had to make sure it didn't lead her down the wrong path.

It didn't matter. She couldn't get him out of her mind and had persuaded Jonny to bring him in. Right now, he sat in the interrogation room while they watched him through the 1-way mirror.

Graham, the suspected puppeteer of this horrifying spectacle, tapped his fingers on the plain white table. His eyes flicked nervously around the room. Moira had looked into him. He was not slow as the teacher had thought but a highly intelligent man with a good job. His suit was nice and expensive, and he looked polished and in control. She could understand that his round face and chubby build could lead people to underestimate him. She would not do that. The man was an accountant, respectable and well-paid. He spent most of his time looking over ledgers and balance sheets. His initial confidence was eroding to reveal an underbelly of fear. Was this because he had something to hide?

"Ready?" Jonny asked.

"I think so. I think he's percolated enough."

They entered the interrogation room together and sat at the table. Graham's eyes flickered anxiously between Moira and Jonny, the usual twinkle of intelligence replaced by a desperate terror.

"What is happening here?" Graham asked.

Jonny held up a finger, shushing him before pulling a chair out for Moira.

"Such a gentleman," she said and sat down. Jonny sat next to her, slammed a folder on the table, and then touched a button on the edge of the table. "Interview started with Graham Lawrence at 11:15 am Detective Inspector Jonny Chandler and Moira Foster in attendance."

"What am I doing here?" Graham asked.

"Why do you think you're here?" Moira asked him.

Something flickered behind his eyes, a dirty secret he wanted to keep. He hid it well and shrugged his shoulders. "I don't know. I explained about the bench. It's a nice sunny spot. I was tired. What more do you want from me?"

Jonny opened the folder and pulled out a picture of the doll. It was the one that was found with Sophie. He slapped it on the table.

Graham cringed, and his lip curled as he looked at it.

Jonny took another picture out of the folder and did the same. This was the doll found with Mandy, only they had photoshopped a red velvet dress onto the doll.

Moira noticed that Graham gasped as he took in the doll. His pupils grew large, and his tongue licked his lips.

"Do you recognize this doll?" Moira asked.

Graham folded his arms across his chest and leaned back in his chair. "No, should I?"

Moira stared hard at him and knew Jonny would be doing the same.

"Don't lie to us," Jonny said. "We will find out the truth, and then you will go to jail. Soon we will be coming to search your house. What will we find?"

Panic crossed Graham's face, but he clenched his jaw and shook his head. "You won't get a warrant. I have nothing to hide."

The fact that the warrant came first in his thought process was telling to Moira, but he was right. Was this man the killer or just a guy with a fetish?

The buzz of voices outside the door snapped Moira out of her thoughts. A reporter, thirsty for the juicy scoop, had managed to infiltrate the crowd of uniformed officers. "I hear accountant Graham Lawrence has been taken into questioning..." his voice echoed, the sentence hanging unfinished in the air as the door to the interrogation rooms shut behind someone.

In the confines of the interrogation room, Moira pushed the damning photographs toward Graham. As he glanced down at the pictures of the dolls, a strange sort of calm washed over his face. His fingers gingerly reached for the images, tracing the outline of the dolls with an intimate familiarity that sent a chill down Moira's spine.

"What does it mean, Graham?" Moira probed, her voice slicing through the palpable tension in the room. Graham, however, remained unnervingly silent. His gaze was fixated on the images, a disturbing affection lighting up his eyes.

The sudden intrusion of a solicitor disrupted the standoff. He strode in, bearing a court order like a knight brandishing his sword. "Mr. Lawrence, you are free to go," he declared, a smug grin plastered on his face.

Graham left the station, his steps shaky, his usual composed demeanor shattered. Moira watched him leave, her gut twisting with the knowledge that this was far from over. She had pulled at the puppeteer's strings, and the unraveling had just begun. If he was their man, would this make him strike again?

THE DOLL MAKER'S FURY

CLARA SAT in the dank room, her worn hands clasped tightly around one of her precious dolls. Her blue eyes bore into the porcelain face, a stern reprimand lurking within their cold depths. "You naughty girl," she hissed, her voice scratchy as if seldom used. "Why did you betray me?"

In the corner, Peter cowered, his eyes wide with fear. The storm of Clara's wrath was a familiar sight, but the terror it instilled never seemed to diminish. He hunkered down further into the shadows hoping to be invisible.

An ancient television sputtered in the corner of the room, the picture lined and flickering. It cast an eerie glow on the faded wallpaper. The news reporter's voice echoed hollowly in the musty air. Each word about the dead girls stabbed Clara's heart like a rusty knife. *Why did this happen?*

As she looked at the picture of the girls and heard that the first one was Sophie, she knew that it was her child. Her precious child that had let her down. Sophie, in the meticulous green dress, was already in trouble. She had pushed Daisy, or was it Edith? Clara was struggling to remember. But now, Sophie dared to do this, to die in a way that would bring people to her home.

"Why did you do it?" Clara shook the doll. She knew she shouldn't do it. From a long time ago, a memory came into her mind. A stern man towering over her, his face red, his eyes wild. "Did you shake the boy?"

She had shaken her head, hiding the smile that shaking that thing brought her. Quickly she pulled her mind back to the present. She had to get on top of this. Maybe, she would go out tonight under the cover of darkness. She would see if she could find Sophie and teach her a lesson. No, don't go out, danger, fear, bad things.

She shook the doll. "Why?"

Don't shake her. She's delicate; she will break. She pushed the thought aside. Sophie deserved to break after what she had done. Sophie deserved it. She had gone out and got killed. That was unforgivable. The picture on the screen showed another girl, but in Clara's mind, it was still Sophie, the doll in her hands which threatened to bring intruders into their home.

"Dead girls, dead girls. You've caused too much trouble," Clara scolded, her eyes fixed on the doll, her grip tightening until her knuckles whitened.

In the corner, a grunt pulled her eyes. It was there. Why was it there? Clara turned her eyes to her son. "Get out, go and do the shopping. We need food."

"But... don't like the way folks look at me," he said, his voice thick and slurred. If she didn't know better, she would think he was drunk. That thought piled fire in her gut. "Out!" she screamed.

The lump lumbered to the door, light filled the room, and then the door closed behind it. Clara let out a sigh of relief. It was as if the light had washed away the darkness. She could breathe. Her eyes turned back to the child in her hands. The naughty one.

"Didn't I tell you not to die on me?" she screamed, her voice reaching a feverish pitch as it reverberated through the room. "Now, the police will come. Why did you die?"

The air grew thick with Clara's rage as she hurled the doll across the room. It hit the peeling wallpaper with a soft thud before tumbling down onto the worn-out carpet. A silent cry of despair filled the room as the doll's glassy eyes stared emptily into nothingness.

The TV blinked, and the screen faded to black. It had overheated again and would not work for hours. Now she wouldn't know if trouble was coming. She wouldn't know if Sophie had done more evil.

The room fell into a chilling silence, save Clara's heavy breathing. She slumped back into her chair, her energy drained by her outburst. Her trembling fingers picked up a card from the cluttered table nearby, her knotted joints struggling against the simple task.

HER HAND HOVERED over the card, her eyes lost in thought before she started scribbling on it.

The scratching of the pen on the card echoed hauntingly in the room.

A sigh of satisfaction escaped Clara's lips as she glanced at the card. Alice. £10. She carefully placed the card on the grimy window ledge, her trembling hands smoothing out the crumpled paper.

Her attention then turned towards the scattered dolls, her gaze finally resting on a particular one. Picking it up gently, she dusted off the dirt from its face before placing it next to the card. Her fingertips traced the doll's face, a disturbingly sweet smile tugging at the corners of her lips.

The TV flickered, coming back to a grey buzzing snow, giving the room a sinister hue, the dolls' lifeless eyes reflecting the eerie light, the silence telling tales of a demented love.

Clara sat back in her chair, her gaze fixed on the doll by the window, a whisper of a song playing on her cracked lips. She was the doll maker, and this was her unholy sanctuary.

They would never find her, never discover her secret. She was too clever, too sneaky. Never again would she be held, imprisoned, and punished. Never again.

THE DREADED CALL

THE BUSTLING CITY of Lincoln was once a vibrant tapestry of life, warmth, and camaraderie. But now, it had transformed into a chilling portrait of fear, every face painted with the stark hues of dread. Everyone was waiting, with bated breath, for the next horror. They clutched their children close, hoping to beat the specter that haunted their dreams.

A sharp trill cut through the oppressive silence of Moira's home, the jarring ringtone of her phone echoing off the walls. She picked up the phone with a sigh, her heart heavy in her chest. It was Jonny. She wasn't sure if she could take this again, but she knew she had to. Her knowledge could help the case. What it did to her was immaterial.

She answered the call. "Yes."

"We've got another one, Moira," Jonny's voice was a murmur of grim urgency against her ear. The words sounded like a death knell. The terse information chilled her to her core as she took it in. A third young girl, only recently blooming into adolescence, had vanished into thin air, shrouding the city in an even denser cloud of apprehension.

Moira swallowed hard, her mind whirling. She was needed at the scene. That much was clear. She knew, deep down, that they wouldn't find anything new, no groundbreaking piece of evidence to finally crack the case. But duty called, and with a single glance at her loyal partner, Rose, she was on her way. She could feel the Boxer's keen gaze on her, the canine's intelligent eyes reflecting her own apprehension.

Dusk was falling. It was earlier than the last two cases. Was this because the killer was getting more desperate, or was it the parents calling them home sooner?

Driving through the quiet streets, the once vibrant Lincoln seemed a mere ghost town, the creeping horror snuffing out its light one by one with each girl taken. It was quiet as if holding its breath. If only the dark streets could talk to her.

As she navigated the path, Moira was swallowed by her thoughts, a whirlpool of doubts and self-recriminations. Her fingers gripped the steering wheel tightly, her knuckles white against the worn leather. The image of Graham Lawrence flashed in her mind, the man who had been clutching a doll just days ago. Could he be the monster behind these heinous acts?

Graham had been infuriatingly difficult to read, a tightly shut book that refused to give away its secrets. His alibi of being alone at home was sketchy. However, there was CCTV around his home, and they hadn't found any evidence that he had left his house on the nights of the two previous abductions. Moira knew that meant nothing. Graham was intelligent. He could work out where the cameras were and avoid them.

She remembered the way he looked at the doll's picture. Hungry, desperate, or was that just all in her mind. Maybe. But there was something unsettling about him, a disquieting air that gnawed at her instincts.

An image of the little girl, forever frozen in time on a merry-go-round, flashed in her mind. A stab of guilt pierced her heart. If she had been more aggressive with Graham, could she have prevented this? She shook her head, trying to clear her thoughts. 'What ifs' were dangerous, she knew, a downward spiral that led to nowhere.

As she parked her car near the search location, a rush of bleak desperation hit her. She wanted, more than anything, to find something. To find a shred of hope, a sliver of a lead, something that would point them in the right direction.

With Rose by her side, she trudged across the sprawling field, her eyes scanning every inch for signs of the missing child. The air was thick with anxiety, the tension almost tangible. She could smell the wet earth beneath her feet and hear the soft rustling of leaves in the wind, but all her senses were on high alert for any hint of the girl.

This time there was little to say to Jonny. They nodded, and Moira got straight to work. Rose was put into her harness, the article, a teddy dropped on the stark cold pavement, and Rose was on the trail.

The dog's tail wagged as she worked. Eager to hunt down the unsub and not knowing that this was anything but a game. Moira envied her. The peace the dog brought was a help, but to live in her world, where the only problem was which spot was the most comfortable. For a moment, Moira wished life could be so simple.

The teddy was clear in Moira's mind. Fluffy and sweet with a pink heart on its chest.

Rose was working diligently, her nose close to the ground, her ears pricked for any sound out of the ordinary. Moira watched her, admiration flooding her chest. Despite the bleak circumstances, the dog's determination was unwavering.

However, Moira couldn't shift the memory of that teddy. No child should ever go missing. Moira didn't know why the teddy was affecting her so badly, but the image of the cute bear was tearing at her heart. Such innocence should never be destroyed. They had to stop the beast that was doing this.

The time ticked by, and Moira felt that this time it would be better. That Rose would take them to the girl, that it would just be a mistake. She would be at a friend's house. However, once again, Rose stopped at the side of the road, a whine escaping her. The dog paced back and forth, trying to reestablish the scent, but eventually, she gave up, dropping to the ground. Moira bent down and stroked her soft broad head. The brown eyes seemed unsure. "It's okay, girl, you did good." Moira pulled the tub of food from her pocket and gave Rose her reward. Turning to Jonny, she shook her head.

Jonny nodded and squeezed her arm before he walked away. For just a moment, she wished she could fall into his arms. Lean her head against his chest and let the tears fall. Coppers were combing the street, knocking on doors, checking everything. Hours slipped by as the search yielded nothing but heartache. The sinking sun cast long, mournful shadows over the landscape, adding to the gloomy atmosphere. Moira's frustration bubbled to the surface. Why couldn't she find anything? Why was this happening in her town to these innocent children?

There was nothing more she could do. She slid into her car, her body numb from the long, fruitless search. As she cranked the engine to life, a pang of grief washed over her. She thought of the missing girl. She had asked for no details and still had none.

It was best to not think of her, and yet her mind filled in the gaps. She could imagine her bright eyes now another face on a missing poster, her laughter a fading echo in the silent streets.

And in the depths of her despair, the image of Graham returned, more potent than ever. His face, his hunger, his doll. A gnawing doubt had taken root in her mind, blossoming into a full-blown suspicion. What if it was him? What if she had let a predator walk free?

With that troubling thought echoing in her mind, she drove away from the scene, leaving behind a field of dread and a city crying out for answers. The weight of guilt bore down on her, pressing onto her shoulders with an invisible force. She couldn't help but wonder if she could have done something, anything, to stop the terror that had descended on Lincoln.

DISAGREEMENT

THE OLD STATION house was ablaze with an eerie tension. The usually bustling office seemed caught in a moment of strained calm, the quiet punctuated by the soft hum of the overhead fluorescent lights and the occasional ring of a telephone. In the middle of it all, Moira and Jonny stood, their intense gaze locked in a silent battle of wills.

Moira's fiery hair was a stark contrast against her worn jeans and earth-toned t-shirt. She stood with her arms crossed tightly over her chest, her knuckles white from the intensity of her grip. Her hazel eyes flashed green with determination, a relentless spirit that never backed down. "We need to bring him back in," she insisted, her voice echoing in the silence of the room. The mention of Graham Lawrence instantly thickened the tension, painting a clear picture of the disagreement at hand.

"You should go home and get some rest," Jonny said, running a hand through his thick hair and pushing it away from his face.

"I feel it in my bones. He is involved."

Jonny, the seasoned detective inspector, stood tall, his hardened eyes a testament to years of dealing with the law's rigid complexities. His own scruffy attire belied the TV programs that always showed the detective in a suit. Jonny liked to blend in, and his worn jeans and faded black t-shirt helped with that. He would make an effort when dealing with parents. He kept a black jacket in his car, but most people appreciated the human touch he brought with him. Jonny was real and understood them. Despite his harsh appearance, they could tell he cared. "Moira," he sighed, his voice carrying an undertone of weary patience. "We don't have anything solid against him. We can't just drag him back here based on a hunch."

Despite the words, his gaze held a touch of respect. He knew Moira's instincts were sharp, honed by her unique training in serial killers and her ability to see things that others couldn't. But he was bound by rules, a soldier in the rigid ranks of the law, forced to operate within the system's stringent boundaries.

The room seemed to hold its breath as Moira met his gaze, her stance unyielding. "He's hiding something, Jonny," she said, her voice dropping to a near whisper. She could feel the truth of it in her bones. "I know it, and deep down, I think you know it too." Moira felt tears pushing at the back of her eyes. She had let this girl down, and she hated it. The feeling of powerlessness was too much to bear, but what could she do? The thought of shaking Graham, of forcing him to speak, was one that gave her some pleasure. Even as she knew that coercion rarely gave good answers. People panicked and said anything, but she had to do something. What?

Jonny's gaze flickered away for a second, an internal battle playing out in his eyes. His duty and his intuition were at war, and for a moment, he seemed lost. But he was quick to mask it with a firm nod, "You might be right, but we have to follow procedure,

Moira. We can't afford to harass him without solid evidence."

Moira nodded, her jaw set in grim determination. "Then I'll watch him," she declared, a flicker of resolve dancing in her eyes. "I'll find the evidence we need."

The declaration hung in the air between them, an irrevocable decision. Jonny regarded her for a long moment before he finally broke the silence. "You want company?" he asked, the slightest hint of a smile tugging at the corner of his lips. It was a subtle show of solidarity, an understanding that they were both fighting for the same goal.

Moira let out a sigh, her shoulders dropping slightly as she looked at Jonny. "Yeah, Jonny," she replied, a small smile mirroring his own. "I'd like that." It felt good to be doing something, and the fatigue fell away. She would go straight there and see if he was home. If he wasn't, then the next time he left the house, she would follow him and hopefully find the missing girl.

"I have a few hours of work to still do. Text me where you park, and I'll join you as soon as I can."

The tension seemed to dissipate, replaced by a shared resolve. They would do whatever was needed to catch the predator. For now, though they disagreed on the methods, their shared determination bound them together. After all, they had a girl to save.

Moira took the long drive across the lonely city, all beneath the watchful gaze of the cathedral. Its eternal presence stared down at her, and tonight she believed it was filled with disappointment.

She parked across the street from Graham's house. Far enough down to cause no suspicion. At an angle so that she could see both doors. There was no light on in the property. Either he was tucked up fast asleep in bed — with his dolls, as that creepy thought came to her mind, she shuddered — or he was out doing God knows what to Amelia.

Moira could see the girl in her mind.

Amelia White was a vivacious girl of just thirteen. She had curly auburn hair that fell in cascading ringlets, reminiscent of the dolls. They framed her freckled, elfin face. Moira flicked to the image on her phone. The photo the parents had provided with shaky hands and tear-stained eyes. Amelia's eyes were deep and chocolate-brown, like her mum's. They were filled with curiosity and innocence that made her appear younger than her years.

At barely five-feet tall, she was petite and slender, an agile gymnast who loved to dart around with unbridled energy.

Moira remembered her mother's choking words as she explained that they had arranged for a taxi, but it was late. Amelia was always the one with a ready smile, popular among her peers and teachers alike, and admired for her vibrant personality and creative flair. She was always at the gym, practicing her tumbles and full of energy. She was never able to stand still, and that would be why she would have made the short walk home.

Moira felt the shock of her disappearance and knew how hard it would hit everyone who knew her, leaving a profound void in their lives, each of them grappling with the terrifying reality of her sudden vanishing. Her parents, heartbroken and disbelieving, were left to hope against hope for her safe return.

Moira fought back her tears and stared at the phone screen for what seemed like forever.

A rattle on the window jerked her awake. With her heart in her mouth, she looked up into Jonny's smiling face. He had brought coffee. She let him in, not wanting to admit how glad she was to see him.

TANGLED IN GUILT

IN THE FAR REACHES OF Lincoln, on the outskirts, where back-to-back houses were replaced by industrial units, factory lines, and grating machinery, Darren Wilkinson sat proudly in his office. It felt good to be at the helm of a successful business. Darren, a hulking man, was used to commanding both respect and a touch of healthy fear from his employees at the electroplating facility. It was good to get away from the shop floor and review this month's figures. Things were looking good.

He has deep-set eyes, a strong jawline currently obscured by stubble and hands calloused from years of labor-intensive work. His hair was cropped short, more out of convenience than fashion, and he carried an aura of stern authority.

The phone rang, and he felt a touch of annoyance. He wanted to finish his report and get down to the shop floor. Flicking his eyes at the phone, he thought about ignoring it, but in the end, he pushed a button putting the call on speaker. "Yes."

"It's a policeman wanting to talk to you," Janet, his secretary, said.

His heart pounded in his chest like a drum at war as the silence stretched between them. "Did he say what he wanted?" Darren knew he had no reason to be afraid. No one could know his secret, and yet, fear curled in his gut like a slimy snake.

"Yes, some information on cyanide."

"Cyanide!" Darren knew his voice was loud, but did it contain a tremor."

"Yes, should I put him through, or do you want one of the line managers to take this?" Janet asked, her voice as always confident and polite.

It didn't matter how much he lost his temper. She was always on his side. She would deflect the call if he wanted her to. Swallowing, he thought about doing just that, but the last thing he needed was for his line managers to look into things that didn't concern them.

"No, I'll take it. I was just hoping to get these reports finished," Darren managed and then realized that it was out of character for him to make an excuse. Bosses should boss, and not everyone needs to know the reason for every decision. That was what he hated about the modern world. This sense of entitlement. Everyone thought they had the right to know everything.

"It's Detective Sergeant Griffiths. I'll put him through."

Darren's hand shook as he reached out to pick up the handset. There was no reason to do so. His office was away from the others and above the factory. No one could hear the call.

The voice on the other end was sharp and official. Detective Sergeant Griffiths of Lincolnshire Police. Is that Mr. Darren Wilkinson?"

"Yes, DS Griffiths, how can I help you?" Darren thought that he had kept his voice steady, using the power he commanded over the factory to project confidence. Even though it was not something he was feeling.

"We are checking all the businesses in the city that might use cyanide. Do you use it?"

Darren's office, once a sanctuary, was instantly transformed into a prison cell by his surging anxiety. The hum of fluorescent lights overhead was his only company in the otherwise silent space. The furniture bore the brunt of years of use, the veneer desk chipped and stained by spilled coffee, and the ergonomic chair worn at the edges. Out of the broad window, the view of the steel-clad factory stood stark against the fading afternoon light.

"Yes...yes, we do use it...for electroplating," Darren managed to stammer out, his usual eloquence evaporating under the heat of the questioning. "But we have strict controls. It's all accounted for. I can show you the records if you wish."

Darren was tall and broad, always a formidable opponent on the rugby field before a busted knee forced his retirement. He was used to people respecting his stature and his status. He carried a presence that filled a room, his prematurely greying hair lending him an air of authority that belied his middle-aged status. Today, however, he felt smaller, defeated, and his usual confident demeanor had dissipated, leaving behind a shell of the man he was. The news on the radio this morning had unsettled him. Another girl missing - the third one in so little time. A thought almost stopped his heart. Was that why he was being asked about cyanide?

"No, that is fine. We are just checking that all the necessary paperwork is in order, and we wanted you to check to see if anything has gone missing. Could you do that?"

Darren let out a breath that he hoped sounded like a laugh. "I don't have to DS Griffiths. We run a tight ship here, and I can assure you that I would know instantly if anything went missing, let alone something as critical as cyanide."

"Then can you explain how it is stored and used,"

Darren sighed, his gaze drifting to the closed drawer on his right. Inside, a sheaf of paper lay, a secret hidden in plain sight. A guilty secret that sent a chill down his spine every time he remembered its existence. Blackmail. He had been blackmailed to supply cyanide, a substantial quantity. It was a while back, under duress, and he had tried to forget about it, shoving it into the farthest corners of his mind. But now, it all came rushing back like a tidal wave, threatening to drown him.

Was it his cyanide, his decision, that had led to the deaths of these girls? The thought pierced his heart like a hot knife. His breath hitched as an invisible vise tightened around his chest. His palms were clammy against the cold receiver, his shirt sticking to his back in the chill of the air-conditioned office.

He had been weak. He had made a mistake, cutting corners in goods sent abroad to keep his company going. To keep his family in the comfort they expected. When it was found out, he thought it was over, but the inspector simply said that they could do each other a favor. The man had told him he had a rodent problem and needed cyanide to get rid of it. If not, the paperwork had to be turned in.

Darren had taken that as a threat to his livelihood and a threat against his family. He had thought he was protecting them, and it didn't seem a big thing. Cyanide was easily traced. No one would use it to do harm... would they. A cold sweat ran down his back. Had his actions endangered other innocent lives instead? His guilt turned into a physical ache, a throbbing in his temples that wouldn't recede.

The detective's voice on the other end of the line seemed distant, a murmur against the thunderous guilt in his mind. "Mr. Wilkinson, did you hear me?"

He answered mechanically, his thoughts elsewhere, his heart heavy with remorse. "I'm sorry, I'm in the middle of something, and I missed what you said."

"Can you explain how it is stored and used," the DS repeated.

"Yes, each batch is tagged. It is scanned at each stage from arrival on the property to final use. Only myself and my line managers can get access to it, and if any was missing, say, for example, a spill. Then paperwork is filled in and reports filled. It has to be confirmed by three managers." Only it didn't that time five years ago.

"Has a spill ever happened?"

"Let me think...." Jesus, wouldn't this guy leave it? "Once, many years ago, but it was seen by me and a whole shift load of men. Unless you had ground up the cement floor, it was gone for good." He managed a laugh that sounded almost plausible. "Is there anything else you need?"

"No, thank you for your time."

The call ended, leaving Darren drowning in a pool of silent dread. He sat there, paralyzed by fear and guilt, his gaze unseeing. The view outside his window blurred, the steel structures of his factory looking like skeletal remains of his conscience against the backdrop of the dying light.

Suddenly, his office felt too small, the walls inching closer with each passing moment. But there was nowhere to run, no place to hide from the monstrous guilt gnawing at him from inside. Darren Wilkinson, a titan of industry, was reduced to a trembling wreck, his secret threatening to consume him. The horrifying realization dawned upon him - he was trapped in a web of his own making.

IN THE HEART of the Portland Electroplating Ltd office, surrounded by walls of cold steel and glass, sat Darren Wilkinson, a looming figure cast into a world of confusion and dread. The harsh fluorescent lights overhead buzzed like a swarm of discontented bees, an undercurrent of tension adding to the palpable atmosphere. The blinds were drawn tight against the encroaching darkness of night, turning the office into an insular world fraught with secrets and apprehension.

All day he had struggled over what to do. Should he tell the police what he knew, or should he forget it? In the end, he had to confront the man who had turned him into a criminal, for that was what he felt like just now: a crook, an aider, and an abettor. Someone who would be shunned rather than treated with respect, and the more he thought about it, the more his ulcer ate away at his guts.

He cradled the phone against his ear, his pale fingers clenched tightly around it. His usually neat hair was disheveled, and droplets of sweat clung to his forehead like morning dew on a leaf. His eyes darted to a family portrait on his desk, the smiling faces of his wife and two beautiful daughters staring back at him, their innocence and happiness gnawing at his insides. His eldest, Sophia, was thirteen. The news reports come to his mind. Darren never watched the news, but even though he had heard this, the first victim was Sophie, her name so like Sophia.

Vomit erupts from him, and he only just has time to turn and grab his bin. A stream of hot liquid comes out and all over the paper, carrots, and all. Swallowing, he closed his eyes, and as he wiped his mouth, he picked up the phone.

"What do you want?" the dead voice on the other end said.

"The police called me, looking for cyanide." Darren takes a swig of cold coffee. It does nothing to settle his stomach as the eyes of his wife and daughters stared at him across his desk.

"So!"

"I need to tell the police," he insisted, his voice quivering. "They called asking about cyanide going missing. If you just used it for pest control, it will be fine. I need to tell them."

On the other end of the line, a voice, cold and unfeeling, cut through Darren's pleas like a blade. "You know that's not an option, Darren," the man said, the barely veiled menace in his tone causing a chill to trickle down Darren's spine.

"They will find out." Darren ran a hand through his hair. The phone felt so heavy, and he just wanted to close his eyes and shut out the world.

"You know the secret you're hiding, Darren," the voice cooed. "We both know what happens if it gets out. People died because you cut corners. It would ruin your... perfect family. The last thing you want is to endanger your family."

A cold lump of fear formed in Darren's stomach. The way the man drew out the word 'perfect' sent tremors of unease echoing through his bones. He saw, with chilling clarity, the underlined threat. A danger not just to him but to his family. To his daughters. His mind conjured images of his eldest, the same age as the girls who had disappeared.

A strangled gasp slipped from Darren's throat. His breath hitched. He felt like a deer caught in the glow of oncoming headlights. The threatening undertones, and the insidious sibilance of the man's voice, were all designed to remind Darren of his position.

"I have to tell them..." even to him, his voice sounded weak.

"Think about your daughters, Darren," the man said. "Think about your wife. They wouldn't want to be dragged into this mess, would they? Can you imagine them taken, locked away, in fear? The scandal would ruin their lives. All over, a few dead rats. All because I wanted to clean up the streets. It's best if we both keep quiet. For everyone's sake."

The words twisted a knife of fear deeper into Darren's heart, the sheer terror choking him. He was being blackmailed, forced into silence. His secret, the reason he was ensnared in this nightmare, was being wielded against him like a weapon. But there was more. The words held an underlying threat against his family. If this man had killed more than rats, then he knew where Darren lived, knew where his girls went to school. No one was safe, and he would not do anything to put his girls at risk.

"I... I understand," he stammered, his heart pounding against his ribcage like a trapped bird. He knew then that he was entangled in a web of deceit and danger from which he could see no escape.

As Darren put down the phone, his hand shaking, he slumped back into his leather chair, his face a pallid mask of fear. The cold, impersonal office seemed to close in around him, a silent witness to his despair. His gaze fell again to the photo on his desk, and the smiling faces there seemed to accuse him, condemn him for the danger he had put them in. His secret, his weakness, could end up costing more than he ever imagined.

His nightmare was just beginning.

THE LONG NIGHT

THE WORLD around Moira was still. She sat in the van, her only companion, the Boxer, Rose, dutifully curled up on the bench seat beside her. The dog was as happy here as at home and had been snoring loudly for the last hour. Moira was agitated. The ticking clock in her head grew ever louder as the 4th morning since Amelia was taken grew nearer. Was she doing the right thing?

There was no way of knowing until something happened. Her tired eyes were trained on the neat two-story house where Graham Lawrence lived his quiet, methodical life. Or so he would have others believe. Moira kept her mind on the way he licked his lips and the hunger in his eyes. He was up to something, and he was creepy enough to be the monster she was hunting.

The early hours of the morning blanketed the world in an ink-black shroud. The occasional headlights would drift by, but they were few and far between, fleeting specters in the consuming darkness. The inside of her van felt cold, a physical manifestation of the chilling emptiness that lay over her soul. Despite the dog's gentle snores, it was cold and lonely. She wanted someone to bounce ideas off.

Her mind drifted, its wandering path leading inevitably to Jonny. She found herself craving his warmth, his strength. His steadiness was a rock she longed to anchor herself to amidst the tumultuous sea that her life had become. The memory of their time working together stirred an old longing, a tender ache for something more than stolen moments and fleeting solace. They had never taken it further than friendship, but sometimes she wished they had. Could it have gone all the way? Could they have shared a life, both understanding the horrors they must face or would it simply make working together too awkward?

With a sigh, she shifted in her seat, her hand unconsciously reaching out to stroke Rose's silky fur. The Boxer stirred, turning to look at Moira with an expression that mirrored her own tired frustration. She knew Rose felt it too – the oppressive sense of stagnation that came with waiting and watching, expecting, and dreading.

The strain of the past few days weighed heavily on her. Each second that ticked by echoed in her mind, a stark reminder of Amelia's growing absence. The restlessness gnawed at her insides, and she knew she needed a respite, however brief, from the car's confinement. With a deep breath, she nudged Rose, signaling it was time for their customary walk.

The streets were eerily silent, devoid of their usual cheerful bustle. She relished the tranquility, the resounding quiet, soothing her frayed nerves. The scent of dew-kissed grass filled her nostrils, momentarily washing away the stench of fear and uncertainty that clung to her.

She didn't go far, simply around the school. That way, there were only a few moments when the house was not in her view. The last thing she needed was for Graham to sneak out while she wasn't watching.

Upon her return, she reclined in the driver's seat, her body aching for rest. Rose settled next to her, the dog's rhythmic breathing a lulling symphony to her wearied senses. She gave in to the pull of slumber, her mind still clinging to the silent vigil.

The early morning light woke her, its soft glow casting an ethereal sheen over Graham's house. Her heart pounded as she saw him step out, immaculate in his gray suit, briefcase in hand. A wave of panic washed over her. Had she missed something during her brief reprieve? Had she let the girls down? Fear and bile rose in her throat. Was that why Lily had died because she was too lazy to stay awake. Sweat had formed on her forehead, and she took a deep breath. Guilt would not help, she knew it was unfounded and pointless, but it was so hard. There was too much evil in the world and not enough of them fighting it.

She shook off the tendrils of sleep, her eyes narrowing in on Graham. Every nerve in her body was on edge, strung like a tight wire. He looked so normal, just a slightly podgy guy off to the office.

This was the third morning since Amelia had disappeared, her absence echoing ominously throughout the town. The worry gnawed at Moira, an insatiable monster feasting on her every thought. She knew she had to silence it, replace it with unwavering determination.

Graham looked normal, but he was early. It was only just 7 am. Where was he going at this time, surely not to the office?

As the town awakened to a new day, Moira steeled herself for another bout of surveillance. She wasn't going to rest until Amelia was found and her town was safe again. Despite her exhaustion, her resolve shone bright, a beacon of determination in the dark sea of uncertainty. She would follow him and hope he led her to Amelia and hope she was in time.

MOIRA EXPECTED GRAHAM TO WALK. Didn't he say he had been walking home from work the other day? However, he jumped into an aging Vauxhall Astra. It was a 59 plate making it a 2010 vehicle. Once a sharp shade of midnight blue, the color had since faded under years of exposure to the sun and now more closely resembled a muted navy.

Moira ducked as he drove past and noted that the paintwork bore the typical scars of a decade's worth of motorway stone chips and supermarket car park scuffs. The minor imperfections were etched into its character.

The car did not suit his persona, and where was he going? She felt her pulse kick up a notch. Could this be it? If so, what state would she find Amelia in?

With one eye on Graham's retreating vehicle, she turned around and followed. There was little traffic on the road until she got closer to the bypass. There, the commute had already started. She maneuvered into the slow-moving traffic, two vehicles behind him, her focus unwavering. Rose, perched alert on the bench seat, her gaze trained on the car ahead.

The morning was painted in pastel hues of orange and pink, the tranquility of dawn betrayed by the pulsating fear lurking just beneath Moira's determined facade. Her senses were heightened, each detail etched vividly in her perception—the thrum of the car's engine, the fleeting whiff of exhaust fumes, the warm, earthy scent of Rose beside her.

As she followed, she wondered about the car. It made no sense. From his house, he was precise, ordered, and particular. This vehicle was anything but. Then it struck her. It wasn't a vehicle that would turn heads but rather one that blended effortlessly into the background — an asset for a man not keen on drawing attention to himself.

Graham didn't take the direct route to work. His vehicle went two roundabouts along the bypass before turning off. Now he weaved through the familiar streets. He was almost back to where he had started. Only the one-way system and the cathedral and castle would make it difficult to drive directly here. Even so, had he taken the shortest route time-wise but not in distance? She doubted it. It was strange to drive all this way and end up near where he started.

The walk would have taken him 20 minutes, whereas the drive took him nearly as long. They were getting closer to his work. From her research, Moira knew he worked at Imp Construction Ltd. The local firm named after the famous Lincoln Imp was now a huge enterprise with branches spread across the country. However, as they got closer, Graham turned off the route. Moira could see no reason. She dropped back a little had he spotted her?

No, she didn't think so. He took a side street and then another, and then as she turned to follow, she noticed he slowed his car. It was as if he was looking at something. Was this where he had hidden Amelia?

Moira let the distance between them lengthen, not wishing to crowd him if he decided to stop. A flash of brake lights. Moira held her breath. Should she call Jonny? Then he was driving away. He turned left and was moving quicker than he had throughout the journey. Moira waited for him to turn and then hit the accelerator, pushing her van to quickly catch up.

She slowed where Graham had. Was he looking at the last house on the block? It was smaller and less well cared for than the others. Moira saw something in the widow, but she could come back. Right now, she didn't want to lose Graham.

She followed for three more turns, and then Graham disappeared into his workplace. Moira circled back to the street where he had paused.

The world seemed to still as she parked her van across the street. Time hung heavy around her, the air thick with anticipation and dread. With Rose's reassuring presence beside her, she got out of the van and crossed the road.

Moira's gut clenched. The house was a morbid landmark, its faded facade bearing silent witness to unspeakable horrors. From her distance, she could make out the chilling display of dolls in the window—a tableau that sent shivers down her spine.

Though they were dressed in Victorian garb and finery, these were the dolls that were left with the unveiling. Or as near as could be.

Moira reached for her phone. She should call Jonny, but she was drawn to cross the road. Three dolls were in the window, each with a card next to them. Two at £20 and one at £10, though she could see no difference other than color.

Each doll seemed to carry a life of its own, their glassy eyes filled with secrets only they knew. As she approached the house, she could almost feel their hollow gazes piercing through her, their silent whispers filling her mind with haunting images. The old wooden door seemed a barrier between the world of the living and the ghosts of the owner's morbid obsessions.

Through the window, she could see an old woman, hidden by the faded yellow net curtains, sitting in a chair.

Her hand reached for the door, and her heart pounded in her chest. The breeze seemed to stop, and the birds were no longer singing. It was as if the world was holding its breath, waiting for her to cross the threshold. But as her fingers brushed the cold doorknob, her phone rang, jolting her from the eerie trance.

Moira fumbled for the device, her heart thundering in her chest. Each ring seemed to reverberate in the silent street, a reminder of the real world she had almost forgotten. She could not just walk in. What had she been thinking?

The caller ID flashed Jonny's name, and her pulse steadied, relief flooding through her. With a last glance at the haunting dolls in the window, she retreated to her van.

Every fiber of her being screamed to go back, to explore the secrets the house held, but she knew better than to act on impulse. There was a method to this madness, a meticulous plan that she must adhere to. And that included answering the call that might lead her one step closer to uncovering the face behind the horror that gripped her town.

DOUBTS AND DECISIONS

ONCE SHE WAS BACK in the safe confines of her van, Moira answered the call.

"We've got a lead," Jonny's voice was excited. "A local drug dealer spotted near where Amelia was last seen. We've got him on CCTV, and we're bringing him in. We could use your insight during the questioning." His words were like a cold splash of water, jolting her out of her current thoughts.

The dolls, the scruffy house across the road, the one she found because of Graham's peculiar interest. This was a lead. Amelia could be inside that house. "I have one too. Graham led me to a house. The dolls are in the window."

There was a brief silence on the line, followed by Jonny's steady voice. "Good, we'll look into that. But right now, our priority is Amelia. Let's focus on the dealer first, all right?"

Moira felt her heart tugged in two different directions. What if the girl was here, in this house, praying for help?

"I want to check this out," she said.

"I know, but... trust me. My gut tells me I'm on to something. I promise as soon as we talk to this guy, we will check out your house."

Moira did trust him, and so she agreed, her gaze lingering on the dolls as she snapped a quick photo before she revved her van back to life. But the seed of doubt was sown, and the question itched at her mind. Was she looking in the wrong direction?

"Okay, but let's make it quick. The clock is ticking."

"He's here now. We'll check out your lead as soon as we're finished."

As the call ended, she took a moment to regroup, her gaze lingering on the doll-filled window. Graham's detour past this house could not be a coincidence, but she was not one to jump to conclusions. The puzzle pieces were falling into place, but the picture they were forming was far from clear.

Resolving to return to the doll house later, she pulled away from the curb. Her thoughts spun, a whirlwind of uncertainty, fear, and determination. Her eyes strayed to Rose, the loyal Boxer's steady presence a comforting constant in the chaotic tapestry of her life.

As she sped away to join Jonny, she couldn't shake off the nagging sense of uncertainty. She had made a crucial decision. To let the dolls go for now. With Amelia's life hanging in the balance, the weight of her decision felt heavier than ever.

This was how an investigation went, she reminded herself. The chilling image of the dolls was seared into her memory. They were not the same. These were dressed in old-fashioned dresses, not the modern-day clothes of the victims. She had to choose, and she prayed that Jonny was right.

Moira navigated the winding streets, a silent promise hardening in her soul. No matter how dark the path got, she would illuminate the shadows and unmask the monster that lurked within. The safety of her city depended on it, and she wouldn't let them down.

For now, she had to concentrate on the best way to get information out of a drug dealer. A life depended on it.

THE INTERIOR of the Lincolnshire police station was uncharacteristically quiet, the somber atmosphere of the missing girls' case looming heavily over the heads of everyone there. There was no idol banter, no bad jokes, and no casual gossip. Everyone was serious and, most of all, tired. They were focused on one thing only, and that gave the place a somber feel.

Moira sat next to Jonny in the interrogation room, their gazes locked over the table on the man seated across from them. Known in the underworld as Snake Eyes, he was the town's main drug dealer and their potential lead.

Snake Eyes was a man of intimidating stature, his six-foot frame hunched over in the chair. His dark, greasy hair was slicked back, revealing a jagged scar that traced a dangerous path down his forehead to his cheekbone. His sharp, angular features were hardened, lending him an air of cruel nonchalance. But it was his eyes that truly unnerved Moira - icy and emotionless, they held an uncanny resemblance to his namesake, a piercing gaze that bore into you with cold calculation.

Looking into that icy gaze, she had no difficulty believing he could kill these girls. However, she didn't believe he would do it in the manner of their cases. This man would not be playing with dolls. Acid curled in her stomach as she wondered where Amelia was. Had she left her in that house? Was she dying while Moira wasted her time on the piece of scum before her?

Take a breath, she told herself. She was here, and she had no doubt that the man in front of her was a killer. He pedaled filth that took countless lives each year. Maybe he was their guy. And yet, her gut screamed no, hurry!

The room was permeated by a tense silence, the only sound the low hum of a fan. These rooms could reach horrific temperatures, and the building was too old for air conditioning. Not that the UK had much air conditioning. Summer never lasted long. Moira felt a shiver of unease course through her as she studied Snake Eyes, taking in his rigid posture and the way his fingers drummed a monotonous rhythm on the steel table. He was not in the least bit bothered by being here. He was confident, calculating and thought he was in control. He hadn't even asked for a solicitor.

Lying in the corner of the room, Rose let out a loud snore. Moira was pleased to see that it caused Snake Eyes to jump. She had noticed that he eyed the dog when she came into the room. Could Moira use that to their advantage?

"Snake Eyes, or should I say, Fred Parker?" Moira began, her tone steady despite her growing anxiety.

A flash of annoyance crossed the big man's eyes.

"We have you on CCTV, close to where Amelia was last seen. We need to know what you were doing there and where she is."

The man across the table only shrugged, his nonchalant demeanor doing nothing to dissipate the tension in the room. "I go a lot of places, detective. Doesn't mean I've got anything to do with your missing girls."

Moira wanted to point out that she was not a detective, not anymore, but she knew that she was procrastinating. It made no difference. She shared a look with Jonny, his calm presence providing a counterweight to the unease bubbling within her. As Jonny continued with the interrogation, Moira felt her thoughts returning to the dolls, the house, and Graham Lawrence. She was torn between the current lead and her intuition, each passing moment twisting her insides in a vice of dread and panic.

"What, were you doing there 3 nights ago?" Jonny asked, his voice like a whip in the quiet room.

Moira had seen hardened criminals quake under Jonny's glare, but this man didn't even blink. He answered Jonny's questions with dispassionate responses. "I was visiting a friend. I can give you his name, so you can check on the timing. I'm sure you will find I have a rock-solid alibi." There was a sneer on his lips that turned Moira's stomach.

Anger surged through Moira. Why wouldn't this idiot cooperate? She knew this was fueled by worry. How long did they have? Had she made the wrong decision? Despite her escalating worries, Moira knew she needed to stay focused. She forced her attention back on Snake Eyes, her eyes hardening with determination. Despite his cold demeanor and his position as a drug dealer, she began to believe he wasn't involved in the kidnappings. But she needed to be sure.

The questions continued, each denial from Snake Eyes deepening Moira's unease. Each passing minute was a potential minute lost in finding Amelia, and as the interrogation went on, her worry turned into a rising panic. But even in her anxiety, Moira was left with a stark realization: if Snake Eyes wasn't involved, then she had made a terrible mistake, and Amelia's time was running out.

"Look, you two don't scare me," Snake Eyes said, leaning back and folding his arms. The smirk on his face said he believed he was in control.

"Do you think this is funny?" she said through gritted teeth.

He smiled and winked.

How she wanted to wipe that smile off his face. "A girl's life hangs on the line, and you want to waste our time. Stand up."

Jonny shot Moira a glance, but she raised her right hand just enough for him to see. Asking him to go with her. He leaned back in his chair, relaxing. Snake Eyes hadn't moved.

Moira stood and kicked his chair. It hardly moved, but it shocked him enough to have him rise to his feet. Moira signaled to Rose, and the dog leaped to her feet and came to heel.

Rose had done a lot of training since Moira had rescued her. Some of this had been in protection work. In this game, the dog was taught to grab a sleeve that a so-called criminal was wearing and, if that criminal moved to keep them still by barking. In Rose's mind, it was all fun. She did not consider she was attacking. However, she was a big dog, and her broad head and heavy jawline could look most threatening. Her teeth were large and white, and when she barked and stood her ground, it took a brave man to face her down.

"Where is Amelia?" Moira demanded, and at the same time, she applied pressure to Rose's collar. This was to illicit opposition reflex from the dog. This was something first discovered by Pavlov. If you pull or push a dog instinct, he called it freedom instinct, it will cause the dog to do the opposite. Moira was conditioning Rose for the game to come.

"I don't know, no, Amelia."

"Listen, Fred, if you think I'm kidding, think again. I need answers, and I need them now, so you talk to me, or you talk to...." Moira looked down at Rose.

The dog was straining against the hand that held her. She was excited about the game, but that expression could look mighty scary to someone frightened of dogs, and Moira was betting that Fred was terrified despite all his bravado.

Fred shook his head. "I told you where I was. I don't know anything else."

Moira almost believed him, but she had to be sure. They were running out of time, and she was not a cop. She didn't have to abide by the rules.

Under her breath, she whispered, "Helper." It was Rose's command to stop a criminal. The boxer's muscles rippled under the lights as she launched herself at the man. Stopping just inches from him, she bounced on her back legs, spittle flying as her jaws came within inches of Fred's face as she barked again and again.

The man cowered back against the wall. Moira let Rose continue. The dog thought this was a great game and would continue for as long as was needed. Moira heard Jonny move his chair back. Would he intervene? Strictly speaking, this was intimidation, it could get Moira thrown off the case, but Rose wouldn't touch the man. He was safe. He just didn't know it.

"I know nothing," Fred shouted. The look in his eyes told Moira he was telling the truth. "Call the dog off, I was just delivering product, and I saw nothing."

"Here," Moira shouted, and Rose stopped and came to heel. "Good girl, bed." Rose returned to her place on the floor, and Moira threw her a biscuit for getting the information. "Sit," Moira said, only this time she was talking to Fred.

Returning to his chair, he was a lot less cocky. The bravado had vanished from his eyes.

"Now you know how Amelia feels," Moira spat the words.

He nodded.

"What we need from you is to go to all your people and tell them to help us. What did they see? Who did they see? Get them to write down anything that could be relevant and to keep doing so, and then we will believe that you are a helpful citizen with these children's best wishes at heart. Can you do that? She held her breath, expecting him to laugh.

"If it is all off the record. If nothing is held against us, then I think we can do that."

"Agreed," Jonny said, and he pointed to the door.

As the drug dealer walked out, now a set of eyes on their side, Moira's mind played out the worst-case scenarios. Each tick of the clock echoed ominously in the room, amplifying her worries. Amelia was in danger. Every second they wasted was a second lost in finding her.

THE MOTHER

FOR LONG MOMENTS Moira stared at the worn table in the interrogation room. She felt frozen, unable to move, and not knowing where to go next. Only this wouldn't do. They had Fred and his organization to help. If they stuck to their word, it was a big win. His people moved in the dark underbelly of the city. They saw things that most others never did.

"What now?" Jonny asked, "Should we call it a night?"

Moira remembered the house and the dolls. How could she have forgotten them? Of course, it was night after night with hardly any sleep. "We need to go look at the house with the dolls. I have a bad feeling about it."

"That again." Jonny shook his head. "It's late."

"Yeah. Tomorrow is the 4th morning."

Jonny was instantly awake. "Is it? Where did I lose a day?"

"You've been working too hard. We all have. I need you to see this," Moira said, her voice just above a whisper. She handed her phone to Jonny, a picture illuminated on the screen. The image displayed three dolls, eerily similar to the ones found with the girls.

Jonny took the phone, his brow furrowing as he studied the dead eyes staring back at him. The harsh light from the screen cast deep shadows on his face, making his normally warm features seem cold and severe. "Where did you get this?" he asked, looking up from the screen to meet her gaze.

"The house, remember. I followed Graham. He went out of his way to go down this street and slowed down opposite the house. I was just about to knock on the door when I got your call," she replied, her hands unconsciously wringing together.

Jonny paused. "Let's go to my desk." They walked out of the room, down the corridor, and into the main area. There were plenty of desks with people still working. Dealing with the numerous phone calls or looking through CCTV. It was a hard time for all of them.

Jonny's desk was next to a window on the right. He pulled his chair up to the screen. "What's the address?"

"13 East Gate," Moira said.

Jonny tapped on his keyboard with single fingers. Despite his years in the force, he was useless with keyboards. His face looked brighter, and his eyes were more awake, but then the fatigue came back. "It's owned by Clara Sutton, a 66-year-old woman. Do you think she's involved?" He gave Moira a sarcastic look.

Moira shrugged, uncertainty gnawing at her. "I don't know, Jonny. But the dolls... they look just like the ones found with the girls, don't they?" Moira handed him her phone. The awful pictures of the dolls brought back the images of Mandy and Sophie and soon Amelia if they didn't hurry. Bile rose in her throat, and she swallowed hard. How she wanted a cup of tea.

Jonny was silent for a long moment, his gaze fixed on the image on the screen. When he finally looked up at Moira, his eyes held a hint of shock. "It's uncanny," he admitted, handing the phone back to her. "Even the clothes are similar, well, equally as well made, just different in style."

He rubbed his face, fatigue etching itself onto his features. "I agree, Moira, it's worth a look. Let's pay Clara Sutton a visit. Maybe she has a relative."

As they made their way towards Clara's house, Moira felt a sense of dread coiling in her gut. The wind whistled eerily through the empty streets, adding to her sense of unease. The house came into view, its façade ominously illuminated by the streetlight. She parked on the road across from the house. The window was dimly lit as if they had hardly any light on inside.

They got out. Rose was in the back of the van, safe in her crate and away from prying eyes. She had done enough today.

As they walked across the street, a chill wind snaked its way through the narrow streets of Lincoln, nipping at Moira's face as she stood in front of Jonny. Her breath was visible in the cold night air, each exhale forming a cloud of vapor that quickly disappeared into the darkness. Around them, the town was steeped in an uneasy silence, the events of the past few days casting a dark shadow over the otherwise quaint historic town.

A shiver ran down Moira's spine as she took in the darkened house. The dolls' uncanny resemblance to the ones found with the girls was unnerving. Their still smiles and glassy eyes seemed to hold a secret she was yet to uncover.

Inside her coat pocket, her hand tightened around her phone containing the picture of the dolls. A sick sense of anticipation welled within her as she approached the front door with Jonny at her side. Could Clara Sutton, an elderly woman, be behind these kidnappings? Or was it merely a disturbing coincidence?

Each step towards the house was an exercise in nerve-wracking suspense. As they stood before the front door, ready to confront the woman inside, Moira couldn't help but wonder if they were too late. Would they find Amelia inside? Or would they be walking into something far more sinister than they could imagine? Each second that passed heightened her anxiety. Every beat of her heart was a loud drum in her ears.

"Ready," she asked.

Jonny shrugged, but she could see from his face that he was on edge. Could this be it? Would they find Amelia, and would she be alive?

Moira knocked loudly on the door to Clara's house. Her heart almost stopped as it swung away from them with a nerve-breaking creak.

The eerie silence that followed amplified Moira's growing dread. It was a quiet that seemed to hold its breath, a suspenseful pause that promised to shatter under the weight of what lay ahead.

UNHINGED

NIGHT HAD FULLY DESCENDED, wrapping the old house in a cloak of darkness as Moira and Jonny approached. They both noticed how the streetlights seemed to avoid the house as if the light itself was afraid to expose the secrets within. Leaving Rose in the van, Moira followed Jonny across the street to Clara Sutton's door, her stomach churning with a cocktail of dread and uncertainty.

Jonny and Moira stood before Clara's humble brick house, the night's darkness lending an eerie hue to the scene. The house had the weather-beaten look of something forgotten by time, the bricks aged and worn, the paint peeling, the dirty windows reflecting the dying embers of the sunset.

"Ready," she asked.

Jonny shrugged, but she could see from his face that he was on edge. Could this be it? Would they find Amelia, and would she be alive?

Moira knocked, and the door creaked open, followed by silence, but before Moira could enter, Clara's frail hand appeared around the door, beckoning them in.

The scent of mildew and old age wafted out, heavy and suffocating. Moira fought back a grimace as they stepped inside, her eyes taking in the poorly lit room. The floorboards groaned under their weight as if the house itself were protesting their presence.

Their eyes adjusted to reveal Clara Sutton, her pale blue eyes darting quickly between them, her thin lips pursed in a worried line. Her cheeks carried a permanent flush, indicative of the heightened alertness that seemed to be her default state. There was a palpable nervous energy about her like a creature perpetually prepared to bolt.

A halo of soft white curls crowned her head, restrained by a dirty-looking ribbon. Her dress, a faded floral print, clung to her frail form, giving her the look of a forgotten character from a bygone era.

But it was her hands that caught Moira's attention, the skeletal fingers bearing the scars and nicks of years of painstaking dollmaking.

Stepping inside the house was like stepping into a different world. The musty air was thick with a peculiar sweetness, an undercurrent that made Moira's senses tingle with apprehension. As they stepped into the living room, they saw that the house was filled with Clara's creations, dolls perched on every possible surface. Their glassy eyes seemed to follow their movements, lending a chillingly lifelike quality to the inanimate figures.

As they ventured deeper into the room, lit by a single dull lamp, they were met with a chilling sight: a cabinet filled with dolls. Their glassy eyes seemed to follow them as they moved around the room. In front of it was a miniature tea party, the dolls seated around a tiny table, a tableau that would have been charming if not for the circumstances.

It was creepy. Moira wanted to run through the house, ripping open doors until she found Amelia.

Clara returned to her chair in the window and picked up a doll. Her skeletal hand pointed to the window, to the dolls for sale. Her eyes darted from her dolls to the two of them and back again. Constantly moving. Full of fear and paranoia. Moira would not want this woman behind her on a dark night. Though she looked weak, something about her gave Moira the heebie-jeebies.

Despite the creepiness and the apprehension, Moira and Jonny stood their ground, determined to unravel the truth hidden behind those darting, anxious eyes and the silent, watchful gaze of the dolls. They had ventured into Clara's peculiar world, and there was no turning back.

Clara was talking to the doll in her hands, the soft sibilance of her voice barely discernible over the silence of the house. "Told you not to. Knew you was bad. One more chance."

"We'd like to ask you some questions, Clara," Jonny began, his voice slicing through the silence.

Clara nodded, her eyes never leaving the dolls. She talked to them softly as if they were her children. Each whisper sent shivers running down Moira's spine.

"Miss Sutton, Clara," Jonny said. "We found two of your dolls at crime scenes. If I show you pictures, can you tell me how they got there?"

"They would be bad girls," she said, her voice a hiss. "I hate to do it, but the bad girls have to go."

Throughout their visit, Clara would often lean in to whisper to her dolls. Each hushed word, each secret shared with her inanimate companions, only served to add to the aura of creepiness that cloaked her.

Jonny handed her a tablet with the first picture of the doll showing. The black leggings and the pink hoody. "Did you make this doll?" Jonny asked.

Clara stared around the room as if expecting someone to jump out at her. She shrunk back into her chair and then moved forward. Shaking the doll in her hand. Her eyes flicked from them to the dolls to the tablet.

"That would be Mary. She always spilled her tea. She had to go." Clara rocked in her chair. It was as if she was unable to keep still. Her eyes flicked to the dark corners of the room, full of fear and paranoia.

"Did you make these clothes for Mary?" Moira asked.

"No." Clara laughed a grating sound like a cackle that set the hairs on the back of Moira's neck on edge. "Mary was in a pale blue gown, beautiful with lace and only a little tea stain. She had to go. You can't have bad girls; they spoil the batch."

Yet, beneath the paranoia, the unsettling habits, and the nervous energy, there was a palpable sense of sadness that clung to Clara. As Moira looked at her, this lonely old woman living in a world populated by dolls, she couldn't help but feel a twinge of sympathy. Clara was a living testament to a traumatic past that had seeped into the present, painting her reality with its grim hues.

The dolls were her escape, and though she wanted to find Amelia here, Moira already knew that she wouldn't. Clara was far from harmless, but she was not one to go out and stalk girls on the street. Moira wondered if she had even left the house at all in many years.

A grunt in the corner had Moira and Jonny almost jumping out of their skins. They turned, their eyes now accustomed to the gloom, and spotted a man huddling against the wall alongside another easy chair.

It was the first time that Moira realized they weren't alone. He was a figure swallowed in shadows, his presence going unnoticed until that moment.

"Who is that?" Moira asked, angry, for she could see that the man looked afraid.

"We don't talk about him, no, No, NO." her voice rose to a shrill scream. "Don't look at Peter. Never look at the lump, never, never." Clara's face was screwed into a mask of horror, and she rocked faster and faster, squeezing the naked doll against her chest.

The doll she was holding was not yet clothed and missing an arm. She clung to it as if it was the most precious thing in the world.

Moira turned her eyes to Peter. Now she knew he was there. It was hard not to shudder. There was something wrong with him. She knew that was politically incorrect, but Peter was not all there. It was clear that Peter had a cognitive impairment or cognitive disability. From the way he held himself, she suspected that his mental capacity would be that of a very young child and one who had, no doubt, suffered the wrath of his mother. Could he be the killer?

What had happened between these two? Moira could only imagine that Peter was unwanted and reminded Clara of a trauma. Had she been raped? It made sense. That was why she had retreated to her dolls. Female, safe, and her children that she couldn't have. A symbol of a loving relationship that she had never experienced.

She could see he was Clara's son now. Moira raised a finger to her lips to ask Jonny to keep quiet while she looked at Peter. Moira smiled. Peter Sutton, Clara's middle-aged son, was a significant presence in their old, cramped house. A large, hulking man with a heavyset build, and she imagined a shuffling gate. His features were an odd mix of his mother's - he had her wide, pale blue eyes, but they were hooded and possessed a disconcerting stillness.

Peter's face was thick with an unkempt beard, and his dark hair looked greasy and was hanging across his face. He peered through it like a child hiding in the bushes.

"Hello Peter, have you seen a young girl?" Moira asked gently.

"Not seen, no one," Peter said. His voice was a deep, throaty mumble, barely intelligible. His presence, much like his mother's, was unnerving – he was not overtly threatening, but there was a palpable aura of unease that surrounded him.

Moira could feel her heart racing, but she doubted that Amelia was here. These two were no doubt capable of awful things, but they did not have the ability to hide from cameras and pull off such intricate crimes. Amelia was not here. Still, they had to look.

"We'd like to search the house, Clara," Moira said, trying to keep her voice steady. Clara turned her gaze from the dolls to look at Moira, her eyes sharp in the dim light.

"No," she said, her voice as brittle as old parchment. "My children would be disturbed."

"Well, we can make you. And if we do, there will be twenty policemen, all with heavy boots," Moira said.

Clara hissed at them and shook the doll in front of her. "My children will eat you."

The droning hum of silence hung heavy in the air of Clara Sutton's living room, disrupted only by the muffled sounds of the passing cars and the occasional grunt from Peter seated in the corner, a hulking shadow almost lost amidst the clutter.

"Clara," Moira began again, her tone respectful yet firm, "do you know a man named Graham Lawrence?"

A bony finger traced the porcelain cheek of the doll, the light touch eerie in the semi-darkness. "Graham Lawrence?" Clara echoed, her tone distant as if pulling a name from the fog of her memories. Her gaze wandered to Peter, who gave a low, inarticulate grunt, a sound that somehow felt like punctuation in the stilted conversation.

"No," she finally said, shaking her head. "No, my dear. Clara doesn't know any Graham. Isn't that right, Betsy?" She cooed at the doll, brushing its artificial hair with surprising tenderness. The doll, seated in Clara's lap with her glassy eyes reflecting the muted light, sat in perpetual silence.

Jonny, ever the observer, carefully scrutinized Clara's reactions, his eyes narrowed. "Graham works at the Imp Construction Company. You might have seen him around, possibly in your area?" His tone carried an undercurrent of urging, hoping to coax something useful out of Clara's meandering thoughts.

But Clara merely shook her head again, chuckling softly under her breath. She shifted her attention to another doll, cradling it in her thin arms. "Did you hear that, Margaret? These nice people are asking about a man we don't know." The doll stared blankly at them, its painted eyes a stark contrast to Clara's animated ones.

A rush of frustration was building in Moira, but she clamped down on it, maintaining her calm facade. "Clara," she said, "We're looking for a little girl, Amelia. We're very worried about her. Do you know anything about her?"

Peter stirred, mumbling something that sounded remotely like 'Amelia.' Moira turned her attention to him, her senses heightened. "Peter? Do you know Amelia?"

But the man retreated into himself, producing a low guttural sound, his eyes flitting nervously towards Clara. Clara, in turn, shot an angry glance at Peter before speaking softly to her dolls, "They're scaring Peter, aren't they, Susie? These strangers with their questions... we like it when Peter's scared. He keeps quiet then. We can forget him and have our tea."

The air within the room seemed to grow heavier, the light of a passing car casting eerie shadows around. Despite the sheer uncanniness of it all, Moira and Jonny couldn't shake off the nagging sensation of a puzzle piece clicking into place. But the complete picture was still maddeningly out of reach.

"Clara, who buys your dolls?"

"Never, no, rehome the bad girls. Have to punish the bad girls."

A shiver ran down Moira's back. Was she punishing Amelia? Was that what had happened to Sophie and Mandy? They had been punished?

They pushed a little harder and a little longer, but Clara would not let them search the house, and she gave them nothing intelligible.

Leaving Clara's house felt like emerging from a nightmare. The cold night air filled Moira's lungs as they stood outside, Clara's front door closing behind them. She could still feel the eeriness of the house clinging to her. The image of the dolls burned into her mind.

"I'm not sure we could get a warrant to search the house," Jonny said, his voice heavy with frustration.

He ran his hand through his hair, his gaze lost somewhere in the darkened street.

"I don't know what to think, Jonny," Moira confessed, her eyes never leaving the house. "She doesn't seem capable... but those dolls..."

The image of the tea party was seared into her mind, a haunting vision that sent a chill running down her spine. She could still hear Clara's voice in her ears, the way she spoke to the dolls as if they were her own children. It was a twisted parody of motherhood that left Moira with a sour taste in her mouth. Especially as she was so cruel to her actual child... son. Poor Peter. What had he been through? Moira intended to ring social services, but she was not sure it would help.

As they walked back to the van, the house seemed to loom behind them, a silent witness to the mysteries within. It was a puzzle that needed to be solved, a riddle that demanded an answer, and Moira couldn't shake off the feeling that the dolls were key.

"Should we look around?" Jonny asked.

Moira got Rose out of the crate and pulled out a sealed bag labeled Amelia. She quickly went through the routine and got the dog to search all around the small house. Rose found nothing, and it confirmed Moira's gut feeling. Clara was creepy as hell, but she was not guilty of these crimes. That didn't mean she wasn't involved somehow. Those dolls were too much of a coincidence.

As the van pulled away, Moira cast a final glance at Clara's house. She didn't know what to make of the elderly woman, but one thing was clear – there was more to this house and its inhabitants than met the eye. And she had every intention of finding out what that was.

AN UNLIKELY ALLY

JONNY AND MOIRA WERE EXHAUSTED, but they returned to the office. They were not stopping this evening until they found something.

When they got back, a man was waiting to see them. He now sat across from them, looking like he'd walked straight off the cover of a punk rock album. His head was shaved to a gleaming sheen, reflecting the harsh overhead lights of the police station interrogation room. His nose sported a ring, gleaming silver in contrast to his weathered skin. His muscular arms, decorated in a mosaic of tattoos, were folded on the table, veins throbbing subtly under the inked skin.

For all his rough exterior, the man's voice was surprisingly gentle, like a soothing lullaby undercutting the harsh percussion of his appearance. This was a member of Snake Eyes' gang, a man who lived on the fringes of law and society, and yet, at that moment, he was their best lead.

"We've got this charity bloke, right?" he began, his voice melodious, making a stark contrast with his gruff appearance. "Name's Samuel Fletcher. Always around the area where the first two girls were taken."

One of the junior PCs, stationed at a desk piled high with scattered notes and case files, perked up at the mention of the name. His hand scrambled around the chaos, finally pulling out a crumpled piece of paper, his face a mask of shock.

"Here," he said, his voice almost a squeak as he passed the note to Jonny. His eyes darted nervously between the senior detective and the man across the table. "A member of the public called in about a man fitting his description. The night Sophie went missing..."

A thick silence followed, punctuated only by the steady hum of the fluorescent lights. Samuel Fletcher, a charity worker, someone dedicated to the service of others, was now under suspicion.

Jonny and Moira shared a glance. There was a chill of uncertainty in the air, the disturbing thought of a charity worker potentially being involved. But they knew they had to follow every lead and tread every possible path, however unlikely.

"Bring him in," Jonny said finally, his voice a low murmur, resolute and unwavering. In the ruthless pursuit of justice, no stone could be left unturned. No matter who was hiding beneath it.

THE ROOM WAS a study in neutrality—cream walls, stainless steel table, plain-backed chairs. One lone florescent tube flickered above them, casting stark shadows over the current occupant, Samuel Fletcher. He sat, tall and lean, his thin beard lending him an air of distinction, his warm eyes rimmed with the signs of a long day.

In the corner, Rose lay curled up, her normally alert eyes drooping with tiredness. Her presence was both a comfort and a reminder of the urgency of their mission.

Moira and Jonny sat across from Samuel, their expressions were as neutral as the room, yet their eyes betrayed the exhaustion of a long, fruitless day. So far, he had given them nothing, and they had very little else to ask.

Samuel broke the silence, his voice echoing in the spartan surroundings. "I wish I could help you more, detectives. I really do." His words hung in the air, echoing Moira's own wish. But wishes weren't what they needed. They needed facts.

"Samuel," Jonny began again, "you say you saw nothing unusual the night Sophie went missing?" His tone was professional and detached, but the underlying urgency was clear.

Moira wondered how he did it. She knew her jaw was clenched with every question. Her fists matched her jaw but sat on her knee in case they gained a life of their own and flew at the man.

"I didn't," Samuel replied, regret painting his features. "I usually finish my rounds by that time. If only..." He let his voice trail off, a potent mix of regret and helplessness settling in his eyes.

Moira seized the opportunity, her eyes fixed on his. "You were in the vicinity, though? Around the time she was taken?"

Samuel nodded, swallowing visibly. "About thirty minutes earlier, I'd say. I didn't see Sophie or anything out of the ordinary."

Moira's heart sank. So close, yet so far. Another dead end. The frustration bubbled up, but she kept her tone steady. "Samuel, do you know anyone who might harm these girls?"

Samuel's eyes hardened, a flash of anger rippling across his benign facade. "I hate the scum who walk these streets. I wish I could clean up this place and keep it safe. But what can a guy like me do?" His voice held an undertone of bitterness, a hint of a battle fought and lost. "I wish the children would stay in their houses and be safe."

"Me too," Moira whispered, and the air seemed to seep out of her as well as the hope.

Moira and Jonny exchanged a glance. It wasn't the break they were hoping for, but Samuel's information could still be useful. "Promise us you'll keep an eye out," Moira said, her voice softer now. "Any little thing could make a difference."

"I will," Samuel responded, resolve steeled his voice. "For Sophie. For Mandy. For Amelia. For all the girls."

The promise echoed in the bleak room as they rose, their bodies echoing the weight of another day passing without a lead. They released Samuel, their exhaustion mirrored in his weary departure.

Outside the interrogation room, Moira turned to Jonny, her voice hoarse from too many questions. "What now?"

"We keep looking," Jonny replied, determination replacing the fatigue in his eyes. "We don't stop until we find Amelia. You want coffee or your normal tea?"

"Coffee. Grab me a bucket full."

A RAY OF HOPE

THE FROSTY MORNING was punctuated by the piercing cry of a blackbird, breaking the silence of the early dawn. It was day four of Amelia White's disappearance. Four days since, the lively girl, with a halo of auburn ringlets and a contagious smile, had vanished. An empty chasm was left behind, swallowing the hope and laughter that used to radiate from the small and vivacious gymnast.

Moira couldn't imagine how the girl's parents must be feeling. The agony they had gone through. She had spent the night with Jonny and many others going over everything, but nothing helped. All Moira kept thinking about was the dolls. Were the dolls a clue?

Because of that, she hadn't gone home. Instead, she was parked further up the street from Clara's house. Waiting, hoping to see something, anything that could help. During the few hours she had been here, she had gone from alertness to sleep to panic that she should be watching Graham.

Dawn was rising, and soon the city would wake. The cathedral still glowed above her, above them all. Little it helped.

Moira's heart pounded against her chest as if trying to break free. Her gaze was fixed on the house, but in her mind, she saw the now infamous path where Amelia was last seen. The gym from which she'd departed would look hollow without the energetic presence of the thirteen-year-old.

Bringing her mind back to the task at hand, she stared at the street. Clara's house seemed to skulk in the shadows of those near it. The street, usually abuzz with life, felt eerily quiet, haunted by the absence of the one who was no longer there.

"Stop it," she told herself, causing Rose to lift her head. "Sleep, girl." Moira stroked the dog's silky ears.

The cold had seeped into the van, the chill a physical manifestation of the fear that held the town captive. Moira's breaths fogged up the windshield, each exhale a silent prayer for Amelia. The wait was agonizing, the dread growing with each passing second. Would they find Amelia today?

Suddenly, her phone vibrated against the dashboard. Her heart felt so heavy, her arms almost unable to reach for it. This was the call she had dreaded. It was Jonny.

Slowly she picked up the phone, closing her eyes for a second and fighting back the tears, she answered.

"We found her," he said, his voice choked with relief. "Amelia is alive."

The weight that lifted from her heart was almost physical, a rush of relief that momentarily left her lightheaded. Alive. The word echoed in her mind over and over. Alive! The void in her chest filled, overwhelmed with a surge of relief.

She raced to the scene, the usually tedious drive blurring into a mere moment in her urgency.

The dawn was just breaking, the early morning sun casting long, inky shadows that seemed to stretch endlessly as Moira pulled up on the street where Amelia's parents lived. The girl should soon be home.

Moira walked along until she stood outside a nondescript semi-detached house. A crowd had gathered, their faces grim, eyes anxious. Amidst the hush of the onlookers, the buzz of the press, and the murmur of the police radio, there was an undercurrent of tense anticipation. This was the house where Amelia White had last been seen. The house where her parents had waited, fearing the worst.

The crowd parted as a BMW drove up. It was decorated in the Battenburg squares of florescent blue and yellow with the police insignia, a crown on a blue circle with a grey star behind it, and Lincolnshire Police in the circle. Moira felt her heart stutter. Could this really be the happy outcome they had hoped for?

As the car pulled up to the curb, its tires crushed a can that popped. The crowd jumped, all turning, expecting the worst. As the vehicle came to a halt, the house door opened, and Jonny and the parents came out. Moira's eyes returned to the police car. The back door opened, and out stepped a female officer, Judy Parsons, her face worn but eyes glittering with an unfamiliar hope. Behind her, a petite figure with curly auburn hair emerged, her face pale but unmarked. Amelia.

A collective gasp ran through the crowd. Some cried in relief, and others stood stunned. But no reaction was as visceral as that of Sarah and Paul White.

Sarah, a petite woman with the same auburn curls as her daughter, seemed to crumple where she stood. A hand flew to her mouth, her eyes welling up with tears that spilled unchecked down her cheeks. "Amelia," she whispered, the name ripped from her soul, a sob and a prayer all in one. "Amelia, my darling." She stumbled, and Jonny grabbed her arm, helping her stay upright.

Paul, a broad-shouldered man with streaks of gray in his hair, staggered a few steps, disbelief etched on his weathered face. A large hand clamped over his heart, his eyes filled with the reflection of his returned child, and a choked sound, somewhere between a sob and a laugh, escaped him.

Without a word, they both rushed forward. The crowd parted, letting them through. Moira looked around and could see that even hardened journalists had tears in their eyes.

As Paul and Sarah reached Amelia, they collapsed to their knees, and Amelia fell into their arms. The family folded into each other, a tangle of limbs and tears, their cries of relief and joy punctuating the stunned silence.

The crowd around them fell away, their raw emotion creating a bubble that no one dared to intrude on. Tears flowed freely, salty tributes to the fear and despair that had held them, hostage for days on end. For this family, it was over, and their prayers had been answered. Moira was overwhelmed. She was so pleased to see this scene that she never imagined happening.

Moira stood to the side, her heart pounding in her chest, as she watched the tearful reunion. The sight of Amelia, safe and back in her parents' arms, ignited a spark of hope within her. Perhaps this was the turning point they had all been waiting for.

As the family wept, huddled on the pavement in the early morning sun, the world seemed to hold its breath. It was a scene of relief, of returned hope, and of a fear that was slowly beginning to recede.

At that moment, Moira knew that their fight was far from over. But for the Whites, this was a new beginning, a second chance that they had been granted, a ray of hope in their world that had turned bleak.

Moira watched as Amelia was ushered toward the house. She knew she could have gone with her. But she also knew that too many people would make it harder. Jonny was good at his job. He would get the information they needed. Amelia was there, bewildered and disoriented but unharmed, her brown eyes wide with confusion and fear. Her parents were holding her tight, their bodies wracked with sobs, their relief as tangible as the cold morning air. The press crowded around them, their flashing cameras creating a surreal backdrop against the tear-streaked faces of Amelia's family.

Moira retreated to her van to wait for Jonny to come and see her. Once inside, she closed her eyes and let the tears fall. One girl came home. It was a start. Now she had to make sure that no more dolls were found, but how?

Moira must have fallen asleep, for the next thing she knew, Jonny was climbing into the van and moaning because Rose was curled up on the seat.

"How did it go? Any leads?" she asked,

He shook his head, but even so, he looked better than he had since Amelia was taken. "Everyone is overjoyed."

Moira understood. The joy of the reunion was palpable, and yet a sense of dread hung in the air.

Jonny quickly explained that Amelia was confused and had a disjointed perception of time. "Luckily, she seems oblivious to her ordeal. That has to be a bonus. I imagine she was kept drugged. All she remembers is waking up in a tight space. She was frightened, kicked, and screamed, and then the boot of the car opened. She was so tired, but she climbed out and began walking. She doesn't know how far, but she thinks she rested three times and that she might have fallen asleep. Luckily, she was seen by a bus driver going home from his shift. He stopped and asked her if she was all right. Then he recognized her and called the police, keeping her safe on his bus until they arrived."

Moira closed her eyes. It was a story to warm the heart. The brave girl had escaped. "Did she see what car it was?"

Jonny shook his head.

"A registration plate."

Again he shook his head.

"I don't suppose she got a street name?"

"I think when she woke up, a spark of adrenaline from the fear helped her kick the boot catch. Then she was too groggy to think. We're just lucky he didn't find her."

"Yeah."

"She thought only a day had passed. She wasn't even sure if it was that long. She remembered something over her face and then waking in the boot. Frightened, cold, and hungry, and not knowing where she was."

It was as though Amelia had lost three days of her life, a blank void in her memory. The unsettling details reminded Moira that the culprit was still at large. However, the sight of Amelia, safe and alive, triggered a torrent of conflicting emotions within her. Elation that the girl was found. Fear for the unknown, for the danger that still lurked in the shadows. Relief that they had saved a life. But also, a chill down her spine as she wondered: was it over? Had they scared the predator away? Or would the compulsion drive them to strike again?

She shared a glance with Jonny, the question hanging in the air between them. For now, they could revel in their success, in the joy of a family reunited. But the task was far from over. The predator was still out there, and they would not rest until justice was served.

And that alone was enough to strengthen Moira's resolve. As the sun climbed higher in the sky, she turned her mind away from the reunited family. It was already whirring with plans and actions. The fight continued, and she was more ready than ever to face it head-on.

A TOUCH OF NORMALITY OR TIME TO BREATHE

THE WEEK EBBED AWAY SLOWLY. Moira felt as if she was immersed in the thick syrup of normalcy. She found herself back in the world of divorce cases, sifting through infidelity claims and unraveling the tangled skeins of marital discord. It was something she hated, and she longed for a case that was interesting, but then her guilt poured acid into her stomach as she didn't want another missing child.

The days were either boring or uncomfortable as she snuck around with her camera. She often took Rose with her. Sitting on a bench with a dog, no one took too much notice. She was just another woman out walking her pet. At least Rose kept her grounded.

Nights, however, held a different rhythm. Within the eerie silence of her office, she would meticulously scrutinize the evidence pertaining to the dead girls, hoping to unearth some hidden clue. To find an overlooked detail that could shed light on their grim fate. Her companion in these hours of relentless pursuit was the unwavering tick-tock of the clock and the click-clack of Rose's nails on the hardwood floor or the thump of her tail on her bed.

A rendezvous at the garden center café, midway through the week, provided a welcome respite from the grim investigations. It was Jonny's suggestion, and Moira had welcomed it. The café, nestled in verdant surroundings, had a tranquil lake with tables on its edge. Two black swans adorned the lake. Their dusky feathers and serene grace seemed to calm her. The sun-dappled water and the relaxed quacking of ducks imbued the setting with an ambiance of serenity, a stark contrast to the tumultuous world she was embroiled in.

They sat under the dappled shade of an old willow at a wooden picnic table, a checkered cloth spread before them. Plates laden with golden chips and hearty slices of pie were very welcome while a cheerful clatter of cutlery echoed around them. The lake sparkled in the afternoon sun, the occasional quack of a duck adding to the serenity of their surroundings. Rose was sprawled nearby, her eyes closed, basking in the tranquility.

Jonny speared a chunk of the pie and waved it playfully at Moira. "You've got to admit, this is miles better than those microwavable meals you've been surviving on."

Moira chuckled, picking up a chip and brandishing it in return. "I don't know, I'm rather partial to my microwave spaghetti Bolognese."

"Ah, the culinary heights of investigative work," he quipped, his eyes crinkling at the corners in amusement.

There was a companionable silence as they continued to eat, the comfort between them evident. Jonny's gaze softened as he looked at Moira. "You know, it's been a while since we've had a moment like this."

Moira looked at him, a playful smile on her lips. "What, eating pie and chips by a lake?"

"No," he said with a warm laugh, "Just us, talking about something other than a case. It's... nice."

His gaze held her eyes a moment longer than he needed to. His thick dark hair curled over his blue eyes. It made him look young and carefree and very handsome. The scar simply gave him character. What was she thinking?

"Nice, huh?" Moira echoed, her gaze steady on him. There was a faint blush on her cheeks, her eyes sparkling with a mixture of curiosity and anticipation.

"Yeah," he said softly, reaching across the table to gently cover her hand with his. "And I'd like more of it. Maybe with a pint or a glass of wine next time?"

Moira was silent for a moment, but then a small smile played on her lips, and she gave a slow, almost imperceptible nod. "You know what, Jonny? I think I would like that too."

They relaxed back to eating; enough had been said for now, and neither of them wanted to push their luck.

Rose, ever so faithful, lay sprawled by her side as Moira and Jonny settled into the quiet rhythm of the garden center café. The light breeze carried the aroma of fresh blossoms and coffee, creating an enchanting blend that gently eased her senses.

The pie was finished, and a waitress collected their plates. Moira leaned back to drink her tea, pouring another cup from the pot.

Jonny, in his usual casual attire, leaned back into his chair, his face partially obscured by the shadow of the tree. His playful gaze flitted from the ducks to Moira, a teasing grin highlighting his features. "You look like you could use a treat, something to take your mind off all the detective work," he remarked, reaching across the table to offer her a freshly baked scone from his plate.

Moira chuckled, accepting the scone with a grateful nod. The week's accumulated stress seemed to melt away in the sunshine. "You might be right, Jonny."

Throughout lunch, Jonny's light-hearted banter and flirtatious remarks left a warm flutter in her stomach. She found herself laughing more freely, her eyes lingering on him a fraction longer than they used to. The idea of sharing a drink with him, once a distant thought, seemed more appealing now.

She sliced the scone and spread jam on both halves, followed by cream, then she handed half back to him. His eyes lit up, she knew it had been hard giving away his sweet treat, but that was why it warmed her heart so much.

As they wrapped up their lunch, Jonny, ever the gentleman, helped her to her feet. Their eyes locked for a moment, and there was a promise of things unspoken. A soft sigh escaped her lips as she collected Rose's leash, ready to navigate back into her world of divorce cases and dead girls.

Yet, with Jonny by her side and the fleeting promise of something more, the journey didn't seem quite as daunting. She found herself hoping, against all odds, that maybe this was the beginning of something new within the chaos.

After all, even in the darkest times, life has a way of surprising you.

DISAPPEARANCE

THE MORNING SUN hung low in the sky, casting long, gloomy shadows over the quiet neighborhood of Poplar Street. Moira stepped out of the unmarked police car, her heart pounding an ominous rhythm against her ribcage. It was two weeks since Amelia White had been found, two weeks of false relief, false hope. Now, a fourth girl was missing. Maybe it was nothing. But there was a curl of dread, cold as a morning frost in Moira's stomach. It was starting again.

Emily Dawson, just eleven, a firecracker full of life and laughter, had vanished from her own home. A small and delicate creature, she had strawberry-blond curls and green eyes that sparkled out of the photo with a vivacity that reminded Moira of Amelia. How she hoped that this would end with the same joy. Maybe, this was something else. Emily was younger than the other three and had been taken from her home.

Standing in front of the Dawson's home, a modest semi-detached dressed in a coat of beige, Moira took a deep breath and glanced at Jonny. His face was a grim mask, etching the hard reality of the situation. Rose was by his side, her intelligent eyes conveying a solemn understanding of their task.

Stepping inside, they were greeted by Emily's parents, Grace and Henry Dawson. The room was filled with a hollow silence that was punctuated by Grace's soft sobbing and Henry's quiet murmurs of reassurance. The walls of the living room held frames full of Emily's photos, her vibrant smile frozen in time, a chilling contrast to the sorrow that hung in the air.

As Moira began to speak, she took in the parents' raw fear and desperation. Grace was a frail woman with ginger hair, her eyes puffy and red from crying. Her slender hands constantly wringing the ends of her cardigan as she listened to Moira. Henry, a burly man with a receding hairline, sat stoically next to his wife, his large hands covering hers in a futile attempt to offer comfort.

"She was just in the garden," Grace said through her sobs. "Who would think? We used to let her play with her friends. They sat outside the shop sometimes...." Her voice broke, and she sobbed. "I should have kept her in the house."

Moira knew that Jonny would have already asked the questions, but she couldn't stop herself. "Could she be with those friends? Could she be being rebellious?"

Grace's eyes opened wide for a moment, filled with hope.

Henry shook his head, and Moira watched as Grace was crushed. She felt mean.

"We already checked," Henry said, a choke in his voice.

The search began. Rose followed the scent just 15 feet along the road and then lost it. Moira was not going to give in. She set the dog to searching again and again, leading them through the city's various hideouts and alleyways and finding no trace of

Emily. The day seemed to grow colder, the sun hidden behind an army of ominous gray clouds. Moira felt the creeping tendrils of dread seeping into her heart, a familiar echo of the past abductions.

"This is different," Moira said.

Jonny was behind her. "I know, but my gut doesn't like it. I think there is more opportunity during daylight hours."

Moira closed her eyes and prayed they were wrong. They walked on and on, following the dog as she searched, trying to find a scent, but she couldn't. "Okay, Rose." The dog came back to her, and Moira took off her harness and popped it in her rucksack. They would keep looking, canvassing. There was little else to do.

As they traversed through different parts of the city, Moira noticed empty charity bags lying on several doorsteps. Their bright colors stood in stark contrast against the dull, stone pathways. Her eyes lingered on the logo printed on them - the same charity where Samuel Fletcher worked. The sight stirred an odd feeling within her, but she pushed it aside, her focus anchored on the grim task at hand. Her mind kept going back to the dolls, Clara, her strange son, and

Graham Lawrence. Somehow they had to be involved, and yet her gut told her that they weren't the killers. How did she square that circle?

The day wore on, and their search turned up nothing. Moira felt the weight of dread growing heavier with each passing hour. Her fingers tingled with cold and anxiety, her breath fogging up in the biting chill.

As evening fell and they still hadn't found Emily, despair began to gnaw at Moira's hope. A thought fluttered around her mind like a trapped bird. Another innocent life would soon be lost, and another family would be shattered. The relentless, chilling pattern was repeating itself.

As she looked out into the darkening city, the image of those empty charity bags flashed in her mind again. She couldn't shake off the unease it sparked. But why? Thousands of them were posted every day. Many were left on the doorstep for months, and it had never bothered her before. Still, it was a loose thread in the grim tapestry they were entangled in, something that didn't fit.

But for now, all she could do was continue the search. As the city descended into the inky darkness, the cathedral stood above them, lit up in all its glory.

It made Moira want to weep. This was her city, and she loved it. No one had the right to spread such terror. Looking away from the glowing golden triumph of architecture, Moira held onto her dwindling hope. Praying that Emily Dawson would be found alive, that she wouldn't be another name added to their grim tally.

They arrived back at the station about the same time as a dozen other teams. Everyone's face was weary and defeated. No one had found anything that could help. How could this man, this killer disappear into the day without being seen? He had to be known by each community and be trusted, but Emily lived five miles from the last victim.

For a moment, she wondered if it was a priest, or was he wearing a uniform, a policeman, or a telecom worker? Then again, how many of us know our neighbors nowadays? Did we even notice people? Everyone was so busy, all living fast lives. Was that why this man just faded into the background? Unseen or unnoticed by all?

"What next?" Moira asked. "There has to be something we can look into?"

Jonny shook his head. "I need to speak to the teams and coordinate everything. Go home, rest for an hour, and I will call you if we have anything."

"She wanted to tell him he needed to do the same. His skin was looking decidedly pale, and deep blue smudges sat beneath his eyes. Jonny was working harder than her and no doubt getting less sleep. How did he keep going? Moira knew he would insist, and she realized she hadn't eaten all day. So she nodded and watched him walk away.

Before she left, she nipped to the canteen and grabbed him a sandwich, a chocolate bar, and a coffee. Hoping the coffee would still be warm by the time he got back to his desk.

"Come, Rose, let's go home."

The boxer's tail wagged with joy. Oh, what it must be like to live a life as uncomplicated as the dog!

SHADOWS OF THE PAST

AS THE EVENING painted the city in hues of deep indigo, Moira took Rose for a run at a local park. There were not many people around, and she set the dog free. Rose would not go far, but it did her good to just run, play and be a dog. She liked to carry a ball and had her favorite pink squeaky ball clutched in her mouth.

As they walked, Rose occasionally came back, squeaking and then dropping the ball. Moira threw it for her, and she raced after it. Moira's mind, however, was not here but had drifted back in time. She was trapped in the memories of a day she had spent years trying to forget. The day they found Lily.

It was a cold winter day when the call came through. A missing girl, barely fifteen, last seen practicing her singing in her garden. Lily, with her beautiful voice and joyful laughter echoing through the telephone line as she spoke to Moira just a day before she was taken. Lily, the beloved daughter of Sarah, Moira's friend.

The case had been different from this one, but it echoed it in many ways. The loss of a child. The dreadful, heart-rending wait, the terrible conclusion.

Moira could still recall the chilling grip of dread as she'd pulled on her uniform that day, praying that Lily would be found safe and sound. The scene at the local park was chaotic; police vehicles with their pulsating blue lights, huddled officers with their grim faces, and a sniffer dog, its nose to the ground, searching for a scent.

The memory of the moment she saw Lily's small, lifeless form under a tree was as fresh and raw as if it had happened yesterday. The world had stopped. A guttural cry had torn through her throat, an echo of the terrible truth she was staring at. Lily was gone. But the brutal way she had been treated. That was seared in Moira's memory forever.

Overwhelmed by guilt and grief, she had tried to work, to lose herself in the sea of faces and names that swirled through the police station. But every call felt like a ghostly reminder of Lily. Every missing child case was another potential Lily. She couldn't cope with the thought of letting someone down the way she felt she had let Sarah down.

The aftermath was a blur of therapy sessions and sleepless nights. She remembered the hollow eyes of her reflection in the mirror. The endless days when getting out of bed seemed like an insurmountable task. The blue uniform hanging in her wardrobe became a reminder of her failure, a trigger that led to panic attacks and fits of crying.

That was when the letter came. They believed it was from the killer, for it was written in Lily's blood. It was addressed to Moira at home. All it said...

It's your fault.

It had been too much. She and Jonny were close. Almost close enough to become an item. He tried to help, but she lashed out. Saying awful things. Blaming him, and then she left, shedding her identity as a police officer like a snake shedding its skin, hoping to outrun the ghosts of her past.

She'd found refuge in mundane divorce cases, building a wall of routine and safety around herself. Then she came upon Rose and began to train the dog for search and rescue. The occasional excitement helped her cope with the mundane. But the haunting memories of Lily were not so easily escaped.

Her thoughts were jerked back to the present as Rose squeaked the pink ball and dropped it at her feet. With a smile, Moira picked it up and threw it. The boxer's muscles rippled as she leaped after it, full of joy.

The dog had a way of snapping Moira from her bitter reverie. They were almost back to the entrance to the park. The streets of the city stretched ahead, empty and silent. She could see the cathedral silhouette in the distance, framed by the distant city lights.

She felt a kinship with the place. With her training, she had a unique knowledge of the horror they were facing. The weight of the terrible discoveries hung heavy on her shoulders. She feared she was facing the same nightmarish reality over and over.

A shiver ran through her, not just from the biting cold but also the gnawing fear that, once again, she would be too late. But this time, she wouldn't run.

This time, she would face her fears and fight for the victims, just as she should have fought for Lily.

Steeling herself against the cold and her rising fears, she stepped forward, a determined figure under the haunting city lights. Somewhere out, there was a young girl who needed them. Emily Dawson was not going to be another Lily, not if she could help it.

UNRAVELING THREADS

WALKING into the bustling police station, Moira felt the familiar knot of apprehension in her gut. *Why was she back here?* She left this all behind for a good reason. Because you let Lily down, and now she was letting more girls down. For a moment, she almost turned and walked away. But it had taken her long enough to pluck up the courage to come, and she was going to see this through.

She scanned the room, her gaze falling on Jonny hunched over his desk, immersed in a pile of paperwork. Looking up as if sensing her, a hint of surprise crossed his face, quickly replaced by a warm smile.

"Moira, what brings you here?" He got up, pushing aside the towering stack of paperwork; warmth filled his brown eyes.

"Thought you might need a break, Jonny. How about lunch?" she suggested, a playful glint in her eyes.

His surprise deepened, his eyebrows arching slightly. "You're asking me out? Now, that's a first," he said, the corners of his mouth lifting in a lopsided grin. "I'm not going to turn it down."

Before she could respond, his radio crackled to life, a voice booming through the static, "We have Clara Jones in custody."

Jonny's smile faded, replaced by a serious look. "Darn, it. I thought they were collecting her later." He turned to Moira. "Moira, we've brought in Clara, raincheck on lunch. Do you want to sit in on the interview?"

Moira felt a rush of adrenaline. Clara, the eerie old woman, and her dolls... and Peter. What did she call him... the lump. She nodded, feeling a strange blend of excitement and dread. "I'd like that, Jonny. But you know what I think..."

"That Clara's not guilty? She's too weak, and her profile does not fit the crime?" Jonny finished her sentence for her. His gaze was intense, serious. "What about Peter? The boy could be the one."

Moira pursed her lips, looking at him thoughtfully. The idea was unsettling, yet it made a perverse sense. The frail woman and the silent young man, bound in some sick, twisted dance of death. But her gut was telling her otherwise. With his problems, she could see him being easily led, but she could not see him acting independently to be able to pull this off.

"I'm still skeptical, Jonny. But let's do this," she replied, her voice laced with resolve.

She closed her eyes for a moment, letting the hum of the police station fade into the background. She thought about Clara, her hushed conversations with her dolls, her fearful glances, and Peter, a man trapped in a child's mind. Could they be capable of such heinous acts?

An idea began to take shape, unorthodox yet potentially revealing. Opening her eyes, she looked at Jonny, her face set in determination. "I have an idea on how to approach this, Jonny. It's a bit unconventional, but it might just work. Let's have that lunch... after the interview."

He nodded a smile on his lips, probably one of the few genuine ones since Emily went missing.

As they walked towards the interrogation room, Moira felt the heavy weight of uncertainty lifting slightly. There was a monster out there, snatching innocent girls off the streets, and she was going to do everything in her power to stop them. She had failed, but she had done her best, and that was all she could do. Clara and Peter might just be the missing pieces in the haunting puzzle they were struggling to solve. And for the first time in a long while, Moira felt hopeful. Hopeful that they were on the right path, hopeful that they could prevent another tragedy.

She did not know what the interview would bring, but she was ready. Ready to confront the darkness, ready to fight, ready to unravel the truth, no matter how horrific it might be.

DARREN WILKINSON PACED BACK and forth in the empty expanse of his office, his heart pounding against his chest like a maddened drum. Despite his size, he felt like a gaunt figure, worn down by guilt and fear. Sleep was an elusive phantom, and food was repugnant; both pushed aside in favor of his relentless self-torment.

He had a terrible choice to make, and it was eating him away.

His factory, once a symbol of his achievements, had morphed into an abattoir of innocence, its cyanide products seeping death into the city. He was certain of it. His weary eyes drifted to the factory floor below, its machineries of death that required that cyanide were uncaring monsters. Just like him? This had become his personal albatross. It weighed around his neck and stank of death.

His fingers trembled as he picked up his phone, dialing the number of the man who had pushed him into this sordid mess. When the man answered, Darren's voice was barely more than a whisper. "I can't do this anymore...," he said, "I have to turn myself in."

The response was immediate and cold, devoid of any human empathy. "No, Darren. Give me more cyanide, or I go to the police."

"No. Are you him? The killer. The evil that is taking these young girls." Darren found he was sobbing, and tears were streaming down his face.

"Of course not, but if I was, remember I know where your family lives. I wonder what Karen's lovely Chestnut locks would smell like. I wonder if Sophia and Emma would like to meet me; what do you think?"

Darren felt sweat break out on his forehead. "No, don't you dare!"

"Then do as I say."

The line went dead, leaving Darren with the echoing threat. The walls of his office seemed to close in on him, the air growing heavier, tainted with a lethal secret. In a surge of adrenaline, he slammed the phone down and turned to his computer. With shaky hands, he began to type out a confession, his fingers stabbing at the keys with frantic urgency. He had to stop this. How could he be part of such evil? Bile rose in his throat, and he rushed to find the bin, letting a stream of hot liquid pour from him. How could he have been so stupid? How could he have been so weak? Now he would pay.

Back to his keyboard, he read the confession, telling them who had blackmailed him and who he thought was responsible for the girl's deaths. A vision of them flashed before his mind, and he sobbed again.

But what about my family?

He added a note that his family needed protection. That this was the reason he had been so weak. That would do it. Once he finished, he sent it to the printer. Crossing the office, he pulled the confession from the printer, his grip on the paper so tight it crinkled. His hands scrawled "Police" on an envelope and placed it on his desk.

It was time. His gaze fell on a bottle of cyanide on his desk – the harbinger of his own impending doom.

With trembling hands, he uncapped the bottle and tipped its lethal content into his coffee. The crystalline grains swirled, dissolving into his dark liquid fate. He lifted the mug to his lips, a grim toast to his guilt and fear. As the toxic brew slipped down his throat, a wave of panic surged through him. His heart hammered against his ribs, his pulse erratic, and he dropped the mug, its shattered remnants mirroring his fragmented life.

This was it, the end, and he had done the right thing. His gaze fell on the letter. A new wave of terror washed over him. The thought of his family – vulnerable and exposed – filled him with dread. Would the police do enough to help them? Would their help be in time?

In a desperate, last-minute decision, he stood and staggered across his office, a hand clasping the cold metal of the filing cabinet. He opened the middle drawer. Not feeling strong enough to open the top and fearing he would collapse if he tried the bottom one. It slid open like a gnawing maw to swallow his courage. He pulled the files aside and dropped the confession in the bottom of the drawer, praying it would be found by the right hands and at a time that would make everything okay.

"I'm sorry," he said and slid the drawer shut. He stepped away and changed his mind again. He should call the police and leave the confession on his desk. He tried to open the drawer, but his mind could not think why.

His world spun and contracted, narrowing to a pinpoint as the cyanide began its deadly work. His breath came in shallow gasps, each one a desperate fight for life. His body convulsed, limbs thrashing wildly as if trying to shake off the invisible specter of death.

In his last moments, a single, terrifying thought gripped him. Would his death seal the fate of his family? Would the killer strike them next? Would he presume that Darren had told them? "No!" He had made things worse, it could be weeks before the confession was found, and the police would not connect him to the crime. The killer was free to slaughter his family. He reached for the cabinet. It was too far.

His body slumped to the floor, his dying gaze falling on the filing cabinet. He reached out an arm, pointing to where his confession lay hidden. The room faded into darkness, Darren Wilkinson's life extinguished under the crushing weight of his guilt and fear, his last breath a silent plea for his family's safety.

THE DOLLMAKER'S SECRETS

THE INTERROGATION ROOM was dimly lit and uncomfortably close, its air thick with a tension that pressed heavily upon Clara. Her eyes darted around the room, and she clutched herself as if she was hugging an invisible child. Her interrogators, Moira and Jonny, wanted to push her, but not too far. They did not want her fractured mind to break. They had to find how to peel away her layers and uncover the information to save Emily.

Clara sat hunched in her chair, her body swaying rhythmically as she muttered indistinguishable words under her breath, her fragile sanity teetering on the brink.

Moira, perched on the edge of her seat, she studied Clara with a sense of empathy. Hoping that she could see something to help them both. She needed to do this. Clara's trembling hands, her distraught face, and her anguished voice tugged at Moira's heartstrings. Her maternal instincts surged to the fore, and she found herself desperate to offer comfort and support, but not at the risk of Emily.

"Clara," Moira began, her voice soft yet firm, her eyes never leaving the broken woman in front of her, "We want to help you. To help you get back to your children."

At the mention of her children, Clara's rocking ceased abruptly. She lifted her head, her eyes - wet and wide - locked onto Moira's. A glimmer of hope sparkled in the depths of those haunted orbs.

"You can help me?" Clara asked, her voice barely above a whisper. "I can't find my children. Have they all been bad? Have they run away?"

"No." Moira shook her head and held her gaze steady and reassuring. "Your children have all been good. They asked you to come here to help the other children. The lost girls. Can you help them, Clara?"

"You have to help me!" Clara sat up looking petulant, her eyes wild.

"I will, but for us to help you, you have to help us first." Moira gave her what she hoped was a gentle smile. She hated that it felt a little desperate. "Who buys your dolls...." Moira noticed the confusion that crossed the woman's face and cursed her mistake. "Your children, who gives them new homes when they are naughty?"

In her fragile state, Clara began to unravel the knots of her bewildering existence, her words tumbling out like beads from a broken necklace. "Three... three good homes," she murmured, her eyes distant. "Buy every time a child is naughty." She let out a cackle of a laugh.

Moira felt Jonny move in the seat next to her. He was getting fed up and likely to spoil things if he pulled Clara out of her fantasy world. Under the table, Moira grabbed his arm. He looked at her, and she shook her head.

Jonny took in a breath and nodded. He was not happy, but he would give her a little longer.

"Where do you send your children when they are naughty?" Moira leaned forward, putting on a conspiratorial expression.

"Oh, I see, you want the home. Not sure I should. No, Not telling. You steal my homes."

Moira bit down her frustration. "If you don't tell, I can't take you back to your children." Moira sat back and folded her arms. "Will they be all right alone?"

Clara's eyes filled with tears. "No, not with the lump. He doesn't like my girls."

"Then tell me."

Clara thought for a moment, her eyes flicking around the room. She was hunched in the chair like a little old witch, but then she smiled. It chilled Moira's blood. "Graham, the hungry one," she continued, a shiver coursing through her body. "I don't like him much, but the children do."

Moira and Jonny exchanged a glance, their shared excitement palpable. Graham had to be Graham Lawrence. Could he be the man they hunted? Moira didn't think so, but she had made mistakes in the past. Had she made one now? There was no time. She had to keep Clara talking before her bubble burst. "Who else, Clara?" Moira gently coaxed.

Moira leaned forward, resting her arms on the cold steel of the table, her eyes searching Clara's. The weak fluorescent light from the ceiling cast long shadows on their faces, adding an eerie atmosphere to their exchange.

"There's Margaret; she can't walk well." Clara chuckled, a sound like a raven cawing.

"Tell me about Margaret, Clara," Moira requested, her voice laced with an undercurrent of urgency. "You said she can't walk very well now. What happened to her?"

Clara's face scrunched up as if in deep thought, her frail fingers tracing an invisible pattern on the table. "Margaret... she's old," she started, her voice trailing off. "Her legs ain't no good. My children, they try to help her. But the bad girls... they ain't so kind. Bad things will happen if they all die?"

A chill crawled down Moira's spine at the vague yet menacing statement. "Who are the bad girls, Clara?" she asked, trying to keep her tone neutral. "And what will happen if... if they all die?"

Clara paused, her lips quivering as if holding back a scream. Her eyes widened, haunted and desperate. "They'd be lost, my children," she whispered. "Lost without their friends. And the bad girls... they'd come for me. They always do when there's no one left."

Her words hung heavy in the air, a chilling echo bouncing off the stark, drab walls of the interrogation room. Moira and Clara held each other's gaze, both drowning in a sea of confusion and desperation yet clinging to the thin strand of hope that maybe, just maybe, they could find a way out of this dark labyrinth.

"Alice," Clara said, her voice choked with grief. "You see, Alice died, and the children didn't come back to me. They should have come back."

The mention of Alice sent an icy chill down Moira's spine. Her mind raced, attempting to decipher the cryptic pieces of Clara's world. "Clara," she asked softly, "How did Alice die, and what happened to the dolls from Alice?"

"Alice was old; her ticker stopped. It could have been the bad girls, the ones I gave her, who scared her to death!"

Moira was starting to understand. Clara thought that some of her dolls' children were bad, so she sold them or, in her mind, rehomed them. She thought they would come back and hurt her. Clara was looking down at her hands, a low moan coming from her. Moira knew she didn't have long. Clara would fall into her own nightmare, and they would get nothing more out of her. Excitement tingled in Moira's gut.

"How many children had Alice rehomed, and what happened to them?"

Clara looked up and counted on her fingers. The nails were filthy and long. She counted on one hand, again and again, mumbling beneath her breath. "She took 19 children and gave them a loving home. I sent each with a note saying how bad they were, listing the trouble they had caused me and saying that they needed cleaning up."

"What happened to the children?" Moira asked. She knew her breath was catching in her throat. This was it. This was the clue they needed.

"They went to the charity shop. How can children be sent to such a place," Clara said with a sigh of profound sorrow. Tears ran down her face dripping to land on the scratched table. "My poor, poor children."

A tremor of realization passed between Moira and Jonny, an unspoken understanding of the depth of Clara's delusions and the terrifying implications they held. The interrogation room, once a silent sentinel of justice, now echoed with the broken ramblings of a woman lost in her own distorted reality. And somewhere within these fractured narratives lay the key to understanding the unfathomable darkness that had fallen upon their city.

But Moira had a clue, one she expected Jonny to support, and yet, looking at him, she could see he thought they had got nothing. He looked so weary. Should she tell him?

THE SUSPECT

THE QUAINT GARDEN center café was bathed in soft, dappled sunlight that seeped through the lush green canopy overhead. They had chosen a table under the shade of a maple tree. Its ornamental leaves, a burnt brown, cast dancing shadows on the glass table. A soft chatter of birds in the background and the scent of roses filled the air. Yet, the idyllic surroundings felt jarringly discordant to Moira and Jonny, their minds far removed from the serene surroundings.

The food was delicious, hearty portions of pie and chips, but each bite was an effort, weighed down by the heavy silence that hung between them. Jonny's brow was furrowed, his gaze distant. He was usually the heart of any conversation, his charismatic charm lighting up the room. Moira had half expected a little flirting as, after all, she had invited him for lunch. But today, his usual joviality was replaced by a somber, downcast demeanor. He'd lost his usual spark, a visible representation of their seemingly fruitless quest.

Moira could sense the despair radiating off Jonny, and she was on edge, wondering if she should share her theory. She knew he blamed himself for the stall in progress, and he hadn't picked up on the same thread she had. Why?

The food finished, his hands clenched and unclenched around the mug of coffee, a physical manifestation of his internal turmoil. She was feeling the pressure, too, the burden of failure pulling her into the abyss of desolation. Yet, she found herself excited by what Clara had revealed. Was she just clinging onto a lifeline, an unexplored path that gnawed at the corners of her mind?

"Samuel Fletcher," she broached, breaking the thick silence. "I can't help but think... the coincidences are too many to ignore. I feel he could be our guy."

Jonny looked up, his eyes narrowing slightly at the mention of the charity worker's name. "Sammy?" He said, disbelief coloring his words. "Moira, he's been nothing but helpful, always ready to lend a hand."

Moira met his gaze, determination flaring in her eyes. "Maybe that's the problem, Jonny. He's always there, near all the scenes. And those dolls, he could have got them from the charity shop."

But Jonny was shaking his head vehemently, his gaze hardening. "You're barking up the wrong tree, Moira. It's Clara and Peter. I'm sure of it." His eyes held accusation. Was he blaming her for not getting a confession?

The conversation had reached a stalemate, each firmly believing in their own theory. Yet, Moira couldn't help but feel that a crucial piece of the puzzle was slipping away. She needed a scent article from Samuel. But how to get it without raising the alarm? She found herself trapped in a maze of ethical dilemmas and logistical complications. She let out a sigh. It was useless. Samuel would not have left anything with his scent on at the station. Why would he?

Moira had not finished her food. It felt heavy in her stomach, and she wasn't sure she could eat much more. Her fork clinked against her plate, the sound echoing her inner turmoil. Her eyes flickered towards Jonny, seeing the same despair mirrored in his eyes. The clock was ticking, and with every passing second, Emily's fate seemed increasingly bleak. Their lunch had done little to alleviate their worries, but it had brought a new, disturbing possibility to the fore. They were not on the same page. Could they still rely on each other's support?

As they stared at their half-eaten meals, the cheerful chirping of the birds now seemed to ring hollow, echoing their gloom. Their jovial lunch meeting had become a somber gathering, the ducks on the lake, their silent spectators. In the midst of the beautiful garden, the scent of flowers and the tranquil hum of nature, they felt the chilling grip of fear, slowly but surely tightening its hold.

"We need to talk to Peter and Clara again," Jonny said, leaning back, his face hard.

"What's holding it up?" Moira hated the thought of Peter in the interrogation room. She doubted he would understand it, and she was sure he would be afraid. She already had a guess on why he hadn't been interviewed. He would have to be assessed for mental competence. That meant that a psychologist would be in the interview with him. She felt a flush of excitement. That gave her the excuse to miss the interview. She could work her own lead. She knew Jonny would come around if she got more evidence. What if I'm wrong? What if I'm wasting Emily's time?

"He's being assessed at 3. Then we can take a crack at him." Jonny smiled.

She knew he was offering an apology with that smile.

"That's good." She hoped this would soften the coming blow. "I'm gonna miss this one. Rose has been home all day, and with you and the expert, I think another person in the room will shut him down."

Jonny's eyes widened just a fraction, but he nodded. "I guess you're right. I would like to speak to Clara after. If I don't get anything, we will have to release her soon. Do you want to be there?"

Moira sucked in some air and contemplated. She had already decided she needed some time alone, but she couldn't let Jonny see that. It would hurt him. "Try her without me, but don't go too heavy. She is a fractured mind, and something in her past scared her badly."

He nodded. "Okay, if you think it is a good idea."

"I do. If I'm there, she will be back in her little world. Thinking of nothing but her children. Try to coax her mind away from them, but don't call them dolls or deny they are real."

Jonny laughed. "I'll do my best." He pointed two thumbs at his chest. "Old bull in the china shop here."

Moira laughed. They were back on even ground. "You can be sophisticated when you want to be." She raised her eyebrows. "Or did I mean tyrannical?"

He threw a napkin at her but fluttered like a dove and landed in the middle of the table.

"Crickey, I can't even sort you out. Come on, let's get back to it."

They walked back to the car on much better terms. She guessed he had an inkling that she would do her own thing, but he would trust her enough to do it. That was good, and it didn't need them to say it in so many words. They were partners like they used to be.

WHERE DOES THE SCENT LEAD?

AFTER MOIRA HAD LEFT Jonny at the station, she went home. Rose was pleased to see her, and she took the dog for a quick walk. The cool breeze as they walked in the woods behind her house was comforting. Though the mornings and nights were frosty, the day was surprisingly warm.

Once they got back, Rose took her squeaky ball to her bed, and Moira sat alone in her office. The blinds were drawn to keep out the sun, and the dim light from the desk lamp cast long shadows around the room. Rows of files, and transcripts of interviews, sprawled across the desk. On the wall was a convoluted map of connections. Her very own murder board.

Each thread of information led to a dead end, or did it? The air felt stale, heavy with desperation, and a fear that was creeping closer with every passing moment. But, buried beneath the anxiety was a tiny spark of hope, a hunch she couldn't ignore.

Samuel Fletcher, the benign charity worker, kept popping up in her thoughts. His consistent presence around the crime scenes, his ready availability to help, and his possible access to dolls through his work for charity shops - it was a path that demanded exploration.

She had to be careful. Clara was not a reliable witness. Even if the dolls had gone to charity, there was no proof that it was one of Samuel's shops. Even if it was, there was no proof that he had them. She closed her eyes and thought about him. Did she get the killer vibe?

No, he seemed ordinary, and he wanted to clean up the streets. To get the bad men off the streets. Had he said, men? They had both presumed drug dealers, bullies, and pervs... what if he meant the girls? Now why would that be? She needed to look into his past. Was there an altercation with a woman? Why wasn't he married? Or had his wife died? She slapped her head; he could be gay; she must be careful. If she made the wrong presumption, he could scream to the press, and an innocent mistake could blow up in her face. She knew of really bad people who had got off because the police went asking questions without enough evidence. The wrong word was said, and the thug screamed to the media. She would not let that happen.

Moira thought for a few moments, then with a smile on her face, she picked up the phone and dialed the first charity shop Samuel worked for. Her voice was steady and professional but tinged with urgency.

She explained that she was working with the police on an urgent case and let that sink in. She heard the woman gulp, but she didn't elaborate. She had to be careful. They had held back the dolls from the media.

"Do you remember any dolls coming through your store lately? I'm looking at a large number from one property. Maybe 15 or 20? I'm interested in dolls from a house clearance..." She tried to keep her voice casual, not wanting to alarm the person on the other end of the line or push them to tell anyone about this.

The voice on the other side was hesitant and slightly cagey. "We get so many donations, it's hard to keep track... but we haven't had more than a few in one go."

"Thank you, that is a help. I'm looking for Samuel Fletcher. I just need to ask him a couple of questions. He's been helping us out. Do you know where he is?"

The woman hesitated, and Moira heard her tapping on a keyboard. "I'm afraid Samuel isn't on our shift today."

Moira thanked her and hung up.

Each call was a replica of the last, confusion and defensiveness shielding any real answers. Persistence, however, began to pay off. On her fourth call, she struck gold.

"There were a number of dolls in a recent house clearance," a woman's voice admitted. "One of our guys took them for his niece, but I can't remember who."

This was the thread Moira had been searching for, a tangible link. She pushed forward. She didn't think Samuel had a niece, but he was hardly likely to say I want to leave them with the bodies of my victims. "I'm with the police," she explained. "I just need to ask Samuel a question. He's helping us as he is out and about so much. Do you know where he is today?"

There was a pause on the line, hesitation seeping through. Then, "Yes," the woman confirmed reluctantly. "He's on the Birchwood Estate today."

The call ended, leaving Moira tingling with excitement. There were still so many questions. Why had Samuel taken the dolls? Why was he killing? It didn't matter; her gut told her she was on the right track.

She thought about the Birchwood Estate. It was a large area. If she remembered rightly, it had over 8000 residents on the last census. They were reasonably modern houses built on the Second World War airfield of RAF Skellingthorpe, which once hosted No. 50 and No. 61 Squadrons. A shiver of apprehension traveled down her spine. It was a big area to search. Could she find Samuel, and could she get Rose to take his scent? Was this the breakthrough they needed? Or was it another blind alley?

Her mind raced with the possibilities, the implications of her new lead. Samuel Fletcher was now not just a peripheral figure in her investigation but a central suspect. Her heart pounded in her chest, and her senses heightened. This was the game-changing moment she'd been seeking, or at least she hoped it was!

As she prepared to leave the office, her fingers brushed against the files, the faces of the girls looking up at her - Emily, Sophie, Lily, Amelia. She took a deep breath, the gravity of the situation hitting her all at once. She had to find him, whoever he was.

THE WIND WHISTLED through the empty streets as she stepped outside, the city holding its breath in anticipation. She was embarking on a path that could potentially lead to the killer. And yet, as she moved closer to the truth, she could not shake off a feeling of dread. The stakes were high, the risks even higher.

Armed with this new information, she set off for Birchwood. Rose was in her crate in the back of the van. She didn't want Samuel to see the dog if they passed him. She could do this, and as she drove, she thought of ways to get Samuel's scent.

Her mission was clear - she needed to find Samuel Fletcher and prove he was involved. For the girls, for their families, and for her own peace of mind, she had to uncover the truth, no matter how dark or unsettling it may be.

THE SCENT OF SUSPICION

MOIRA FOUND herself navigating the winding streets of the Birchwood Estate, driving her van slowly, looking for any sign of the charity worker. The quaint charm of the area was in sharp contrast to the disquieting mission that brought her here. Small houses adorned with manicured gardens dotted the streets, interspersed with a church, a modest shopping center, and a dentist's office. Her heart pounded in rhythm with the rumble of the car's engine, every turn amplifying the knot of anxiety in her stomach as she searched the empty streets.

She was on the hunt, a hunter tracking her prey in a game where every second mattered. But this was a large area, with winding streets and quiet cul-desacs. It would be easy to follow Fletcher around, always missing him or crossing a street when he was just around the corner. Her breath caught in her throat as she thought about Emily. How long did the girl have? Where was she? At another junction, she peered both ways. Should she turn left or right? Moira would usually listen to her instinct, but this area was too large. She had to be methodical and follow a preordained route. Left, that was the way she had planned. The street was clear, and she gasped as her mind screamed for her to hurry, but this was police work. Long, methodical checking. Going through the motions was often torture, but it was the best way.

Another turn, nothing. She cursed and hit the steering wheel. How long had she been at this? It seemed like forever, but when she checked the clock on the dashboard, it was only 40 minutes.

The sun cast a warm glow over the area, and in the midst of the domestic tranquility, she spotted him. Her breath caught in her throat. There he was. Samuel Fletcher, her quarry, was visible in the distance, his tall figure striking against the backdrop of the setting sun.

Her pulse quickened. The moment of truth had arrived. She turned her van into a side street, maneuvered it around, and parked it discreetly. With practiced ease, she unbuckled the seat belt and exited the vehicle, the weight of her mission settling heavily on her shoulders.

Rose, her loyal canine companion, was immediately alert, sensing the change in her handler's mood. Moira had never done something quite like this, but she hoped the dog would learn the game quickly. Rose's striped body rippled as she jumped from the van, her eyes bright. She knew they were working. Moira attached her tracking harness but put on a short lead. If she looked to be tracking the dog, that might alert Samuel. The last thing she wanted to do was make him panic. If he did, he could kill Emily early. No, she had to be careful.

She walked out of the side street and across the road. Samuel was still ahead of her. Walking down the driveway of each house, popping his charity bags through the letterboxes, he had not got far. Moira's gaze never left Samuel's retreating figure. She began to walk toward him. The dog whined, her eyes darting between Moira and the distant man. Rose was confused. Why had she not been given a scent?

What were they tracking? Her intelligent gaze discerned the tension in the air.

"Right," Moira said, her command for the dog to walk on her right, away from the road. For a moment, Rose was confused. This was not what she did with her harness on. Moira hoped she wouldn't damage the dog's training, but she had to trust that Rose would understand.

With a nod of encouragement from Moira, Rose launched into action, her agile form bounding down the streets, her nose taking in the scent from the air. Moira clutched a fluffy dog toy in her left hand. It was new.

As they closed the distance, Rose let out a bark. Samuel turned. A look of surprise crossed his face as he took in the sight of the approaching duo.

"Do I know you?" His voice held a touch of uncertainty, his gaze darting between Moira and Rose.

"Take," Moira whispered, and Rose sniffed the man in front of them.

"Do you?" Moira replied, her tone nonchalant. She reached down, stroking Rose's back in praise. "Oh yes, I remember, Samuel is it?"

He nodded, grinning now.

"I was just out walking the dog. I think she remembers you." She gave Rose a treat, her gaze never leaving Samuel. As she did, she dropped the toy. "Oh gosh." Moira made it look as if she was struggling to bend.

"Let me," Samuel, with a flourish, bent easily and picked up the toy. He squeezed the soft fur, and it squeaked. That made him chuckle as Rose bounced and then sat, her eyes on the prize.

Thank you." Moira reached out and took the toy by a leg. Looking at Rose, she smiled. "After your walk, remember."

The dog woofed as if she understood.

"Have you seen anything that could help us?" Moira asked as they walked to the next house.

Samuel shook his head. "It pains me, but no." He pointed down the driveway. "This is my next house."

"Of course, you know how to find us. Keep those eyes peeled."

He nodded as Moira walked away.

When he was out of sight, she pulled a plastic bag from her pocket and put the toy in it. Hopefully, this and Rose taking his scent would work.

Moira walked along and down a side street. She hoped she could do a circular route back to her van.

"Good girl, Rose." Moira's voice was a quiet murmur, the words laced with gratitude and affection. She crouched down, her eyes tracing the path Samuel had taken, her mind whirring with questions, scenarios, and possibilities. The stakes had been raised, and the game was on. Did she have enough? She knew this was a long shot, and even if it worked, she would struggle to persuade Jonny that she was right, but what else could she do?

CHASING SHADOWS

AS DUSK FELL over the city, the lights on the cathedral came on. It sat there, never changing, and it felt like a good omen as Moira drove to the playground. Moira and Rose were set on a chilling pilgrimage, revisiting the hauntingly familiar scene where the girls' bodies had been found. Each scene where they had gone missing.

The air hung heavy with the bittersweet scent of flowers against the crime of exhaust fumes and the smells of humanity. How could the dog find an old scent amongst all this? As they passed a shop, Moira saw a young mother leaning over a pram with a friend? They were laughing and happy. A beautiful scene that could warm the heart, but Moira knew the death that stalked these streets, and she was no closer to catching it. She drove on, the juxtaposition of life's renewal and its brutal endings overwhelming in its poignancy.

She had to be patient. This was the start. If it worked, it would confirm her suspicions, but would it convince Jonny? Moira had wondered about simply following Samuel home, but she doubted she could do it without him noticing. She doubted she wouldn't lose him. The man planned this meticulously, and she didn't want to make him jumpy. That way led to Emily's death.

A shiver ran down her spine. She had to do this. She had to find the girl in time.

They started at the spot where Sophie had disappeared. Moira got Rose ready and dumped the toy on the ground. The dog understood. She no longer saw a toy but a scent, and she circled, taking it in. It had been so long since Sophie went missing. Would Samuel's scent still be here?

Rose searched the pavement, taking long seconds, and Moira's heart pounded against her chest. Please, please let me be right. It's all we have.

At last, Rose tensed and set off. She had it. Moira picked up the teddy and followed. Rose tracked to the curb. Moira checked there was a gap in the traffic. She let the dog continue. Rose tracked as if she was going around a vehicle and then stopped. Cars were coming. "Good girl." Moira eased her back to the pavement and pulled the treat from her pocket. Rose looked a little unsure. That had been short, but Moira was elated. Samuel had been here and only on this spot.

Each location whispered tales of innocence lost, the silent screams still echoing in the somber silence. The grass, the gravel, the empty alleyways - they all bore silent testimony to the atrocities that had unfolded, the stories imprinted into the very fabric of the earth.

Rose, ever attuned to Moira's moods, moved with purpose, her nose diligently tracing the invisible trails left behind. Each scene was a new test, each scent a piece of the puzzle. At each location, the seasoned search dog showed the same reaction: a sudden stiffness, a whine, a focused intensity. The signs were clear to Moira. Rose had picked up Samuel Fletcher's scent. At the playground, the dog tracked for much longer. He had been there, and he had walked from the car park and all around where the girls were left. In her own mind, she had him.

It was a chilling revelation that made her blood run cold, every instinct screaming at her that she had been right. Samuel, the do-gooder, the friendly neighborhood charity worker, had been at each of these murder scenes. The insidious creep of horror was almost paralyzing, but she forced herself to move, to think, to strategize. It wasn't enough, she knew. Not enough to convict, not enough to even accuse. But it was a start, a break in the case that had haunted her sleepless nights and tormented days.

She returned to her van with Rose secured on the seat beside her. Her hands trembled as she ignited the engine. The façade of Samuel Fletcher, the benevolent Samaritan, had been cracked. Behind the mask, she saw a monster, a predator lurking in the shadows of goodwill. She felt a rush of cold fury, a burning desire to rip off the disguise and expose the darkness beneath.

But to do that, she needed more. She needed evidence, hard and irrefutable. A plan started to take shape in her mind. She would have to lure him out, trap him, and make him reveal himself. Or she had to get Jonny on her side. Which could she do?

As she drove away, the crushing realization of her missed opportunity hit her like a punch to the gut. She should have followed him. He could have led her to Emily. Guilt and regret were bitter pills to swallow. She shook her head, dispelling the crippling self-doubt. There was no time for regret. He would have spotted her. She had to think clearly to catch this monster. Every moment wasted was a moment Emily didn't have.

She felt a renewed surge of determination. Samuel Fletcher's days of hiding behind his charity worker persona were numbered. She was coming for him. And this time, she would not be too late.

THE POLICE STATION was a hub of frenetic energy. Uniformed officers darted in and out, phones rang incessantly, and the metallic clatter of keyboards echoed around the room. Amidst this cacophony, Moira spotted a hulking figure hunched over Jonny's desk. It took her a moment to realize it was Peter, his bulky shoulders shaking as sobs racked his body.

Moira walked over to the desk situated near the window. It was dark outside, and the streetlight made Jonny's face look pale. The man was out of his depths, and as he spotted her, his eyes pleaded for help.

Moira nodded. Darn it, this would use up valuable time. She turned to Peter and put a gentle hand on his shoulder. He looked up, his eyes wide with fear. "What is it?" she asked, putting a gentle, encouraging expression on her face and lowering to her knees to be on his level.

"Me mum... me mum's gone!" Peter wailed, his knuckles white as he clung to the edge of Jonny's desk. His face, usually guarded and fearful, was twisted in distress.

Moira looked at Jonny, searching for reassurance, but all she found was unease. His usual confidence had evaporated, replaced by a look of complete bewilderment. Peter's wails were a chilling, out-of-place melody in their procedural world, and Jonny seemed lost on how to mute it.

Moira turned to Jonny. "What's happened?"

"He says his mum never came home, but she left here with information on how to get home. I think this proves my point. She's holed up somewhere with Emily and this... this...." He pointed angrily at Peter. "He won't help us."

Moira took a breath. She knew that Jonny was not normally this biased. It was his exhaustion and his frustration and fear about Emily that was making him react like this. Did Clara's disappearance have anything to do with this? She could have just gotten lost, but could Jonny be right?

No, Moira shook her head to clear her thoughts. Clara and Peter could not have done something as sophisticated as this. They were deranged: she had no doubt, dangerous under the wrong circumstances, but not devious, meticulous killers.

Moira picked up the phone on his desk and made a call. "Hey, where are you?" She nodded at the reply. "Any chance you can meet me at DI Chandler's desk? I have someone who needs your help." She nodded again. "Yes, it's Peter Sutton... Thanks, I owe you one."

Moira hung up the phone.

"What was that about?" Jonny asked with annoyance filtering into his voice.

"I'm getting a social worker to take Peter off our hands."

What, no." Jonny stood, and Peter cowered into his chair, covering his head with his arms and sobbing.

"We need to get the information out of him."

Moira stepped between Jonny and Peter, pushing Jonny back into his chair. "Think you're gonna get much?"

Jonny sighed.

"He gives me the creeps," Jonny confessed, shooting a sidelong glance at Peter. "I can't shake the feeling they're involved - him and Clara."

Moira felt a flare of annoyance at his words. "Jonny, he's frightened, not a suspect." She put a hand on his arm, forcing him to look at her. "Pull it together. We have a job to do."

Just then, Elaine, a seasoned social worker, stepped into the scene. She was a petite woman with kind hazel eyes and streaks of grey in her brown hair. Dressed in a light floral blouse and beige slacks, she exuded a sense of maternal warmth and authority. She was holding a teddy bear. Nodding at Moira, she placed a gentle hand on Peter's arms.

He turned to look at her, and his eyes focused on the bear.

Elaine handed it to him. His big eyes opened wide, and he pulled it to him, hugging the bear as tears slipped down his face. "Can you find me, mum?"

"Peter," Elaine cooed, her voice like a soothing balm. She approached the young man, her hand extended in comfort. "Come with me, dear. Let's find your mum and get you something to eat and drink, okay?"

As Peter was gently led away by Elaine, Moira turned back to Jonny. She saw a flicker of the uncertainty she'd seen earlier, but there was a hard edge to his gaze now.

"You need to remember who we're fighting for," she told him, her voice soft but firm. "Those girls didn't get to go home. Peter might be difficult to understand, but he's a victim here too. And we owe it to all of them to find the truth."

A RIFT AMONGST ALLIES

MOIRA HAD TO WALK AWAY. She couldn't shake off the feeling that the worst was yet to come. That time was of the essence and that she was wasting it. But she couldn't deal with Jonny right now. So she walked to the break room and made two coffees. Usually, she would have had tea, but she needed the caffeine boost. Closing her eyes, she thought of Emily. Taking deep breaths, she reminded herself that Jonny was exhausted and worried. That this was not the man she knew. Ready, she walked back to talk to him. Knowing that the next few minutes could be life or death for Emily.

Jonny's desk was cluttered with reports, coffee cups, and various evidence bags, their contents each telling a part of a story they hadn't yet fully unraveled.

Moira popped the cup on his desk and eased herself into the chair opposite him, her annoyance bubbling just beneath the surface.

Jonny ran a hand through his disheveled hair, his eyes ringed with exhaustion. He turned his chair and mumbled his thanks. An uncharacteristic air of defeat clung to him.

Moira inhaled deeply, gathering her thoughts. "Forget Peter for now. I have new information, and I think... know Samuel's our guy, Jonny," she stated, her voice laced with firm conviction.

Jonny's brow furrowed in confusion, then he let out a bark of laughter. "Samuel? The charity worker? You've got to be kidding me! You're still barking up that tree, Moira."

Moira bristled at his disbelief. "Rose found his scent at each of the scenes. It's him, Jonny."

His laughter was gone, replaced with a gaze of skepticism. "That dog? You're basing your theory on what a dog sniffed out... after all this time?" His words hung heavy in the air, a challenge to Moira's credibility.

A potent mix of fear and frustration clawed at Moira's insides. Fear for Emily, fear for the race against the ticking clock, and frustration at Jonny's stubborn skepticism. She felt a cold rage spill over. "You're a bigot, Jonny!" she hissed, her words like ice shards.

Jonny recoiled, taken aback by her outburst. "I'm just trying to be realistic here, Moira. You can't seriously believe that a dog could still trace a scent after all this time. Especially considering how many people have been over those same spots. This is just confirmation bias. You're seeing what you want to see," he reasoned, his voice laced with the concern of a friend but the stubbornness of a seasoned detective.

Moira bit back her frustration. Why couldn't he see this? It was so obvious to her, and she wanted to scream at him to listen, to hurry. She wanted to tell him that some dogs could detect scent months after it had been laid. That the factors leading to this were breed and the number of scent receptors, training, and, most of all, precipitation. She wanted to say that Rose could do this.

She closed her eyes and took a breath. Losing her temper would not help Emily. "But she did, Jonny," Moira pressed, her voice a whisper. She thought of Rose, the invaluable partner whose instincts had never led them astray. She thought of the 300 million scent receptors the dog had. Then she remembered why she had left the force. As well as her despair at letting Lily down, as well as the letter blaming her, it had been the refusal of the bosses to trust intuition. The reliance on cold facts and figures was essential in court, but in the field, intuition counted. Moira had thought Jonny was different, but now she was beginning to question her judgment.

Yet, amidst the stormy disagreement, a single goal remained steadfast. They both wanted to solve the case, to deliver justice for the girls whose lives were cruelly stolen, and to bring Emily home — alive. They might be at odds, but they were still on the same side, fighting for the same cause.

But as the silence stretched out between them, heavy with unspoken frustrations and growing doubts, Moira could not help but wonder if their shared goal would be enough to bridge the chasm that had suddenly opened between them.

"I'm not listening to this," Jonny said. "I have to find Clara. Either help me or get out of my way?"

Moira nodded and left his desk. "I trust you, trust me," she fired over her shoulder as she walked away.

MOIRA DROVE HOME, the glare of headlights pierced her skull, and she rubbed at her tired eyes. Would this case ever end? It had to. She had to save Emily. A vision of the girl appeared in front of her, and she had to brake suddenly as traffic stopped at a roundabout.

Jesus, don't run into someone!

Once in her house, it felt cold and lonely. Rose whined, and Moira bent down to give the dog a cuddle. The boxer wiggled like a whirling dervish in her arms before running to fetch her ball. Moira threw it while she shoved a curry into the microwave. The next few minutes were taken up by throwing the ball and thinking. How could she find out more? How could she track Samuel and find Emily?

As the microwave pinged, an idea started to form. She would mull it over while eating and then get to work. A bottle of tonic and a gin seemed like a great idea. She reached for the purple bottle, her favorite rhubarb and ginger but stopped. She might need to drive. Instead, she poured a large tonic and added a slice of lime from the freezer.

The food was eaten quickly, her mind elsewhere. With her drink, she retired to her desk. Rose followed her and lay on the sofa behind her chair, occasionally squeaking the pink ball. This one had lasted a long time, Moira noted as she waited for her PC to boot up.

Soon she was clicking through Samuel's digital past, her hands hovering over the keyboard as her eyes darted over the litany of posts, tweets, and status updates. The benign exterior of Samuel's online life began to splinter, revealing a much darker underbelly beneath his offline persona.

She found herself tracing the timeline of his life backward. She still had access to a few of her police apps. A picture was forming, from the seemingly benevolent charity worker to a traumatized child steeped in horror.

Reports of childhood abuse surfaced, recounting tales of a young prostitute mother who locked him up for three days at a time, only to release him on the morning of the fourth. That timing chilled her to the bone. This must have been the catalyst for his behavior, but why the dolls?

His fragmented childhood played out in foster care systems, punctuated by an episode of violence towards his foster sister that led to his time in juvenile detention.

Moira felt a chill crawl up her spine. She couldn't shake off the image of Samuel's childhood, the trauma that had arguably shaped him into the man he was now. She could see his innocence being eroded with every day locked away, with every cruel touch and every scathing word. The child hadn't stood a chance.

Yet, empathy for his past didn't negate the atrocities of his present. And not every abused child turned to murder. In her opinion, something else had to be wrong too.

She had already been certain he was the one responsible for the terror the city was engulfed in. The unspeakable acts against innocent young girls. But with this new information, her certainty became grim determination.

Tucked away in the recesses of his social media history were tweets, and posts dating back years, all echoing the same sentiment – the streets needed to be cleaned up. Many of these posts showed pictures of young prostitutes or maybe just girls he thought were prostitutes. Some of them didn't have tired eyes and beaten expressions. He had twisted all girls into his mother. In his twisted logic, Samuel deemed the young girls not as victims but as sirens luring men into damnation. His posts became manifestos calling for these girls to be 'removed.'

In later years things changed, and his posting became more charitable. The calls to clean up the streets were more vague, and he made himself out to be a champion of the average Joe.

Moira stared at the screen, a cold realization settling in. The shadowy figure tormenting the city had been hiding in plain sight all along. Disguised as a charity worker, he sought to 'clean up' the streets. Her heart pounded in her chest, echoing the ticking clock of the case. Samuel wasn't just a charity worker. He was a harbinger of death, dealing out fatal justice to those he perceived as corruptors.

Her fingers danced over the keyboard, documenting her findings. Her mind churned, piecing together the puzzle of Samuel's past and his ominous intentions. She knew what she had to do. She had to confront this man to stop him before he could claim another innocent life.

She leaned back in her chair, exhaustion washing over her. But there was a spark in her eyes, an unyielding determination that would see her through. She had been right about Samuel, and now she had the evidence to back her intuition. Now, she needed to bring him to justice for the victims whose lives were cut short and for Emily, whose life hung in the balance.

As she tried to decide what to do next, a text notification pinged on her phone. It was Jonny. Acid curled in Moira's stomach. She needed his help. Was he still angry?

THE TURNING POINT

MOIRA'S PHONE buzzed on her desk, the soft vibration resonating within the silence of the room. She glanced at the screen, her heart sinking when she saw Jonny's name. The message lay unopened, a proverbial Pandora's box that she feared to unlock. The weight of the investigation was already bearing heavily on her, and she couldn't cope with any more negativity.

She ignored the text, diverting her attention back to her computer screen, but Jonny's words remained, looming on the periphery of her thoughts like a specter.

Despite the urgency pressing upon her, a part of her longed to talk to Jonny, to share her findings with him. But she pushed the thoughts away, finding Samuel was more important than her feelings.

She scoured the net, but Samuel had been canny. Despite her search, his address remained a mystery that she had tried in vain to uncover. He was a fortress, walls built high and guard perpetually up.

Her phone buzzed again, drawing her attention away from the task at hand. Another message from Jonny. She hesitated, her thumb hovering over the screen. Taking a deep breath, she opened it. It was an apology. No excuses, no justifications, just a simple, sincere apology.

A flicker of warmth bloomed within her, piercing through the icy dread that had taken residence in her heart. She tapped out a quick reply, her fingers swift over the screen:

I need you to listen.

Look at the email I'm sending.

I'm on my way.

I'm sorry too.

With renewed resolve, she turned back to her computer, her fingers flying over the keyboard. She condensed her hours of research into an email, every link, every post, every piece of incriminating evidence against Samuel. She hit send, hoping Jonny would keep an open mind.

The fatigue had dropped off her as the search got closer. It was as if she could scent the sweat of Samuel's deceit, and she wondered if this was the excitement that Rose felt when she tracked. It was intoxicating.

Rising from her chair, she grabbed her coat and keys, shooting one last glance at her screen. The silent room seemed to pulse with the urgency of her task. Samuel's time was running out, and so was Emily's. "Coming?" she called to Rose then they stepped into the chilly night. She could feel the gravity of her mission seeping into her bones. But she was getting closer. She was sure of it.

The drive to the station was a blur, the city lights streaking past in a haze. She could feel her heart pounding in her chest, a frantic rhythm that mirrored the chaotic swirl of her thoughts.

Every passing minute was critical, and as the police station loomed into view, she steeled herself for the confrontation ahead. She had the evidence. She had the drive. Now all she needed was for Jonny to believe her.

THE MOMENT MOIRA stepped into the police station, she could feel the undercurrent of heightened tension, a palpable energy that seeped into the very air she breathed. The rhythmic cacophony of hurried footsteps and hushed whispers echoed off the tiled floor, a symphony of urgency in the face of impending action.

Officers in uniform were everywhere, donned in their protective gear, stab-proof vests tightly secured over their chests. The fatigue lifted from them as excitement replaced it.

Briefings were being held, maps spread out over tables, their detailed markings scrutinized under the harsh fluorescence.

A small prayer slipped past Moira's lips as she took in the scene, hoping against hope that this flurry of activity was due to her revelation about Samuel. She couldn't bear the thought of them heading down another dead-end, not when every passing minute brought them closer to a possible tragedy.

Spotting Jonny among the organized chaos, she navigated her way toward him. He looked up as she approached, his eyes widening in greeting. The apology from his message was now reflected in his gaze, his guilt manifesting as a heavy shadow behind his irises.

"Moira," he greeted, his voice a mere whisper in the bustling room. "I got your email."

He reached out, his hand enveloping hers in a reassuring squeeze. The warmth of his skin seeped into her, grounding her within the storm brewing around them.

She offered him a small nod, her lips curling into a grim smile. She appreciated the apology, but what she needed now was his belief. Her fears were alleviated when she caught a glint of understanding in his eyes, a testament to the fact that he had finally grasped the gravity of her discovery.

"We've got nothing else, Moira. It's worth a shot," he conceded, releasing her hand to rub his tired eyes.

"I've managed to get a warrant. We're preparing for a raid."

Moira felt a surge of relief wash over her, dispelling some of the anxiety knotting her stomach. Their suspect was within their grasp, and they were finally making a move. *Please be in time.* The voice in her head screamed, hurry, hurry.

The room buzzed with a renewed sense of purpose. Every officer, despite their exhaustion, wore a determined expression. They were united by a common goal - to apprehend Samuel and, in doing so, hopefully, save Emily.

As the teams scrambled into their respective vehicles, Moira found herself holding her breath, her heart pounding in sync with the ticking clock on the wall. *Would they be in time?*

The question echoed ominously in her mind as she watched the convoy of police cars and vans peel out of the station and disappear into the night, their flashing sirens cutting through the darkness.

Silence fell over the station, its occupants holding their collective breath, praying for a successful operation. And there, amidst the silence, Moira found herself hoping, praying, that they would not arrive a moment too late.

Jonny came with her, and with Rose on the seat between them, they set off for Samuel's house.

THE RAID

THE FLASHING SIRENS bounced off the somber walls of Samuel's property. It was a small, old detached house on the outskirts of Lincoln. Set apart from the others as if shunned. It was surrounded by large thick hedges and could be easily missed if you didn't know it was there.

In Moira's mind, the hedges cast a predatory glow over the otherwise serene house. As the crack team descended upon the dwelling, their movements were as swift and fluid as a flock of birds engaged in a nighttime murmuration, each member knowing their place and purpose.

Moira watched them from the rear. The shouts of "Armed Police" echoed through the night.

The door was taken down by a battering ram, and they stormed inside. Moira and Jonny followed, staying back to let the specialist officers do their job. Inside, the rooms were bathed in the soft glow of moonlight, disrupted only by the harsh beams of torches slicing through the darkness. The silence of the sleeping house was shattered by the thunderous crash of the doors being breached and the shout of the officers. Armed Police, and clear," echoed through the house.

Led by their adrenaline and training, the first team of officers surged forward, their heartbeats drowned out by the heavy boots thudding against the wooden floor. The element of surprise was their ally, and they intended to make full use of it.

In a matter of moments, they found Samuel tucked into his bed, the very picture of innocence. As he blinked up at them, his face contorted in confusion and terror, murmurs of doubt began to ripple through the officers. Nothing else had been found. The house was empty save for its sleepy owner. Emily wasn't here!

Moira felt her knees give, but Jonny caught her and took over.

Comments of a wasted effort and misplaced suspicion filled the air, their undertones tainted with frustration and disappointment.

Moira stood at the threshold of the bedroom, watching as the muscular figure of Samuel was escorted to the kitchen. He looked bemused, the crease between his eyebrows deepening as he squinted at the assembly of officers around him. The scene felt surreal, eerily calm, and Moira knew they were missing something. There were more murmurs of dissent.

"Come on, lads, make the arrest and let me take over. We will find something," Jonny said.

Samuel was led out, and the officers gradually cleared the room. Moira could see the exhaustion returning. Had she been wrong?

Jonny turned to her, his eyes mirroring her silent plea. They both knew that if this was a dead end, they didn't have a lead to follow. They were back to square one, and Emily would not survive. Moira couldn't remember how many days she had left. They all drifted into each other when you didn't sleep. She had to focus. There was a desperate edge to her voice as she said, "Let Rose search."

There was a moment of hesitation from Jonny, a glance thrown in the direction of the disgruntled officers. But the desperation in Moira's eyes made him nod. He trusted her, trusted her instincts, and right now, it was all they had.

Moira fetched her from the van, and with a signal given, Rose was released. The dog's nose immediately hit the ground, her tail held high and straight, her entire demeanor shifting into work mode. Her nostrils flared, seeking out the scent that had led them to this place.

As the officers watched Rose's focused movements, the murmurs quieted. There was something about the dog's intense concentration, the seriousness of her work, that commanded respect. They watched as she moved through the rooms, her nostrils quivering, her body tense. She found nothing on the ground floor, and Moira and Jonny followed her up the stairs. Room after room, she went and then into the last bedroom. Moira was feeling sick. She had let another girl down.

Rose stiffened, but there was nothing in the room. Still, the dog's movements stilled. Her tail stiffened, and her body coiled as she focused on a wardrobe.

It was a flimsy thing, poorly made and unsubstantial.

Moira's heart clenched in anticipation, her breath hitching as Rose's whine echoed through the silent house. Was Emily in that wardrobe?

"Get that door open!" Jonny's voice cut through the tension like a knife. The officers sprang into action, and for the first time that night, there was hope that they might uncover something from this seemingly innocent house after all.

Moira held her breath, afraid of what she might see.

Two officers approached. One held a gun as the other reached out for the door. The door creaked open under the tense hands of the police officer. It was dark inside; the light from the gun pinpointed the back of the wardrobe. There was nothing there. No clothes, no shoes, but worst of all, no Emily.

Moira let out a wail and dropped to her knees.

"Clear out," Jonny called.

THE LAIR

"ARE YOU OKAY?" Jonny asked as he helped her to her feet and pulled her into his arms. Moira leaned on his shoulder and felt the warmth steady her. They had never been this close, and she wanted to let go, to cry. Instead, she pulled away and shook her head. She wasn't, and she wasn't sure if she ever would be.

"Rose," she called, but the dog was pawing at the back of the wardrobe. Moira felt her heart explode in her chest, and a surge of adrenaline gave her strength. "It's light. Check behind it."

"What?" Jonny asked, and then she saw the light bulb go off in his head. "Guys, get back up here."

Moira and Jonny moved the wardrobe with the accompaniment of pounding boots. They stood back as the guys ran into the room. There was a hole in the wall revealing a dimly lit room, its secrets tucked away in the eerie gloom. The musky scent of dampness and worse invaded their senses, an invisible haze that seemed to cling to their skin and hair.

The room was bare of comforts. Minimalist furniture, a stark contrast to the otherwise ordinary house, gave the space an impersonal, cold feel. But it was the walls that caught their attention and made their hearts skip a beat.

Pictures, hundreds of them, stared back at them from every available surface. Young girls, their faces radiating innocence and joy, were captured in moments of unguarded happiness. A lump formed in Moira's throat as she moved closer, the innocence in their eyes a sharp contrast to the gruesome fate they'd met. Some were scribbled over in black marker, others in red, but most were just there. Some wall of crazy that Samuel was creating.

Every step she took echoed ominously in the silent room, her heart pounding in sync with each thud. Among these smiling faces, she recognized some victims whose lives were brutally snuffed out. She wondered about the ones she didn't recognize. Would they be the next victims? No, there were too many, and some were years old. These were just people he thought were bad. Girls he believed needed cleaning from the street. Moira shuddered.

As the other officers stepped into the room, the atmosphere tightened. The initial shock gave way to a chilling realization. They were in the lair of a monster who hid behind the guise of a charity worker. A shudder passed through Moira, and she clenched her fists, anger simmering beneath her calm exterior.

A gasp from one of the officers drew her attention to a corner of the room. There, strewn haphazardly, were clothes. Not just any clothes, but those belonging to the victims, meticulously stripped and kept as trophies. Yet, Emily's were absent. Was this a silent indication that she was still alive and time was running out?

In another corner were the dolls, each one meticulously crafted, and beautifully dressed, except for one. It was wearing the jeans that Emily had gone missing in. The top was still to be finished. Their lifeless eyes seemed to gaze into the distance, a silent plea for salvation. Moira shuddered again. Where was Emily?

They searched the room. A table where material and a sewing machine stood. A pair of old scissors lying on white material. To make a blouse for the doll, no doubt.

"Look at this," an officer called.

Moira and Jonny went over to the dark corner. Tucked away in an old wooden chest, they found the notes. Each one was meticulously penned, laced with hatred and contempt for the 'bad girls' they were addressed to. As Moira picked one up, her hands trembled at the venomous words. They screamed of warped justice. These were Clara's notes to the bad children she had to rehome.

Dear Jane,

A delightful surprise, isn't it? An unexpected note in your pristine, predictable world. I've seen you, Jane. Your twisted snide smirk, your sneering eyes piercing through the innocence of this world, like a blemish on a porcelain doll. You are one of the bad girls.

We are all children, Jane. Yes, just like the ones you see in a playground, laughing, crying, screaming. They're pure and raw, unaware of their naked vulnerabilities. Isn't it beautiful? Such innocence! But then, there are children like you. Tainted, bitter, cruel. You, Jane, are a malignant tumor, infecting all that's pure.

I am not writing this to preach or to guide you on a path of righteousness. No, Jane. This is not a sermon. It's a verdict. A verdict delivered by the judge, jury, and executioner all embodied within me.

Each child is special, unique. And they deserve love, care, and respect. But the children that misbehave, the unruly ones like you, Jane, need to be corrected, don't they? You remember your mother's scolding, don't you, Jane? Your face still holds the sting of her wrath. Yes, I know all about it, Jane. You need to be shaken, shaken, until you stop.

You've pranced around long enough, like a princess with her imaginary crown. Now it's time for you to understand your actions and your words. They all have consequences. Each child must face their punishment, and so shall you, Jane.

The bad ones must be erased, Jane. Removed. Rooted out, like a stubborn weed marring the pristine beauty of a perfect garden. They must learn the lessons that life failed to teach them. I'm here to provide that education, Jane.

So, sleep tight, Jane. Dream of sugarplums and fairies because when you wake up, it will be time for your lesson. Your nightmare is just beginning. It's time for you to learn, Jane. It's time for you to feel my wrath.

WITH ALL MY SINCERE HATRED,

Clara.

As Moira finished the note, the room felt colder, its walls closing in. This was so like Clara in her twisted world. When he found the dolls, Samuel must have felt he found a kindred spirit in her words. They embodied how he felt. This was his catalyst. This was what made him start acting on the feelings he had held for so long.

Their man, their monster, had been encouraged by these words from a deranged mind stuck in her own nightmare. The officers looked at one another, their eyes echoing the same sense of dread and resolve. The outside of the house seemed to mock their discovery, a picture of normalcy that housed an unthinkable evil.

But still, they were no closer to finding Emily.

As they started gathering the evidence, as the SOCO teams arrived, Moira turned to Jonny. His face was pale, his eyes reflecting a horror that she knew was mirrored in her own. They were so close. They caught him, and they stopped him. But where was Emily?

WHERE IS EMILY?

MOIRA'S HEART pounded like a wild drum in her chest as she watched Samuel Fletcher, the charity worker turned serial killer, being led away in cuffs. His calm demeanor was disconcerting, a mask that hid the monster within. She wondered if he knew they hadn't found Emily yet. It was a thought that gnawed at her heart and propelled her feet to move.

Jonny was already turning to leave, his mind on the impending interrogation, but Moira held him back. "Stay," she urged her voice barely a whisper in the quiet night. He hesitated, studying her face. She could see the questions there, but she didn't have the words to answer. Not yet. "Please, Jonny."

With a reluctant nod, he conceded, his attention now on the house, the crime scene that was already buzzing with activity. But Moira's focus wasn't on the house; it was on the silent figure of Rose, who stood in the garden, her nose to the ground, her body tense.

Moira's hand tightened around Emily's bag, the teddy inside brought tears to her eyes. She clipped the tracking line to Rose's harness and dropped the article. It was a long shot, but she had to try. There was one secret room. There could be others. Or maybe Emily was under the floorboards. They had to find her.

Rose took the scent. "Take," Moira said, knowing she didn't need to the dog knew its job, but her voice was firm despite the dread that twisted her stomach. The dog began to move, her movements methodical and determined. Moira followed her heart in her throat, Jonny close on her heels.

Rose froze and sniffed the air. She was no longer moving forward but stuck. She had lost the scent. Moira felt her heart shatter and tears formed in her eyes.

"We tried," Jonny said. "Let's get back."

Moira nodded, but as she started to turn, Rose suddenly stiffened, her entire body alert. Moira's breath hitched, her pulse roaring in her ears. Rose moved, her paws padding softly down the garden, then across the wild lawn. In the corner was a group of leylandii. Overgrown, their fronds reaching out. There was nothing here.

But Rose went behind them, and as Jonny shone his torch, they saw a small patio. Rose stopped and barked, breaking the silence, and then she was digging, her claws scratching at the patio slabs.

This was unusual, the dog was stressed, but she believed she had found Emily.

"No," Moira said. Were they too late, was she buried here.

"Help me." Jonny bent over and pushed Rose aside. Moira looked and could see that some of the slabs were loose.

Moira moved before she realized it, her hands joining Jonny's, pushing away the slabs. Their desperation lent them strength. The patio slabs gave way to reveal a hidden stairway leading down into the darkness.

Cautiously, they descended into a damp, claustrophobic lockup. The air was heavy, suffocating. As their eyes adjusted to the dim light, they saw her. Emily. Alive. Her eyes were wide and frightened, her body frail from days of confinement.

A sigh of relief escaped Moira as she approached the girl, her heart aching at the sight of her. "Emily," she said, her voice choked with emotion. "You're safe now." Moira handed her the teddy, and the girl began to cry, hugging her toy to her chest.

Moira's gaze shifted to Jonny, his eyes mirroring her relief. Their disagreement felt like a distant memory in the wake of their discovery. But there was also a firm resolve in his gaze. The monster was caught, and he would pay for his crimes.

This was why she did what she did. Why she had missed the force. For moments like these, when they could bring a victim home alive. It didn't erase the horror of the past days or the lives lost, but it was a start. A chance at justice. A chance to clean the streets of the real monsters.

She could hear Jonny on the airwave, telling everyone that Emily was alive. Cheers came back to them as she helped the girl to stand.

THE DRIVE to the Dawson residence felt like a dream. The looming dread that had been their constant companion for days suddenly dissipated. It was replaced by quiet anticipation, the promise of a reunion that everyone had been praying for.

Emily was dehydrated and weak from hunger. She had sores on her legs, and her fingernails were broken where she had tried to escape. But she was alive.

The Dawson home was a humble structure nestled in the heart of the town, but tonight it was ablaze with lights, an island of hope in the enveloping darkness. Even as Moira pulled up to the house, she could see figures moving beyond the curtained windows, their shadows playing out a pantomime of restless waiting.

Grace and Henry Dawson were waiting in the living room, their apprehension tangible. Grace was a delicate wisp of a woman, her normally vibrant ginger hair now faded, the tendrils clinging listlessly to her pale forehead. Her hands, frail and trembling, persistently twisted the hem of her faded cardigan, each wring echoing the beat of her anxious heart.

Beside her sat Henry, a solid shelter against the storm of uncertainty. He was a man of few words, his strength residing not in verbose speeches but in the comforting warmth of his quiet presence. His large hands dwarfed Grace's, holding them in a firm but gentle grip, like a promise, a vow to keep her grounded.

A family liaison officer was with them as well as a paramedic. They would make sure that Emily was all right. They would decide if she needed a hospital and help her get counseling.

As Moira stepped in, leading Emily through the front door, time seemed to slow down. The tension in the room crystallized, a moment frozen in time, and then it shattered, giving way to a wave of emotion so profound it left everyone breathless.

Emily, pale and shaken but alive, stood at the threshold, her wide eyes taking in the familiar surroundings. A whimper escaped her lips, a sound so fragile it cut through the silence, making everyone wince.

Grace was the first to move, rising unsteadily to her feet. She staggered a step, then another, her eyes locked on Emily's. "Emmy," she whispered, her voice choked, the sound barely carrying across the room.

Emily responded to her mother's call, her legs carrying her forward as if on autopilot. She fell into her mother's outstretched arms, a sob catching in her throat. Grace held her, murmuring soothing words into her hair, her own tears wetting the crown of Emily's head.

The room was silent, save for the quiet sobs and murmured comforts, each person immersed in their own relief and gratitude. Henry rose, moving over to his wife and daughter. He wrapped his arms around them, adding his strength to their huddled forms, his silent tears joining theirs.

Moira watched the scene, her heart clenching in her chest. It was moments like these, moments of raw, unfettered emotion, that reminded her why she did what she did. Why she had dedicated her life to hunting monsters and bringing them to justice. This was her reward, the sight of a family reunited, the relief of a town breathing easy after days of suffocating dread.

It was far from over. There was still a monster to prosecute and a town to heal, but for now, this was enough. Emily was home. Safe. Alive. And for Moira, that was a victory worth every tear, every fear, every sleepless night. The town had exhaled a collective sigh of relief, the tension broken, replaced by tears of joy and shared gratitude. And within all of it, Moira found a moment of peace, a tiny island in the stormy seas of her work. Emily was home, and for now, that was enough.

PROMISE FOR THE FUTURE

THE SMALL, dimly lit interrogation room reeked of sweat and tension. Samuel's eyes were glassy, vacant as he stared across the table at Moira and Jonny.

Moira swallowed, she had to stay calm. She could feel the room's oppressive silence, like the heavy, moist air before a storm. She had been involved in interrogations many times before, but this was different. The victims were children and the horror of what Samuel had done was almost unbearable.

Samuel looked different from the arrogant and almost jaunty man they had captured. Sat at the table, his hands trembling slightly, was a haggard man with haunted eyes.

DI Jonny Chandler shifted uncomfortably in his seat, eyes locked on Samuel, analyzing every twitch, every flicker in those haunted eyes. "Why?" he asked, his voice barely more than a whisper.

Samuel said nothing, his face a mask.

"Why did you do it, Samuel?" Moira asked, her voice calm but persistent.

Silence filled the room, interrupted only by the faint hum of the fluorescent lights overhead. Samuel's eyes flickered but remained downcast.

"I said, why?" Moira repeated, leaning closer, her gaze unwavering.

"It's their fault," Samuel finally whispered, his voice thick with emotion. "The girls... they were all mean to me when I was on the streets. Shouting, spitting at me. They needed to be taught a lesson."

"A lesson?" Jonny asked incredulously, his face twisting with disgust. "You killed them!"

"I told them one day they'd find out life is hard," Samuel continued, ignoring Jonny. His voice rose, his eyes wild with a strange kind of fervor. "They were all lost, and I had to teach them."

Moira felt a chill run down her spine as Samuel's words sank in. She forced herself to keep her composure, to dig deeper. They had their confession, but she needed to know why.

"Why did you do it?" Moira pushed, her voice trembling with controlled rage.

It was as if a switch had been flipped. Samuel's face twisted into a sneer. "They deserved it," he spat. "All those girls mean and vile, spitting at me, calling me names when I was doing nothing. Life is hard; I was just trying to survive."

Moira's heart pounded in her chest. She thought of the faces of the young girls, frozen in death, each accompanied by a doll, each life snuffed out in Samuel's twisted fantasy.

"What happened that day, Samuel? The day it all started?"

The room seemed to darken as Samuel's eyes glazed over, lost in the memory. A smile formed on his face, and he seemed to look inside. He was in a place where only he could visit.

"I was doing a house clearance," he began, his voice distant. "There were these girls loitering by the shop next door. They called me a creep and spat at me as I walked into the house, dreading the walk out again. Dreading having to face the insults one more time."

Moira sensed a shift in him, a door opening to the madness within.

"The house was wonderful. It smelt of death, mold, neglect," Samuel continued, his voice trembling with anticipation. "But then I opened a door, and there they were—all the girls who had shouted and spat and mocked me. Standing on shelves, each with a letter, saying how evil they were, how they had to be taught a lesson."

"The dolls?" Jonny asked, his voice shaky.

"Yes," Samuel whispered, his eyes shining with a fanatical light. "I knew I had been led there to punish them. They had been brought to me for a reason."

He continued to explain how the dolls were left just for him. Each with a note telling him how naughty the girl had been and how she needed to be punished. He had spent the night reading the letters and finally he understood. "That was when I tried to find the girls to match the dolls," he said. "I had to punish them, to strip them of their worldly sins and lay them bare for the world to see."

"That was why you removed their clothes?" Moira asked, struggling to keep her voice steady. The horror of it all was threatening to overwhelm her.

"Yes. To make them vulnerable," Samuel replied, his voice almost dreamy. "Make them feel how I felt. To lay them bare before the world. But no parent should have to see their child like that, so I dressed them again. Put their dolls with them so the parents could see the transformation. The lost evil doll transformed into the pure woman."

His face twisted into a grotesque smile, and Moira felt a wave of nausea wash over her.

"How did you choose each doll for each girl?" she asked, desperate to understand, to find a way to make sense of the madness.

"By their names, of course," Samuel replied, his voice filled with a chilling certainty.

Moira's heart froze. Clara had unknowingly caused this. She was not to blame, but she had sparked this madman's killing spree.

"It's over now," Jonny said, his voice thick with emotion.

Samuel simply smiled, his eyes vacant, lost in his twisted world of retribution and salvation. "Yes, I did a good job. There is more work to do. It will be waiting for me when I get out."

As Moira and Jonny left the room, the weight of what they had uncovered settled over them. The man they had interrogated was not just a killer but a deranged soul lost in a nightmare of his own making.

"He's never getting out," Jonny said.

"No, he's not. It's over," Moira said, almost to herself, trying to convince her racing heart. But the cold chill that had settled in her bones refused to leave. The case was closed, but the horror of it would linger, a haunting reminder of the darkness that could lurk behind the most ordinary of faces.

THE CONFESSION of Samuel resonated throughout the town, a chilling crescendo to the macabre symphony that had held them captive. His voice, cold and unfeeling, echoed in the interview room, an unholy confession of twisted justice and warped morality. The air seemed to curdle with his words, each of them staining the sterile white walls of the police station.

Even as Samuel was led away, his cold, steely gaze imprinted in their minds, the townsfolk started to emerge from their chrysalises of fear. The streets, once deserted, started to hum with life again, whispers of relief wafting through the air, mixing with the faint scent of blooming wildflowers.

Moira stood at the edge of this scene, her heart heavy yet content. She had followed the breadcrumbs, danced with death, and emerged victorious. She felt, more than ever, that this was where she belonged: protecting the innocent, hunting the monsters, and ensuring that justice was served.

Yet, as the town sighed in relief, she found her own breath hitching. A niggling sense of unease gnawed at her, a dissonance in the harmonious melody of closure. She couldn't put her finger on it, but something felt off. Maybe it was because she no longer lived in this world. She had left the force, and a slew of divorce cases waited for her on Monday. Did she want to come back? Would she ever be allowed?

The sharp chime of her phone sliced through her musings. The screen flashed with a message from Elaine. Clara had been found at a bus stop, fear gnawing at her fragile mind. Reading further, Moira found out that Elaine was planning to work closely with Clara and Peter, offering them the help they needed. There was something about the woman that raised the hair on Moira's scalp. She would remember her for the future. Something told her that Clara would cross her path again.

A pang of sympathy shot through Moira as she read the message. The tragic circumstances of Clara's disappearance and the revelation of Peter's mental struggles painted a picture of a family in turmoil. A wave of anger surged through her at the thought of how they had been left to their own devices. Elaine had found out that Clara had been raped, and Peter was the progeny of that. She had received no help after her life had been shattered by a monster.

Elaine was doing a commendable job, offering a beacon of hope to a family that had been pushed to the edge of despair. Moira found herself grateful for the social worker, her dedication shining through her every action.

She pocketed her phone, casting a final glance at the bustling town. The sense of unease still gnawed at her, a distant echo amidst the symphony of relief and closure. The monster was caught, and the town was safe, but there were still shadows lingering, whispers of fear that needed to be chased away.

With a final sigh, Moira turned away from the sight, a vow taking shape in her heart. She would be there for this town, for its people. She would hunt the monsters and chase away the shadows. Because this was where she was meant to be, her purpose was as clear as the morning sun. Despite the danger, despite the emotional toll, she would stand as the town's protector, a beacon against the storm.

As she walked away, the town breathing a collective sigh of relief behind her, she knew her work was far from over. She had a monster to prosecute, a town to help heal, and shadows to chase away. But for now, for this brief moment, she allowed herself to bask in the victory, in the relief of a job well done.

And as she did, she knew, without a doubt, that she was exactly where she was supposed to be for as long as she would be allowed to work with the police. That thought was a thorn in her mind.

THE GENTLE CLINK of cutlery against porcelain and hushed conversations set a soothing melody at the garden center café. The aroma of freshly brewed coffee and baking pastries hung in the air, mingling with the earthy scent of flowers and potted plants. Moira and Jonny sat in a secluded corner, a temporary oasis from the cacophony of the world outside.

Jonny slid a plate with two plump sausages across the table to Rose, who perched at his feet, her brown eyes glistening with anticipation. "Never thought I'd see the day when I'd be giving out treats to a dog that helped me crack a case," he said, his tone light but his eyes reflecting his gratitude. The dog's tail wagged, thumping rhythmically against the chair leg.

"Wait," Moira called. "Not all at once." She shook her head. "Men!"

Jonny chuckled, cut a piece of sausage off and handed it to Rose. She snapped it up with gusto.

Jonny then turned to Moira, his smile softer, "I certainly never thought I'd say this, Moira..." His hand reached out across the table, gently taking hers. Her hand was warm, soft, a stark contrast to the calluses of his own. He cleared his throat, the words coming out more sincere than he anticipated, "I won't doubt Rose again. She might have the smallest nose I've ever seen in a dog, but she certainly knows how to use it. It's been great working with you, both of you."

The words hung in the air between them, heavy yet comforting. He dropped her hand quickly, a sudden shyness taking over. He cleared his throat and changed the subject, "The governor... he's offered you a retainer. Wants your insight on cases that might need... well, your expertise."

Moira's eyebrows arched at that, a grin tugging at the corner of her lips, "Oh, so they want me for the weird ones, huh?"

Jonny was taken aback at her response, a nervous chuckle escaping him, "I'm sorry, are you interested?"

Moira leaned back in her chair, a sparkle of amusement in her eyes. She looked at Jonny, at the man who had come to respect and trust her. She looked at Rose, the dog that had become her most trusted companion. She looked around at the bustling café, at the town that was her home. She smiled, her heart full of warmth and determination.

"You bet I am," she said, her voice laced with a new sense of purpose. She tossed Rose another piece of sausage. The Boxer caught it easily, and her eyes searched for more.

As the pair shared a meal in front of the lake, the laughter and chatter around them seemed distant, their shared experiences forging a bond stronger than they had ever expected.

They were no longer just colleagues. They were partners, each bringing a unique set of skills that complemented the other. And as they moved forward, they knew they would face whatever challenges came their way, together.

IF YOU ENJOYED **The Lost Girls** grab Under the Stairs here or join my newsletter for new book announcements and a Free short story in the Moira Foster series.

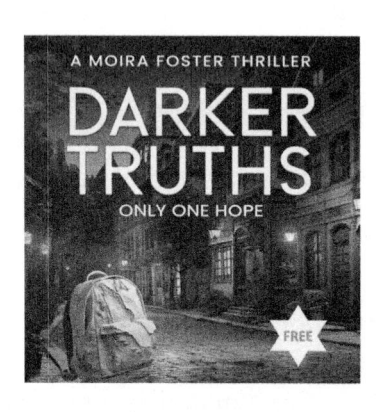

IF YOU WOULD LIKE to join my Street Team fill in this form

Thank you for Reading,

Caroline

BOXERS: THE MULTIFACETED WORKING DOGS

Some readers have been surprised that the dog I use as a tracking dog in these books is a boxer. They are often thought of as the joker of the dog world. They are brilliant at making you laugh and will use any opportunity to do so. However, they are amazing working dogs. Very adaptable and easy to train. I have had 8 boxers over the years and when I wanted to include a dog in my stories, it had to be a boxer.

When one thinks of working dogs, breeds like the German Shepherd or Labrador Retriever might immediately come to mind. However, one of the lesser-known stars in the realm of service and working dogs is the Boxer. With their muscular build, expressive eyes, and boundless energy, Boxers have long been more than just a family companion.

Historically, Boxers were among the pioneer breeds to be employed as police dogs. Their alertness, agility, and inherent protective instincts made them invaluable assets to law enforcement teams. Not just stopping there, Boxers have also played a significant role as seeing-eye dogs (Guide dogs to us Brits), helping to guide the visually impaired, showcasing their versatile abilities to adapt and assist.

But their utility doesn't end in the streets or homes; Boxers have also made their mark in search and rescue missions. Their surprisingly keen scent ability, despite their short noses, allows them to track and locate individuals with precision. This, combined with their love for sniffing, makes them an excellent choice for such critical roles.

Training a Boxer is a rewarding experience. They are fun-loving, eager to please, and remarkably easy to train. Their intelligence and desire to have a job make them not only efficient workers but also loyal partners in various tasks.

My own dogs have done various jobs from obedience, tracking, IPO, scent work, Mantrailing, Hoopers, and a tiny bit of agility. As you can see they are very flexible

In conclusion, Boxers are a testament to the multifaceted abilities that working dogs can possess. Their contributions in various fields, from police work to search and rescue, underscore their adaptability, intelligence, and dedication. The next time you see a Boxer playfully wagging its tail, remember there's more to them than meets the eye; they could very well be one of the canine world's most versatile workers.

Pictures of some of my boxers:

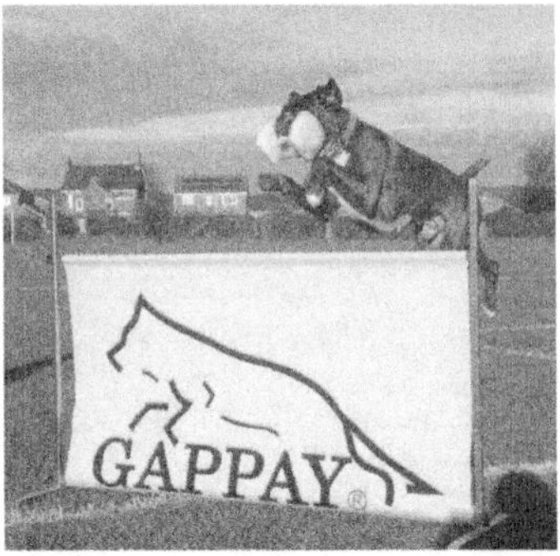
GAPPAY

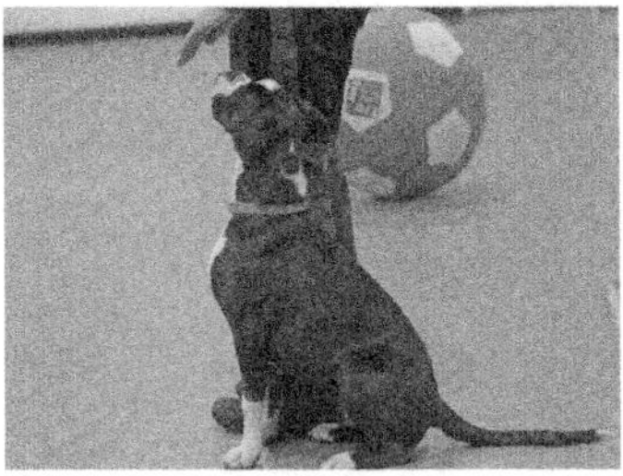

Printed by Amazon Italia Logistica S.r.l.
Torrazza Piemonte (TO), Italy

54333477R00231